Critical Acclaim for
THE RED PRESIDENT

"A FAST READ, HIGHLY DRAMATIC."
—*West Coast Review of Books*

"A FRIGHTENINGLY CONVINCING TALE OF ESPIONAGE AND INTRIGUE. His well-drawn characters, carefully researched plot, and understanding of the Washington political scene all combine to make *The Red President* a sure bet . . ."
—*Library Journal*

"GROSS TELLS HIS TALE WITH AUTHORITY . . . a 'what if' or 'could happen' plot fleshed out with behind-the-scenes glances at factual cloak-and-dagger goings-on at the CIA and KGB."
—*Best Sellers*

"AN INGENIOUS CONCEPT . . . Gross, who has more than a touch of early Robert Ludlum in his style and approach, has produced AN ABSORBING, FAST-PACED BOOK, WHICH AT TIMES IS CHILLINGLY PLAUSIBLE."
—*Orlando Sentinel*

"FASCINATING . . . FAST-PACED . . . AN ENTERTAINING YARN."
—*American Library Association*

"A SWIFT ENDING."
—*Milwaukee Journal*

Continued . . .

Berkley Books
by Martin L. Gross

THE RED PRESIDENT
THE RED DEFECTOR
THE RED SWASTIKA

THE RED
SWASTIKA

MARTIN L. GROSS

BERKLEY BOOKS, NEW YORK

THE RED SWASTIKA

A Berkley Book / published by arrangement with
the author

PRINTING HISTORY
Berkley edition / July 1992

ISBN: 0-425-13330-3

A BERKLEY BOOK ® TM 757,375
Berkley Books are published by The Berkley Publishing Group,
200 Madison Avenue, New York, New York 10016.
The name "BERKLEY" and the "B" logo
are trademarks belonging to Berkley Publishing Corporation.

PRINTED IN THE UNITED STATES OF AMERICA

10 9 8 7 6 5 4 3 2 1

ACKNOWLEDGMENTS

THE characters in this novel are all fictional, with the exception of historic figures and events that are mentioned as part of the plot. These, to the best ability of the author, have been researched and presented with accuracy.

Executive Order 12333 is an actual United States federal document prohibiting assassination. First signed by President Gerald Ford in 1976, it has subsequently been officially reaffirmed by Presidents Jimmy Carter, Ronald Reagan and George Bush.

The technical material on the "Enhanced Radiation Device," or Neutron Bomb, is presented in some detail, but does not violate any classified government information.

The work of German industrialists in providing hardware and methods of mass destruction to Third World countries over the past number of years has been well documented. But the author hopes that any early equivalents of *The Red Swastika* will be crushed before they become unfortunate history.

—MARTIN L. GROSS, 1992

THE RED
SWASTIKA

PROLOGUE

THE pacing did little to relieve his anxiety. The Oval Office, which was so grand in the nation's imagination, now seemed small in reality. He felt frustrated not being able to stretch his legs to their fullest, as if distance would solve his dilemma.

No one on the Hill had been of much help. Both Senator Niles Chase, the chairman of the Select Intelligence Committee and Happy Rider, House Majority leader and fellow Arkansan, had warned him that it was too risky an idea. And what about the repercussions from the same scheme, which had failed so disastrously thirty years before?

President Hawley Briggs, homey and unfashionable at best, square-jawed and stubborn, slowed his pacing as the pressure rose. His feet seemed to mimic his mind. He turned in one direction, then another, treading more lightly as he reached the federal eagle woven into the rug. First came a silent but resounding "no," followed almost immediately by a hesitant "yes." Just as quickly he retreated to the original position.

Did he really have power over life and death? More important, should he? Long torn from princes, this power had ironically been restored by popular democracy. Yes, as President, he could commit his own people to battle, thus to death. But did that include taking the life of *one* specific individual—even an enemy—as if he, Hawley Briggs, were an ancient God-King?

His first official act on taking the oath of office was to endorse Executive Order 12333, the fifth President to do so. The words of the Order left little room for debate, as his friends—and his critics—reminded him. It read: *"No one employed by or acting on behalf of the United States government shall engage in, or conspire to engage in, assassination."*

Wouldn't he be building his own moral gallows if he followed John Davidson's advice? Perhaps even lose his footing in the Beltway political swamp? But his critics had the luxury of commentary. Only he, as Commander-in-Chief, could order the deed.

Briggs broke his path and moved to the soaring colonial window alongside his desk, a massive mahogany piece brought in by Teddy Roosevelt when he built the Executive West Wing in 1905. Palms outstretched, he leaned against the window muntins, slightly chilled on this late spring night. He pressed in toward the panes, then back, repeating the movement over and over like some biblical prophet appealing to Jehovah.

Should he order the assassination—take one life to spare many? Wasn't that his real obligation? But as the thought of the hangman's shadow overcame him, he backtracked just as quickly. One way, then another. Then finally, pressing in and out against the colonial frame, he hissed a soft, satisfying sigh of decision.

The President walked the few steps to his desk and touched the intercom.

"Les, get me John Davidson on the horn. Quick."

BOOK
—1—

— 1 —

BERLIN, MAY 4, 1995, FOUR WEEKS EARLIER

"HELMUT, don't you think it's cold out here on the deck?"

The questioner was Marieanne Luft, a tall, pale-complected woman of thirty with strong aquiline features. She stared imploringly up into Helmut Dieter's ruddy face.

"A bit, Marieanne, but it's invigorating. Especially with you on my arm."

"Flatterer. But who can trust a BND man, in politics, or love?" She laughed. "Helmut, I fear nature is calling. I have to go below just for a minute. Be right back."

She kissed him—Dieter thought extravagantly for such a small parting—then tugged the trenchcoat tighter around her taut frame. Marieanne headed for the ship's bulkheaded stairwell, then stopped for an instant to turn back, waving with her usual coquettishness.

The couple had boarded the passenger cruiser *Ludendorff* just as the night fog crept insidiously across Lake Havel, suspending a moist envelope over that large inland waterway, which eventually emptied into the city's winding Spree River.

The boat was in the misty environs of Spandau Citadel, not far from the razed prison where the Nazi war criminals had been held by the Allies until the last one, Rudolf Hess, had died. The lake had become a tourist site for those reliving the glory days of the Cold War and for secretive lovers hoping to avoid the center of this bustling, affluent capital of four million souls.

Berlin. The aura of intrigue that had once hung over its divided borders had never left it. With unification, that intrigue had shifted from espionage to international competition for money and power. As a prime player, Berlin was straining to outdo New York, London and Tokyo for the title of *Weltzentrum*, the center of planet Earth.

The city had taken on the pride, some said the arrogance, that comes with success. Having finally absorbed its Eastern provinces, Germany had become the unchallenged power of the New Europe. Its strength came not only from the vast untapped markets of the enormous Third World, from North Africa to China, but from that of its neighbors in Eastern Europe, including Russia itself.

Hitler's *Drang nach Osten* no longer spelled the ferocity of the Wehrmacht moving Eastward. Now it marked the relentless drive of the German money machine, sending its exports—from computer-run machine tools to gold-wrapped chocolates—to fill the factories and store shelves from Moscow to Bucharest. The war lost in 1945 had taken a half century to be won, but Hitler's bloodbath had finally paid off, in Deutschemarks.

Helmut Dieter was a soldier in that new Germany. Not in its gray-uniformed army, limited by treaty with the former Soviet Union, but in the inner army of bureaucrats who kept the export machine humming.

Dieter was a plainclothes intelligence officer in the *Bundesnachrichtendienst*, or BND, the tongue-splitting equivalent of the British MI6 and the American CIA. As head of *Ganzfakt*, its super-computerized center, he had spent a decade developing files not only on fifteen million

Germans, but on five million crucial foreigners as well. Originally programmed for crime and espionage tracking, *Ganzfakt* quietly doubled as a tool of German industry. With the CIA sanitized by the US Congress, Americans also found Dieter's intelligence files invaluable—another fine German product for export.

But tonight was not for business. Dieter had brought Marieanne on this evening excursion for reasons of the heart. Marieanne was the latest in a chain of women designed to heal the wound cut by a disinterested wife. But she was different from the others, he was sure. The time was fast approaching, probably within moments, when he'd tell her of his impending divorce and ask her hand in exchange.

What a lovely creature, Dieter thought. Totally apolitical, which sometimes left the conversation barren. But she was loving, and beautiful in face and flesh. And if he wanted to talk business, Marieanne—a broker at the Berlin office of Merrill Lynch—was eager. Talented at handling money, she had doubled his investments during their exhilarating one-year affair.

As he waited for her to return, Dieter walked to the railing and stared out as the *Ludendorff* passed the well-lit Spandau Citadel, home for his own office in the new capital of Berlin. Time had brought things full circle. America was now calling on Spandau for help in their latest tussle with Third World mavericks. Langley had petitioned *Ganzfakt* to work up detailed profiles of those in the inner circle of Mussad, the bombastic North African political and terrorist leader who had become Washington's nemesis after the defeat of Iraq.

Dieter was happy to cooperate. America was picking up the tab and there was profit in intelligence.

Staring into the black waters, Dieter's thoughts returned to Marieanne. Who could figure? One conspired to make life pleasant, then luck, or ill-fortune, made the true decision. With Marieanne, it had been a happy stroke.

"*Bitte*, a light."

Dieter turned, barely making out a bulky presence through the murk. A short man, dressed in a trenchcoat with the hood pulled up around his face, advanced out of the mist to within a yard of him.

"I see you're admiring Spandau Citadel," the man said in a Bavarian drawl.

"Yes, there's history in that building," Dieter answered, fumbling in his pocket for a lighter. Straining, he could finally see the face. It was nondescript with pudgy jowls and a flesh-tipped nose. But the distinctive feature was the eyes, charcoal gray dotted with small flecks, as much catlike as human. "Goes back four hundred years, you know."

"But not all good history, *nicht wahr*?" the short man said. "Just in this century, we lost two wars because of traitors to the German cause. And now we have to settle for a hollow materialism. Little compensation for glory, don't you think?"

Dieter was intrigued. He kept searching for the lighter, hoping not to lose the thread of the argument. There was so little chance to discuss politics, either at the BND, with his wife, or a non-political Marieanne.

"But wasn't a greater materialism always Germany's goal?" Dieter asked the intruder. "In both World War I and II? Weren't we just using military might, under the Kaiser and Hitler for more and more riches?"

The short man stoked his pipe with a steel cleaner. Still seeking the light, he moved the elaborately-carved Meerschaum closer to Dieter.

"More land perhaps, but not for money alone, *mein Herr*," the man finally responded. "Our goal was always the German soul—to make the world one under our superior culture. In that fight, we're still the losers. We have the money, but we're blindly watching American films, dressing like sloppy Californians and dancing to their vulgar music."

Dieter listened, stimulated. How many Germans shared that view? Or was the enormous flow of cash enough to satisfy the raging Teutonic soul?

He dug again, this time into the pocket of his vest. There it was, the miniature lighter. He flipped open the lid and, as the flame came on, Dieter offered it to the short man, still partially hidden in the shadows.

The man moved closer, his smile broader. With one hand, he leaned his Meerschaum into the flame, then puffed on the pipe—once, twice, the tobacco glow lighting the night's inner circumference.

The other hand seemed to disappear for a second before it reappeared, iridescent. Dieter barely saw it. The knife blade glistened in the reflected light, then came at him. First in a clean, straight trajectory to his heart, then once inside, twisted in rage.

"*Mein Gott!*" Dieter screamed, the thought of Marieanne his very last.

The short man extended his palm and shoved the BND officer over the rail, watching the bleeding body inertly somersault into Lake Havel. He sucked twice on the Meerschaum and peered down into the water as Dieter's corpse receded into the boat's white wake.

"American stooge," he muttered, sucking on the pipe. "Lackey," he repeated, the Meerschaum's glow lighting his gray pupils, outlining the satisfaction.

— 2 —

MOSCOW, THE NEXT DAY, MAY 5

THE ugly buff-colored American Embassy on Chaykovskogo Street loomed on the near horizon as Colonel Sergei Naschenko quickened his military stride. The meeting with the Americans was scheduled for 9:00 P.M., and dusk was rapidly closing into dark.

Oh, those Americans, Sergei consoled himself. He had spent most of his career in the MVD, the gray-uniformed Interior Ministry police, fighting Western imperialist influence, and it had taken a wrenching head-twisting to get used to his new job as liaison between Moscow and Washington. Not easy, he reminded himself, to live in a world arranged by Americans.

But Naschenko took orders. During the 80s, he had been pointed in the opposite direction—on loan to a unit training Arab terrorists at the camp outside Bratislava, Czechoslovakia, where he had put PLO people, Syrians, and Libyans through the mysteries of plastique bombing and guerrilla tactics. Part of the Kremlin's plan to become the pro-Arab, anti-American power in the Middle East, the project had since fallen apart with the demise of the Soviet empire.

Naschenko felt like Humpty Dumpty. Instead of inciting Arabs to revolution, he was on his way for a friendly chat with American Ambassador Harry Towers and CIA-Chief-of-Station Charlie Truscott, supposedly their Cultural Attaché. The object? To help America deal with Mussad, the pugnacious North African leader, who sought to lead a fractured Arab world from his strategic position.

The Americans were pressing. High on tonight's agenda was the growing terrorism sponsored by "The Great Mussad," as he called himself. Naschenko was able to identify, maybe even thwart, some of his former students, from one-time Stasi East Germans to PLO killers now serving Mussad in his modern capital of Al Rashon on the southern Mediterranean.

The MVD Colonel nervously checked his watch under a pale street lamp. With only ten minutes left before the embassy meeting, he'd have to hurry.

"A light, Comrade?"

Naschenko swiveled toward the voice, then smartly moved out from under the street lamp, a reflex of intelligence training. In the near dark, he saw the source. A short man dressed in a parka, his pudgy face peering out of the hood, was holding a white Meerschaum pipe. Large gargoyles carved on the bowl made it seem out of proportion to the bearer.

"I lost my lighter—Colonel isn't it?" The man spoke in Russian, but the accent was more Germanic than Slavic. "I'd appreciate your help."

The Colonel checked his watch again, deciding that the quickest course was to give the stranger his light. Addicted to Marlboros made in Russia, Naschenko easily found a lighter in his greatcoat pocket.

"Here. Please hurry. I'm on my way to an important meeting.".

"Of course, Colonel," the man answered, puffing to clear his pipe. "Another moment, please."

Naschenko was put off by the German accent, a reminder of the flood of businessmen from Berlin and Frankfurt monopolizing Moscow's best hotels. Americans had once been philosophical Cold War enemies, but the memory of Nazis dug deeper. As a child, Naschenko had seen his father butchered by Germans in his small town in Byelorussia.

That was a half century ago, he told himself. Germany was now Russia's strongest ally, softening their guilt by pouring in 150 billion Deutschemarks to relieve Russia's economic crises. In return, Russia had thrown open the door to German exports, and the purr of Volkswagens, renamed "Mir" or "Peace," on the streets of Moscow was proof of this new alliance. By repaying with mountains of raw materials, from oil to timber, Russia had virtually become a German economic colony. At least that's what mischief makers ragged.

"Good, the pipe is stoked," the short man finally said, returning the lighter in his extended left hand. "Thank you, Colonel."

Naschenko reached out, but his eyes were suddenly diverted. In a flash of recognition, his pupils widened as the pudgy German pulled a dull steel Beretta from under his coat.

"My God, why . . . ?" Naschenko shouted into the cold night.

The pipe smoker smiled and fired, the launcher-shaped silencer muffling the sound of the 9 mm bullet as it struck Naschenko in the heart.

He fell to the concrete sidewalk just as the lighter left the assassin's hand in an arc, then collided with the Russian's lifeless body.

The man with the Meerschaum waved in the dark. The signal was swiftly caught in the headlights of a waiting

Chaika—Sea Gull—the favorite black limousine of the middle-level bureaucracy.

"*SKOREYE!*" HURRY! the driver rasped in Russian as the Chaika pulled abreast.

The executioner nimbly boarded the car, which raced away with no one in pursuit. From the opened rear window, he called: "Filthy American tool! You're better off dead."

—— 3 ——

JOHN "The Baptist" Davidson woke abruptly, startled by the sound.

He leaned across the Colonial four-poster, a reminder of his seventeenth-century Virginia ancestors, and glanced at the digital clock. It read 5:32 A.M., Eastern Daylight Time. He sat up, alert against the pillow, and focused on the low ring of the phone. Since the number was unlisted, he assumed it was no crank call.

"John?" he could hear the familiar voice on the other end. "This is President Briggs. I hope I didn't wake you."

"No sir," Davidson said, his chuckle soundless. "What's up at the Oval Office?"

"I know your phone's not secure, John. Could you come down to the White House so we can talk? Soonest."

Davidson's grogginess cleared instantly. "Always appreciate the chance to become involved, Mr. President. Be there in forty-five minutes."

Widower of a decade, Davidson lived alone. He traversed the wide pine floorboards of his 1785 farmhouse in Leesburg, Virginia, and after a quick shave out of a blue porcelain bowl, moved to dress. He gave it seven minutes, all he could spare if he was to make the appointment with President Hawley Briggs, four-time former Arkansas governor and friend of decades.

After a quick "tenement" wash down, Davidson sharply parted his full head of wavy, silver hair and donned a gray herringbone three-piece suit, a costume of forty years' standing. Whether in Washington's August dog days or the wet chill of Moscow, he had never been seen dressed any other way. He left it to others to debate if the ascetic former Chief of CIA Counterintelligence had only one suit, or if there were clones which he rotated to keep Davidson-watchers off balance.

Davidson knew he was the object of considerable controversy. He had his well-positioned admirers in the Beltway, but detractors, especially on the Hill, viewed him as a "paranoid Third Man" throwback. He enjoyed the attention, but was candid in his suspicions, not only of certain Congressmen but of some of the brass on the seventh floor at Langley. The Agency, he feared, had always been a sieve for sensitive information. In his own youthful presence, he recalled, Nikita Khrushchev had boasted that when JFK sneezed, the sound could be heard in Moscow twenty minutes later.

His strongest suspicions centered on the Analysis section. Davidson liked to recount how Analysis's Team A had advised President Nixon that the Russians were not arming during the Brezhnev era, advice which had resulted in large cuts in American defense spending. Of course, it was the time of the Soviet's greatest military buildup, as Davidson had futilely warned the White House. Only a review by

Team B years later uncovered the error, or worse. Davidson thought dizzyingly back to the memoirs of a KGB defector who revealed that Brezhnev had contemplated a first nuclear strike against America in the nation's weakest period, the 1970s.

During the tensest Washington-Moscow years, the old spy had won the intelligence brass ring when he enticed a Soviet KGB officer, Major Dmitri Martinov, a secretly practicing Baptist—thus Davidson's nickname—to reveal the identity of thirty KGB agents working in New York, Paris, London and Berlin, thereby gravely wounding Moscow's operation.

Davidson's star rose until he was forced out of the Agency in a purge of 800 "activists" in the guilt-ridden post-Watergate days. But he had kept his hand in through a network of sympatico Agency people, active and retired, who were *nashi*, Russian for "ours" or "trustworthy." Opposed to them were the "disloyals," who Davidson was sure had prompted his early retirement.

But the Baptist had been rehabilitated by time, events and the White House. Today, if Langley-McLean was the center of official Agency operations, Davidson was the locus of the unofficial. Ever since Congressional oversight had made covert action a chancy game, Davidson, now sixty-five, had become invaluable to Chief Executives anxious to avoid less-than-secure "findings."

President Hawley Briggs was no exception.

Davidson entered his peeling forest-green 1976 Volvo station wagon and exited his 27-acre, 300-head small commercial dairy farm—"Davidson's Cows"—which helped pay the bills of his unpaid forays for the White House.

Onto VA 7, Leesburg Pike, in the early dawn, then into Washington across the 14th Street Bridge, he drove cautiously, reaching the North West Gate of the White House

at 6:16 A.M. Davidson parked and was soon ushered into
the small anteroom of the Executive Wing, where he sat
opposite a young Secret Service agent, earpiece in place and
jacket bulging with the standard issue Smith and Wesson
.38 revolver.

"The President will see you now, Mr. Davidson." The
President's assistant, tall, creamy-skinned Leslie Fanning
greeted him. "It's been a while, hasn't it?"

Davidson grinned courteously at the jet-haired Les. Both
efficient and sensual. An admirable, if rare, combination, he
thought.

"Yes. Haven't been in harness for almost a year."

Fanning escorted Davidson down the hallway, then made
a left toward the Oval Office. "That's right, Mr. Davidson.
And I'm sure President Briggs could use some help now."

Davidson walked behind Fanning, entering the political
sanctum sanctorum of the Western world, a room laid
out in a rare, oval shape. Originally built by Teddy
Roosevelt to architectural criticism, it has since been
called one of the most gracious neo-classical chambers in
the West. Davidson's only thought was that it was small
for its large consequences. But he guessed that added to
its charm.

In this cream and yellow room, the Baptist, as most called
him, had been a guest of every Chief Executive since Ike—
nine in all. Yet he was still awed by its heavy presence of
history.

"John." The President beamed, respectfully crossing the
room, then motioning toward two wing chairs set catty-
corner to the alabaster-hued Adams fireplace.

The physical contrast in the men was remarkable.
Davidson was medium-sized, wiry, angular-faced, looking
the sophisticated Shakespearean player, with full silver hair,
bushy black eyebrows, prominent Roman nose and deep-set

dark brown eyes, a genetic mark left by a Hispanic maternal grandmother.

President Briggs had more the shaggy demeanor of a frontiersman never quite acclimated to the city: tall, a touch overweight, his dirty blond hair receding. His clothes seemed to be cut for an even larger man. His face and manner were inexact, but as his enemies in Washington had learned, his folksy, impromptu style was misleading. Behind it was a razor-fine mind supported by dogged determination.

"Turn your chair a little toward the wall, John, and watch this. My newest toy."

As the President pressed what looked like a telephone console, a projection screen dropped into place on the wall next to the fireplace.

"Keep your eyes peeled, John." In an instant, a map of North Africa, stretching from what had been Spanish West Africa on the Atlantic Coast all the way to Somalia on the Red Sea, appeared in crystalline detail. From the Mediterranean on the north it reached down to the United African Republic at the rim of the sub-Sahara. In all, Davidson was looking at the top third of Africa. A small arrow cursor pointed near the center of the northern coastline.

"Sort of my own briefing room," Briggs explained. "This is Al Rashon, Mussad's capital. He's started to infiltrate the Arab Muslim countries near him and he's also going southward into Africa proper. He has a built-in spearhead. Several black nations just below him have a strong Muslim tradition, all the way down to Tombouctou—what we call Timbuktu—in Central Mali at the lower edge of the Sahara."

Davidson nodded, once having served as Agency Chief-of-Station in Khartoum in Sudan, a racially-mixed Arab and black country whose capital was symbolically located at the junction of the White and Black Nile rivers.

"Mussad's been quiet for a while, but now we're getting reports of stepped-up activity," the President confided. "He's learned a lesson from Iraq. His troops are well-armed, but he's not about to pull off any straight aggressions that would bring in the UN. Instead, he's using his oil money—including ours—to bribe and infiltrate both Arab and black African governments."

The President suddenly displayed alarm.

"I'm afraid it's working, John. His largest takeover target, the United African Republic, a mainly black country with twice his population, is shaky. Mussad's people in the cabinet are boring from within. There's also a puppet Arab and black guerrilla army, trained and supplied by him, moving south for attack. I'm sure Mussad intends to use subversion to take northern Africa and much of black Central Africa. Meanwhile, he stands back and denies involvement."

The President stared at his buzzing console.

"I'm afraid to bring the US into what the world will consider civil wars."

From personal sources in Al Rashon and in Harashi, the UAR capital, Davidson knew the President was not exaggerating. Once a week, Davidson held impromptu sessions at the Cosmos Club on Massachusetts Avenue, where journalists, members of academe and the defense establishment called at "his" wing chair in the library to pick the brains of the canny retired intelligence man.

The Baptist had warned them, as he had the President. Within three months, he predicted, Mussad would take over two mostly black, partially Muslim, African nations. After that, he'd turn up his subversive incursions and go after his Arab North African neighbors.

But the President was aware of all that. So why this dawn reveille?

"John, I know you're wondering why I called you so early just to discuss politics. Well, I didn't. Here, take a look at this National Security Agency report. I got it less than an hour ago."

Davidson took his tortoise-rims from his breast pocket and focused on the one-page NSA report. The head read: "FOR LEVEL ONE EYES ONLY. EVIDENCE OF RADIATION BLAST NEAR AL RASHON CONFIRMED BY AIR SAMPLES."

Davidson read on. The radiation blast had been potent, but analysis confirmed it was not a conventional uranium-fission explosion.

"I don't need scientific help on this, John. What I need is your experienced nose. Sniff around and find out what you can. I'm not issuing a finding. Officially, I'm asking you nothing. But I want to learn everything. I'm sure you understand."

As Davidson nodded confirmation, Briggs continued.

"I don't need this kind of headache, John. Third World nuclear proliferation is more dangerous than was the Cold War. In spite of their devilry, the Russians at least proved responsible in that area. With a Mussad, you never know."

The President rose, indicating the end of the meeting.

"My Arabic is rusty, Mr. President. I haven't used it much since Khartoum. But I may not need it. Our friends may turn out to be the villains."

Briggs nodded. "It won't be the first time, John. Good luck on this one. I have a hunch it may be your most trying."

"I don't remember your ever throwing me an easy one," Davidson answered, touching his pale forehead in salute, then turning to exit the Oval Office.

— 4 —

"ALL right, kids, keep it down to a roar and clear those aisles. OK?"

Frustration covered coach Charlie Borden's face as he bellowed into the aging DC-9 charter airliner carrying his charges closer to their destination: Istanbul, Turkey.

The high-spirited teenagers, thirty boys and girls from JFK High in Rockland, Indiana, jostled a basketball across the aisles until the coach brought them to a full stop. Reluctantly, they returned to their seats and took up quieter pastimes— listening to Walkmen, playing cards, reading comic books and paperbacks. A few boys stole prohibited kisses from the coeds.

For the first time, one American high school—The Cornsilkers of JFK—had won both the boys' and girls' national championship. The teenagers, plus three chaperones and coach Borden, were on their way to Istanbul, Turkey, to represent the USA in the International High School Basketball Tournament. They would play against fifteen other countries, from Japan to France, but the Cornsilkers were heavily favored to win the title.

God, I'll be pleased when we land, Borden thought as he checked the subdued chaos. If only he could harness that energy on the court. They'd surely walk away with the coveted trophy, a silver globe inside a hoop.

From his seat, he glanced across the aisle at the girl team's captain, Lonnie Taylor, a quiet, attractive seventeen-year-old reading a school text. At five foot ten, she was as perfectly proportioned as any smaller coed. Her denim skirt and tight white blouse were conservative, but unable to disguise her beauty. Borden checked his own feelings to make sure they were innocent.

"That's better," Borden called out as the youngsters quieted. "You all have school assignments. Use the rest of the time in the air hitting the books. OK?" A soft moan raced through the plane.

Borden removed a large map from his briefcase and folded it to fit on the serving table. With a pocket ruler, he measured the distance from their halfway starting point, the Canary Islands, where they had vacationed for a few days, to Kemel Ataturk Airport in Istanbul, a total of 3,204 miles, and a flying time of six hours and ten minutes. Their ETA was 4:06 P.M. He checked his watch, then measured the remaining distance, simultaneously making a quick sight-check out the window. Below him stretched endless miles of North African desert.

"Whoa!" youngsters called out as the plane suddenly seemed to hit an air bump.

"Fasten your seat belts, everyone!" Borden shouted, turning to make sure all the high schoolers had heard.

But what seemed like turbulence only became worse. The plane first levitated up, then came down. It started to twist erratically on its horizontal axis as well, moving unsurely from side to side.

Borden quickly unbuckled and raced forward toward the pilot's compartment, holding onto the seat edges as he advanced.

"Captain, what's happening?" he shouted as soon as the cabin door opened. "Is it bad turbulence?"

Tie askew, the young pilot motioned to his co-pilot to take over.

"I wish it were, coach. But we've got worse trouble. The hydraulics have just conked out on our controls, and we're flying by wire—manual all the way. Only the damn wires are cranky on this old boat." The captain pulled a shirtsleeve across his sweated forehead. "Do me a favor. I don't want to use the loudspeaker and scare everyone. Go back and tell the kids that we have to make a landing now. Tell them we need to refuel, or any damn thing."

"But where are we going to land?" Borden asked, fear for his charges rising as the plane continued its wild gyrations. He glanced at the co-pilot—desperately pulling, pushing, twisting the foot and hand controls, trying to hold the DC-9 on a sound horizon.

"We're just twenty miles from Al Rashon. I'll get on the horn and radio a request for an emergency landing."

"Isn't that Mussad's capital?" Borden asked. "I hear he's a real son-of-a-bitch."

"Probably worse than that, coach," the pilot answered, strapping himself back into his seat. "But it's better than crashing." He paused, retaking the undulating wheel. "At least I think so."

I think so."

5

THE "Decayed Tooth," as wry Berliners called the World War II bombed-out and unrepaired church on the Kurfurstendamm, so dominated the skyline that it was easily visible from this cramped alley a mile away.

On the Ku-Dam, local shorthand for the bustling main drag, Berlin seemed like the most modern of cities. But in this quaint cul-de-sac, time had been held at bay, both physically and politically. At least those who had just entered the small street liked to think so.

The brass plaque on the door announced the practice of Dr. Hans Koller, *Chiropraktiker*. Office hours, 9 to 6. The sun had set, Berliners had finished dinner, and several of the German capital's most prominent citizens had traveled to his nineteenth-century limestone townhouse for more than a manipulation of the spine.

Beginning at 8:30 P.M., the guests began arriving, greeted at the door by a simple stout woman, Heide Steiner, maid-housekeeper to widower Koller.

"Bundesminister Dollop, welcome," she said, then turned to a uniformed Army officer. "And General Menck, you know the way, of course."

Within ten minutes, Heide had taken the coats of eight citizens of the Federal German Republic, all men except for one attractive woman in her thirties. Once inside, they walked four steps down to a lower level, where Dr. Koller waited in his office.

The suite included a large examining room, perhaps twenty by twenty-five feet, filled with two instructional skeletons, large four-color anatomical charts, and several reclining treatment tables. The chamber was decorated in bare, modern style, with only one anomaly. A large oil painting, a romantic nineteenth-century landscape by Adrian Ludwig Richter, dominated the far wall.

Tonight, the office had been converted into a meeting place. Chairs had been set out and a treatment table doubled as a refreshment stand. Koller smilingly greeted each guest as they milled, offering everyone *schnapps* and small German pastries filled with apricots and strawberries. Dr. Friedrich Olmst, a prominent industrial scientist, smacked his lips. "*Schoen*," he announced.

Physically, Dr. Koller was the least impressive of the group. Five foot six at most, he was some twenty pounds overweight and resembled a cherubic German *Burgermeister*. His features were nondescript. Glasses balanced low on his nose, and receding gray hair, long at the sides, gave him the look of a preoccupied professor. The chiropractor wore a navy-blue, three-piece serge suit, shiny at key points. Surely, no one to elicit great admiration. Merely a journeyman practitioner of a minor medical art, probably with a rather small practice.

But within fifteen minutes, the environment, and Koller himself, had changed dramatically.

The serving table had swiftly become a lectern. Everyone had taken their seats and now stared expectantly at Koller. Among those in the audience were Paul Dollop, a ranking member of the Foreign Ministry; Colonel General Johann Menck; Dr. Olmst, a physicist with the Federal Nuclear Agency; Helmut Zolb, a leading parliamentarian in the Bundestag; and representatives of the BND and several major corporations, including Heinrich Wilhelm, the Berlin emissary from Heinschmann, GmbH, a multi-billion mark Dusseldorf conglomerate.

Dr. Koller rapped a sharp gavel. As eyes turned toward him, the chiropractor's physiognomy seemed to undergo an abrupt transformation. The crystal blue eyes, somewhat sleepy in relaxation, took on a luminescence. His stance shifted from a pleasant slouch to ramrod attention, the muscles stretched into compliance with his expression, one of near ferocity. The small man seemed to gain inches in height as he walked, in short, peppery military strides, toward the landscape painting at the end of the room.

He reached up and turned over the picture. Staring down on the room was now a color likeness of Adolf Hitler, a reproduction of the official World War II portrait.

Returning to the lectern, Koller's demeanor seemed almost to imitate that of his one-time Fuehrer.

"Fifty years ago today, we lost our destiny and accepted another," he began in a resonant baritone that sounded twenty years younger than his person. "It has made us rich, but politically impotent. The world is now cast in a Pax Americana that can only disgust a true German. We did not struggle to create the perfect civilization only to have barbarians from Texas and California rule the globe."

Small clusters of "*Ja, Ja,*" rose from his elite audience.

"Officially, the German government, for all its wealth and rapport with the United States, has no global political power. And worse yet, no aspirations."

His glasses put aside, Koller's eyes focused with the intensity of laser beams. "But we in Red Swastika do have aspirations, and the world will learn of them soon enough. In Moscow, powerful elements of the Army are with us.

When they formally take the Kremlin, they'll advance our goal of a new Greater Germany with glory and empire. The partnership of our talent and capital and Russia's natural resources and arms will be unbeatable."

Koller spoke lower, almost as an aside: "With the Reich, of course, as the senior of the two." The chiropractor paused, leaning into the podium.

"General Barenchenko has already promised to return the German lands—Pomerania, Danzig and East Prussia—stolen by Poland at the end of World War II. That's only the beginning. Leaders throughout the Third World are looking to our technology and financial strength and will join our crusade against the American superpower. Even in the Americas—in Brazil, Bolivia, Paraguay and Argentina—we have friends who will risk everything. Once the world is remade in a German image—the Fourth Reich—they will gain their reward."

Koller paused. "Major Niemann of the BND. What can you report?"

The young intelligence man rose. About thirty-five, tall, taut-bodied and blond, he seemed the archetypical German of Nazi mythology, his voice a reminder of SS arrogance.

"Our operative, the man with the Meerschaum, has eliminated two who tried to block our Mussad project. I'll be following up any other intrusions." Niemann bowed from the neck and retook his seat.

"And Dr. Wilhelm? Anything new on the corporate front? Is German industry with us?"

The emissary from Heinschmann, a stringy man with a scar on his right cheek, stood.

"Has German industry ever let the nation down?" he asked rhetorically. "We were the first to support the Fuehrer. We accomplished impossible tasks despite bombing in World War II, and now we have led Germany to its miraculous recovery. I pledge the same in the future."

Wilhelm smiled his assurance. "Tonight," he said, "I can report that our project in Recife has finally reached fruition."

As they heard that name, Dr. Koller and the entire Red Swastika central cell braced. News from Brazil could alter the configuration of not only the Third World, but the First and Second ones as well.

Koller turned toward the portrait, his eyes lit in admiration. "*Heil*," he said reverently, followed by a similar chorus from the others.

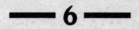

6

LEAVING the White House, Davidson walked from Pennsylvania Avenue to K and 16th, where he entered one of the low-profile office buildings that gave Washington its relaxed landscape, so distinctly un-New York.

He headed for a pay phone, where he dialed a local 202 area code number: 881-7171. "Hello," a pert feminine voice answered in what was obviously a recording. "You have reached a disconnected number of the Central Intelligence Agency. Please call the main number, Area Code 703-482-1100, and ask for your party. I'm sorry for the inconvenience."

Davidson listened patiently. "I'm sorry too. Please excuse the call."

He hadn't used the communications subterfuge in months.

If it was still operating, he had made contact with one of
the *nashi*, any of whom Davidson could trust with his
modest pension. Since it worked on a rotating schedule,
Davidson believed he had reached Mike Bellamy, former
Berlin Chief-of-Station.

The key words were "I'm sorry." A voice imprinter would
verify that the caller was the Baptist, and all he had to
remember was the system. It was Wednesday, and if his
memory served, the rendezvous was at an all-night diner
in Arlington, Virginia. The time: 8:45 P.M. In his mind, he
reviewed the site to be sure he wasn't scheduled for either
the movie house in Bethesda, or the shopping center in
Gaithersburg, Maryland. They were both legitimate meeting
points, but Davidson had been known to show up on the
right day, on time, but in the wrong place.

Home in Leesburg, he spent the remaining hours in his
wing chair, with "Dulles," his affectionate Labrador, by
his side, reading Churchill's two-volume history of the
Second World War. After a short nap, he woke fresh for
the upcoming meeting with Bellamy.

At 7:55 P.M., Davidson entered VA 7, Leesburg Pike,
and headed eastward, driving tentatively. Not because of
the weather, but as a precaution against what he believed
he saw in the rear view mirror. Another Volvo, this one
a new silver 960GL, had maintained the same cautious
distance behind him for several minutes.

Following simple tradecraft, Davidson left the Pike at the
next exit and traveled on a parallel road for half a mile. The
Volvo behind him continued the tail. Ahead, he could make
out a highway entrance and as he got back on the Pike, so
did his shadow.

For ten minutes the two Volvos rode in near tandem on VA
7 en route to Washington. Deciding it was time to make his

move, he rapidly decelerated his wagon. The unsuspecting silver Volvo at his rear braked suddenly, then skidded into the next lane, ending up alongside Davidson.

"Hello, fellow Volvo driver. Enjoying the night air?" Davidson shouted out the opened window. Without waiting for an answer, he pressed the accelerator, soon reaching 80 mph.

Davidson had never enjoyed cars, or even driving, but kept himself tuned for such occasions. Moving into the left lane, he maintained his speed, his eyes following the road and the tail simultaneously. After several minutes, he heard a report. Davidson turned to see a bullet shatter his large rear window into a pile of rounded shards. The bullet itself missed him and was probably imbedded somewhere in the back of his seat.

That wasn't part of his evasion scenario. Now he had to improvise. Davidson hunkered down into the seat and as he approached within fifty feet of the next exit, he swerved the Volvo into a desperate sixty degree turn, ending up in a small ditch on the grass edge of the exit, where he watched the silver shadow race harmlessly by.

The remainder of the trip to Arlington was uneventful. If he had known that his opponents, whoever they were, were so intent on killing him, he'd have listened to worried *nashi* and installed bullet-proof glass in the old wagon. Perhaps he'd still look into it, although the cost was prohibitive, especially for a self-sustaining, basically unemployed intelligence man.

A few minutes early, Davidson arrived at the diner and drove into the parking lot, choosing a spot at the outer edges. He turned the radio to station WGMS-FM and listened to a Chopin piano concerto as he waited for Mike Bellamy.

"Baptist. On time as usual."

He turned toward the passenger side. Bellamy, a stocky

man of about forty-five—more the Chicago policeman than the caricature of a button-down Langley agent—had stuck his head through the front window.

"My God, John. It looks like you were hit by a Marine mortar."

Without responding, Davidson left the car and waved for Bellamy to follow.

"I took a peek into the diner. There's an empty section in the back. I'm in the mood for some fish soup. They say it's good here."

Seated in the diner's rear, Davidson told of the highway incident. Bellamy was surprised that, whatever his mission, Davidson had drawn such a deadly response.

"I understand that they've put you on the German desk since you came back from Berlin," Davidson said. "I'm shocked. It's so rational."

"I suppose I know something about the situation there— if anyone can ever figure out the Germans. How can I help?"

"I'm doing a little something on Mussad in North Africa, Mike. Is there anything going on that you know about? Either on your desk, or elsewhere?"

Bellamy sampled the fish soup. "You're right, John. It is good." He stared up. "Mussad? Yes, something came across my desk yesterday." He leaned down and slurped a quick spoonful, fully-orchestrated.

"Take your time, Mike." Davidson was not one to rush his sources.

"A little item came from Ben Latham. You remember him—my replacement as Chief-of-Station in Berlin. An Ivy Leaguer, but with some guts. He sent me a short report on Red Swastika. A right wing, pro-Nazi group, but with ties to the Russkies, at least the hardliners who want their empire back." Bellamy reached to an inside pocket. "It was the best thing I had so I brought it for you. Doesn't say much, but it does mention Mussad."

Davidson scanned the note, perhaps twenty lines in all. Red Swastika active in Germany? He had heard only rumors about their operation.

Bellamy finished his fish soup, with gusto.

"Get yourself another plate. It's on me, Mike. I've got to take off." Davidson headed toward the cashier.

"OK. But what's it all about, Baptist? I hate to come in in the middle of a movie."

"I'll let you know as soon as I can, Mike. Meanwhile chat with the other *nashi* and learn what you can. You know how to reach me."

— 7 —

BERLIN, MAY 7, 8:00 P.M.

THE night along Berlin's Platz der Republik was festive.

The old Reichstag building showed only minor scars from the great fire of 1933 when Adolf Hitler torched the parliament and falsely blamed the anti-Nazis. Restored to its former glory, except for its missing dome, it was now the official seat of the German government. Spotlights washed its classical baroque façade and bathed a dozen black, red and yellow flags of the Federal German Republic waving alongside the white, blue and red Russian banner.

It was a celebration of the fiftieth anniversary of the end of World War II, concluded on May 7, 1945, and the official beginning of what German newspapers were calling "Eine Neue Welt"—A New World. In that world, Germany and Russia were pledging undying friendship, entering a partnership pundits believed could become the strongest on the globe.

Germany had not left the European Community, which it now dominated, but had turned East as well. The once-hated Germans, grateful for Russia's permission to unify, had poured 150 *billion* Deutschemarks into that crippled nation. Berlin had warded off the bankruptcy of the Russian state.

Of course, the Germans had not rescued Russia out of pure altruism or even guilt. They had moved eastward for the rewards of an enormous market of 350 million people in the former USSR bloc, all hungry for their superior goods. Tonight's celebration was formal recognition of that fact, and of a partnership that insured that Germany would remain *über alles* in the New Europe.

The partnership was logical. Germany had been stripped of military power not only by its defeat in World War II, but by the 1990 agreement to limit its army in return for Russian withdrawal from East Germany. The former Soviet Union had itself lost the first Cold War in 1989. Germany was potent economically while Communism had drained the USSR. But Russia had enormous untapped natural resources and nuclear know-how. Nationalists in both countries dreamed of a combined Germano-Russia alliance that could shape a new superpower. Perhaps someday the greatest.

But to outsiders, the two nations also represented a potentially frightening formula for the twenty-first century. Especially if either, or both, should fall into the wrong hands—for which they seemed to have a tragic propensity.

Inside the remodeled ultra-modern bowels of the Reichstag that union was being fused. Before an audience of 1,000, including representatives of 150 anxious nations, the German Chancellor—tall, bulky Karl Bessinger—mounted the podium.

"History has turned old enemies into new friends," he began. "But there will be no more wars between us. We've come here, exactly fifty years from the end of World War II, to sign the Second Russian-German Pact. This one is different from the one drawn up by Hitler and Stalin. It will not divide Europe but truly unite it."

Russian President Valentin Malinovsky, an angular, high-cheekboned man somewhat reminiscent of Andrei Gromyko, concurred. "What we're witnessing is nothing less than an unselfish German Marshall plan for our nation," he said when he reached the podium. "Without it, we couldn't maintain our system. I don't know what would have happened to us, especially during the tense days of the early 1990s, without Germany. In Berlin, we have a friend on whom we shall always rely."

In the press gallery overlooking the ceremony, an American television commentator, Ezra Jenkins, stared skeptically into the camera carrying his comments back home by satellite.

"No one here has mentioned America, as if that superpower no longer mattered," the popular carrot-haired anchorman began. "With American troops in Europe down to twenty-five thousand, and those few maybe on their way home—if the German peace protestors continue to have their way—I have to wonder."

Jenkins paused, signaling his cameraman for a close-up.

"Here in the Reichstag, we're witnessing two giant nations,

both once the devils of war, come together. Either it's a great day for the planet. Or . . ." Jenkins coughed heavily into his microphone, then signed off, obviously burying his fears.

— 8 —

THE stillness in the tropical forest outside Recife, Brazil, was interrupted by the whir of a helicopter.

A city of nearly two million and capital of Pernambuco State in northeast Brazil, Recife lies at the mouth of the Rio Capibaribe at the Atlantic coast, about halfway between Rio de Janeiro to the south and the Amazon River to the north, distances of over a thousand miles each way in this vast nation.

"Cotrell, SA," read the large blue and orange sign outside the guarded cyclone-fenced perimeter where the helicopter landed. Inside the fence, stretching a mile in every direction, was a swatch of flat open ground cut out of the forest, and dotted with small modern buildings. The area represented everything that could be said about Brazil—the bleak primitive wedded to the ultra-modern and scientific.

The site was Cotrell's main Research and Development facility. Within these grounds, the enormous Brazilian conglomerate—involved in everything from road building to weapons design and production—tested its major electronic and ordnance products. They not only supplied the Brazilian armed forces, but were exported around the world for hard currency to help pay the enormous debt to American banks. Cotrell prided itself on underpricing other arms-dealing nations, including, the USA, France, sometimes even China.

The quality of its products, whether tanks or missiles, surprised the First World. The secret, many believed, was Brazilian-German teamwork, a partnership that had its strength in the sizable Brazilian-born German population, many of them descendants of the Nazis who fled there after World War II. The other base was the scientific teamwork between the two countries, each of which shared a love of unbridled capitalism, following the buck wherever, and however, it could be made.

"Stand back and let the couriers come out," yelled Ernst Vogel, a spare, middle-aged German, a former professor of physics. He was under contract to Cotrell as scientific coordinator of Project Recife, a joint effort of Cotrell and Heinschmann of Dusseldorf, Germany.

Brazil was only part of Heinschmann's worldwide export business, which overshadowed Cotrell's tenfold. Heinschmann was both consultant and fabricator for nuclear reactors, even chemical and biological warfare materials in several African, Asian, and Middle Eastern nations. In Al Rashon, Heinschmann was building Mussad a nuclear reactor, ostensibly for electrical energy creation, at a cost of nine billion dollars.

The German conglomerate's balance sheet was heavily dependent on its Third World exports, and its political sympathies followed the Deutschemark.

"Bring the containers here," Vogel shouted above the chopper noise as he stood alongside a Land Rover guarded by two security men armed with AK-47s.

"Good, good," he called more moderately once the copter engines were shut. "Horstmann, a real pleasure to see you."

Coming toward him was a bulky German, perhaps six foot six, a model of an American fullback, dressed in bush clothing topped by a pith helmet. Wolf Horstmann looked the perfect German colonial, a not inappropriate image.

"Professor Vogel," Horstmann greeted, overshadowing the professor by almost a foot. "The shipment just came in from our people in Akademgorodok. It looks legitimate to me, but I'll leave that to you scientific folk."

Horstmann turned and waved to the copter. Two men in white jump suits opened the cargo door and extracted three large high-pressure stainless steel containers. Each was oval in shape and approximately two foot at the largest dimension. Following behind was a man carrying a small lead radioactive-proof capsule.

"They're both marked," Horstmann explained. "The deuterium is in the large containers, the tritium in the smaller one."

"Good, good," Vogel repeated, stretching to give Horstmann a fatherly shoulder tap. "Now we're getting somewhere. You know, Horstmann, I care nothing about the money. What's important is that this is Red Swastika's first important foreign policy step. Now, let me get the material to the laboratory."

"How long will it take?" Horstmann asked.

"Enjoy yourself in Recife for a few days. I'll call you at the Pernambuco Hotel when I'm ready. We have to put the mechanism together and get the deuterium and tritium into position with the fission trigger. Then we'll load the finished devices into 8-inch artillery shells. When they're ready, the charter plane will land here and you can take off for Al Rashon." Vogel paused. "I think you'll get a proper hero's welcome."

Horstmann allowed himself a beerhall laugh.

"I expect I will, *mein Herr*. I expect I will."

9

HAWLEY Briggs shifted uneasily in the large leather Presidential chair. He sometimes found it too enveloping, even suffocating. Only by restlessly moving about could he deal with the pressures of office.

He had one such pressure drilling into his head right now. On the surface, it was an aviation catastrophe, but it had more troublesome implications. The nation was mourning, he hoped prematurely, the disappearance of a DC-9 charter carrying boys' and girls' basketball teams to an international high school competition. The flower of American youth had been lost, perhaps even killed, somewhere over Northern Africa. If they landed safely in the desert, could they survive? No radio message of any kind had been forthcoming.

There was little he could do except what he had already done—issue orders to the Sixth Fleet in the Mediterranean to search for a downed passenger plane. He had also called each leader of the North African countries to do the same over their land mass. But so far, no word from anyone.

"Mr. President, there's an urgent call from North Africa, from an official in Al Rashon." Les Fanning, his energetic executive assistant, had walked unannounced into the Oval Office. "I told him to call State but he insists on talking personally to you. Says it involves the missing DC-9."

Briggs's fingers eagerly grasped the phone.

"Yes, this is Briggs. Who is this?"

"My name is Abdul Tenasha. I am a counselor to our great leader, Mussad. I have news of your missing teenagers."

"Yes, please tell me." The anxiety showed in Briggs's tone.

"Don't worry, Mr. President. They're safe. The plane had mechanical trouble—hydraulics, I believe—and landed at our modern airport outside Al Rashon."

"Good, Mr. Tenasha." Relief surged through him. "Thanks for calling. I'll dispatch a C-5A from Spain and we'll pick them up—this very evening. Can you arrange everything?"

The pause was long enough to strike Briggs as ominous.

"Can you hear me, Mr. Tenasha? Again, thank you. Will those arrangements be OK?"

"Not exactly."

"What does that mean?"

"Mr. President, it means that your teenagers will not be available to leave. At least not just yet."

"Why is that? They're all American citizens traveling on legitimate passports. We're assuming the cost of picking them up."

Again a silence, punctuated by coughs.

"We understand your concern for your citizens, but we have our concerns as well, Mr. President. You see, we believe the plane was actually on a spy mission—aerial reconnaissance of the patriotic rebel armies moving southward into the Sahara. Their film was probably jettisoned into the desert when they realized they had mechanical trouble.

So, you realize we can't release them just yet."

"Well, when the hell can you release them?" Briggs shouted.

"Shortly, Mr. President, immediately after payment of reparations for spying over our air space."

"What? Goddam you, there was no spying. And remember who you're talking to. I warn you. You better get those kids ready for our plane to pick them up. And I mean now." He sensed his blood pressure threatening.

Again, a short silence. "Please, do not anger yourself, Mr. President. As soon as the payment is made, they will be released. We'd prefer not to harm your handsome American youngsters, especially the young ladies."

"That's outright ransom, Tenasha. We stopped paying tribute to Barbary Coast pirates in the days of Jefferson."

"Yes, Mr. President, but that was before sensibilities were so strong. We wouldn't want your youngsters to die because of your stubbornness."

Briggs tried to talk himself down. You can't deal with this in anger. Think slowly, speak deliberately.

"All right, Tenasha. How much ransom do you want? Not that I intend to pay you bastards a nickel, but I'd like to know your ante anyway."

"Much more sensible, Mr. President. All we're asking is twenty F-22 fighters, that magnificent piece of American technology. Failing that, ten billion dollars in cash— no excuse me—in gold. We wouldn't want bank deposits that could be foiled. You have twenty-four hours before we act."

With that, the phone went dead.

"You son-of-a-bitch!" Briggs screamed into the isolation of the Oval Office, then grasped at his heart.

— 10 —

GENERAL Dmitri Barenchenko stared out the window of his seventh floor executive suite in a suburb cut out of the far Moscow woods. Once a village of small *izbi*, log cabins, it was now home to Moscow white-collar workers crowded into concrete apartment blocks. But the MVD headquarters was still surrounded by pine and birch forests, and as he focused on that typical Russian landscape, he thought of the once powerful Soviet Union he had once known, and swore he would again recognize.

As Deputy Director of the MVD, he had helped preside over the dismemberment of the Eastern European empire, then of the USSR itself. He regretted it, but of course no one cared about his complaints. They were all disregarded by the Presidium as the niggling of bureaucrats unable to understand the strategies required in a more modern world.

Maybe so. But now he had his own strategies for Russia, strategies for which the fax in his hand spelled out a disturbing obstacle. It was from Vlasov, the fanatic Inspector General at Science City—Akademgorodok—in the Urals.

Vlasov had sent him this cryptic message: SUSPECT DISAPPEARANCE OF HYDROGEN ISOTOPE TRITIUM AND NUCLEAR TRIGGERS FROM FUSION LAB IN AKADEMGORODOK. SUGGEST SECURITY OFFICERS ON SCENE BE REPLACED.

He had never liked Vlasov. Now he knew why. Everything had been going well for months, and a mere colonel threatened to undo it. As chief of the Russian arm of Red Swastika, he, Barenchenko, had carefully developed a group of patriotic sympathizers in Science City, men disgusted with the breakup of the Soviet Union, who had cooperated in isolating and delivering the neutron bomb components for reshipment to Recife. Every aspect of the scheme had worked smoothly, from the physicists in the lab, to the pilots who flew the material out of the country. Packed as "machine parts," they were shipped from Akademgorodok to the Caucasus in an Aeroflot cargo plane, then transshipped to Recife, Brazil, hidden in barrels of "cheese." A dozen such shipments had already been made, undetected.

Now Vlasov threatened all. Barenchenko wrote out a message by hand and faxed it back to the Inspector General in Science City:

GOOD WORK. WILL JOIN YOU IN HANDLING INVESTIGATION. ON MY WAY FROM MOSCOW.

"General Barenchenko. I'm honored that you've taken the case under your wing."

Inspector General Arkady Vlasov had met the plane at the military airport, where he picked up the MVD chief and his aide in a black Chaika. "I fear there's a dangerous discrepancy in the inventory of heavy hydrogens in the physics laboratory. Probably a theft, by some insiders, in exchange for hard currency," he told Barenchenko. "But now that you're here, I feel we have an opportunity to . . ."

"Good, good, Vlasov," Barenchenko interrupted him. "And I want you to meet my aide, Captain Kochev. He'll be coming with us. Let's go directly to the facility so we can get started." Barenchenko smiled solicitously. "By the way, Vlasov, I feel muscle-bound after the long flight from

Moscow. Do you mind if I drive? My aide can ride in the back. You can sit up front with me."

The trio, with Barenchenko himself at the wheel of the Chaika, left the airport and took the four-lane highway toward the main research center, a city that once employed upward of 25,000 scientists, from metallurgists to nuclear physicists, but was now being decimated by the Moscow authorities.

"Well, Vlasov, what do you think of the new German–Russian accord?" Barenchenko suddenly asked.

Vlasov seemed surprised by the question. "Why, General, I wouldn't know. These are decisions best left to the Kremlin."

"Surely. I understand. But don't you think that together, and once there are strong governments again in both countries, we can regain some of the power that has been drained from us by the arrogant Americans?"

Vlasov hesitated. Barenchenko sensed the IG had become uncomfortable with the conversation. "Again, General, I am just an overpaid inspector doing my job. But what you say surely makes sense. Although, I repeat, I am only doing my job—which is to track down some missing fusion components. Quite dangerous in the wrong hands."

Silence followed the short exchange, until about halfway to their destination, Barenchenko suddenly swerved the car off the road onto the rough, unpaved shoulder.

"What's wrong, General? Any problem?" Vlasov asked.

"I'm afraid there might be." Barenchenko stopped the Chaika and opened the driver's door. "The car's handling badly. We might have the beginnings of a flat. I'll take a look."

Slowly, Barenchenko circled the car. He kicked at the tires, while Vlasov sat idly, waiting for the journey to resume.

Had Vlasov been more alert, he might have seen the

aide, Captain Kochev, remove a steel wire garotte, about 2 mm in thickness, from his jacket pocket. Slowly, the wire peeked over the seat behind the Inspector General, poised over his head.

In one swift, energetic move, Kochev looped the wire over Vlasov's Adam's apple and gave it a fierce, definitive tug.

The victim's cries came out as choked, muffled whimpers, Vlasov managing only a short gasp before his face turned into a bluish, lifeless mask.

— 11 —

"ALL right, boys on this side of the barracks. Girls on the other," a walnut-skinned, mustached lieutenant in desert fatigues shouted in English.

Borden scanned the bare room, filled only with bunk beds. With the Lieutenant, whose name was apparently Hakim, were a half dozen soldiers carrying AK-47s. Watching silently at the edge of the scene, almost as a spectator, was a European in civilian clothes whom Borden had heard speak in German-accented English. A giant of a man.

"We don't want you to be bored, so we've prepared a little show—which you'll see later on tape," said the North African officer, his voice oozing with false pleasantness. "You three, follow me," he ordered, pointing at Borden and the two pilots, "and you, pretty one." He gestured toward Lonnie Taylor, the captain of the girls' basketball team. "You're part of this play, too."

"Hold off," Borden protested. "We'll go with you, whatever the hell you're planning, but leave her alone."

The butt of a gun glanced across Borden's chin, scraping the skin.

"Just a warning, basketball coach. No more noise, please."

Borden rubbed his shirtsleeve across the bloodied area.

"What's this all about? We're American citizens and we demand to speak to our embassy. If not, we'll hold you all responsible on criminal charges."

"Heroic speech, coach, but your President knows all about it. You're safe for now, but it's up to him if you live or die."

Hakim grinned at Lonnie. "Don't worry, young lady, you won't be killed. You'll just provide us with some entertainment—and show the American people that we're serious."

Two soldiers approached Lonnie, reaching for her arms. She pressed them away. "I can walk by myself."

Four of Mussad's men, one carrying a small black case, took up the rear as Borden, the two DC-9 pilots and Lonnie were led into a bunkerlike room in the rear of the airport terminal. The space was sparsely furnished, with only a metal desk, a chair and some files.

"All of you, against that wall. You—Lonnie, isn't it—at the opposite wall. Quick!"

Borden focused on Lonnie as she slowly complied, impressed with her demeanor but frustrated by his own impotence.

"All right, young woman, take off all your clothes and throw them on that chair."

"What do you mean? In front of all these men?" Lonnie's coolness cracked. "Are you crazy, or some kind of sex maniac?" she shouted, her thin voice finding its timbre.

"Neither, pretty American. We know what we're doing. Take off your clothes or I'll personally shoot you. Right now."

Borden started forward but his way was blocked by a soldier's rifle barrel pressed against his chest.

"Don't play hero," Hakim warned.

Between soft, accelerating sobs, Lonnie disrobed. First her prim white blouse and blue denim skirt, then her shoes. Standing in her underclothes, she shook with embarrassment.

"OK, satisfied now?" she asked.

"No. I said all your clothes. I want you naked. As God made you."

Borden lurched forward, but the gun barrel dug deeper. He tried to look away, but as Lonnie took off her pants and bra, he was drawn to the sight, angered at himself and at the lecherous merriment of Mussad's soldiers.

Lonnie stood nude, desperately trying to cover herself, one hand over her genitals, the other arm unsuccessfully seeking to mask her full breasts. The fifth soldier opened his black case and aimed a camcorder at Lonnie, the soft whir proof that her nakedness was being transferred to video.

"All right, men, take her," Hakim called.

Two soldiers rushed Lonnie and dragged her to a desk, her screams ricocheting off the tight walls. One soldier reached behind and pinned her arms while the other spread-eagled her legs. Lonnie's cries reached a crescendo, then descended into desperate whimpers, her sobs punctuated by an occasional scream.

"HELP ME! HELP ME!"

Borden had momentarily frozen. "YOU BASTARDS!" he suddenly shouted, pushing the soldier's gun from his chest. Arms outstretched, he leapt toward the Lieutenant's throat.

Hakim retreated a step and pulled a Mauser from his belt. He shifted his body and fired. As the bullet entered Borden's right temple, he fell without a sound, his head exploded by the 7.65.

The Lieutenant waved the pistol in the air in the direction of the pilots, one of whom had vomited onto the floor. "Interfere and you'll get the same."

Hakim swiveled toward one of his men, really a boy of about seventeen. "You're perfect. She's just your age. Go ahead, rape her."

The young soldier stared at his officer, his expression incredulous.

"I said, rape her. Or do you want your brains on the floor too?"

Lonnie's sobs were now unrestrained, hysterically soft and whimpering, like the thrum of a wounded bird. As the young soldier took off his pants and approached, she suddenly shifted rhythm and let out a long, unpunctuated wail of pain. The released energy gave her body the power for one enormous lurch. Lonnie broke the grasp of all four hands holding her, then kicked out at the soldier pinning her legs. He took the blow in the chest, falling to the ground, gasping.

Hakim swooped onto Lonnie, forcing her back down onto the desk. Leaning over the quivering girl, the Lieutenant slapped her face, first on one side, then the other.

"No more of this nonsense, do you hear?" He turned to the young soldier, whose expression showed fear instead of pleasure. "I said rape her."

The soldier hesitated for an instant, then obediently pressed himself on top of Lonnie, who was now semi-conscious, her sobs quieter and irregular. The soldier entered and worked his pleasure, only calling out with exhilaration at the climax.

Finished, he dressed and sulked back to his position, his eyes averted from Lonnie, who had mercifully passed out.

The camcorder, which had been whirring through the incident, stopped.

"OK. Take the videotape to headquarters," Hakim ordered. "Have them make a half dozen copies. And tell them to be careful."

He turned to Lonnie, lying prone, her legs still spread, her eyes vacant.

"OK, young woman, you can get dressed. You've done your job."

Lonnie seemed spent, as if in a coma. The Lieutenant approached and felt her pulse. "She's alive," he announced, turning again to the soldier who had assaulted her. "Call the doctor, then help her get dressed."

With that he waved his gun, leading the American pilots, stunned witnesses to the barbarity, out of the room.

— 12 —

THE rendezvous with Mike Bellamy was for Friday at 8:45 P.M., at the shopping center in Gaithersburg, Maryland, Davidson was sure.

Near midnight the night before, Mike had flashed his car lights outside the Leesburg house. The signal had been picked up by a reflector mirror on the second floor and converted to a coded buzz which sounded in Davidson's study. If the old spy wasn't home, it left a telltale beep on his answering machine.

Davidson drove northward toward Maryland that Friday, arriving a few minutes late. He was met by Bellamy, sitting in a red sportscar parked in front of the brightly lit supermarket. Davidson taxied his dented Volvo alongside the new vehicle, back to front, so that the two men could talk through the opened drivers' side windows.

"What's up, Mike?" Davidson asked as matrons with children pushed their grocery carts in front of them. "You woke me with your signal so I guess you've got something worthwhile."

"I've got more than something, Baptist. We've hit the intelligence jackpot." Mike paused, Davidson thought for effect.

"What's that?"

"One of our people, an MIT-trained Brazilian named Alberto Marcolas, is working with the Cotrell people in Recife. He says that they've just gotten in some frightening stuff—deuterium and tritium. He doesn't know from where or for what, but it sounds scary to me, Baptist. What do you think?"

Davidson's thoughts came in a rush. Deuterium and tritium were both heavy isotopes of hydrogen. Deuterium, which is produced from the electrolysis of heavy water, had twice the mass of simple hydrogen; tritium, an expensive man-made radioactive element, was three times as heavy. But both were still among the lightest of elements, and ideal for fusion. My God, the components of an H-Bomb. Could the Brazilians be making one, and for whom? He turned it over rapidly in his mind, then backtracked. No, not even Heinschmann had that capability.

In a rapid reevaluation, he mentally shifted back to an

old friend, Sam Cohen, then of the Rand Corporation. In the days of the first Cold War, Cohen had come up with a simple but devastating weapons concept—an "Enhanced Radiation Device." In journalistic jargon, it had been named the Neutron or "N"-Bomb. For a quarter of a century, Sam had pushed his idea in the halls of the Pentagon, promoting it with words and charts before endless committees. It was the most efficient of all nuclear devices, Cohen insisted, but his theories fell on inattentive ears.

When deuterium and tritium are put in a container under pressure, then placed in the head of an eight-inch artillery shell, or a missile, along with a small fission device, and exploded, fusion of the heavy hydrogens takes place. The result is the spread of deadly high-speed radioactive neutrons over an area of up to a half mile. No enormous explosion takes place and little property is destroyed, but the radiation first paralyzes, then kills, everyone in its path. Silent death.

Most important, it is a relatively "clean" weapon. Unlike an atomic bomb, there is no significant fall-out and troops can safely take the ground within a matter of hours. The N-Bomb, Davidson speculated, was the ideal weapon against troops in the North African topography.

Sam Cohen had fought his valiant, if losing, battle with the Pentagon until Reagan entered the White House. One of the new President's first decisions in 1981 was to order full-scale production of the N-Bomb. Hundreds were quickly prepared as artillery shells and heads for short-range Lance missiles.

Now, Davidson was sure that Cotrell was doing the same, with the help of a supplier of fusion material. But who? And for whom?

"What do we know about Cotrell?" Davidson asked.

"They're big, but not that big." Bellamy paused. "Marcolas

didn't say anything about it, but we've had other reports that Cotrell has been working with a giant German firm, Heinschmann, out of Dusseldorf, on some projects. We don't know which."

"Isn't Heinschmann the company that's building a nuclear reactor for Mussad in Al Rashon?" Davidson asked.

"That's right, John."

The pieces had rough edges, but they seemed to shape a pattern. Cotrell, Heinschmann, N-Bomb, and perhaps Mussad. If so, Davidson asked himself again, who was supplying the isotopes and the triggers? And why?

One part of the pattern was petrifying. "If Mussad's getting neutron devices from these people," Davidson said, "it's potential horror for all of North and Central Africa. Maybe even much more."

"Mike, keep your ears open at your German desk and let me know anything quickest," the Baptist added. Tipping his tweed driving cap in salute, he put the creaky Volvo into reverse and pulled out into the suburban darkness.

— 13 —

"LUNDESBERG, this is Koller."

The phone had just rung in the BND *Ganzfakt* office at Spandau Citadel in Berlin. The operation was now headed by Colonel Karl Lundesberg, replacement for Helmut Dieter, who had died in a freak accident by falling off a lake steamer in a dense fog, the German government had announced.

"Do you have the material the Americans wanted on Mussad's lieutenants?" Koller asked.

"Yes, Herr Koller. It's all been arranged. I did the work myself. No one at Spandau knows of the scrambling."

"Good, Lundesberg. Get the files to Ben Latham, the American Chief-of-Station, their supposed Cultural Attaché. That should get it quickly inserted into their intelligence channels and back to Washington."

"I'm sure it will. It'll also keep them confused."

"Keep up your work, Lundesberg," Koller stroked him. "The Fourth Reich will be your reward."

— 14 —

"WELL, Horstmann, I'm happy to see that you Germans are not just boastful beer swillers. You've come through with your promises, even if your price is exorbitant. Might I even say it's ransom." Mussad laughed. In his long red cape with flowing red and white dotted *kaffiyeh* head cover, he sat in an open armored Mercedes command car, adapted for desert travel, his eyes shielded by dark sun goggles, his face a beacon of pride. "Come on, Colonel, get in and we'll drive out to see our handiwork."

Wolf Horstmann, a former Colonel in the East German Stasi secret police who had defected to Al Rashon during the "velvet revolution" that overthrew the Communist government in 1989, lifted his 270 pounds almost gracefully into the six-seater vehicle. Ahead, he could see the outlines of what looked like army barracks, a compound in the middle of the desert, surrounded by a dozen motionless tanks.

He, Mussad, and four aides bumped over the dunes under a merciless sun, high and hot over them at noon. As they approached the compound, the stillness struck Horstmann as peculiar. Mussad had refused to tell him the reason for the desert trip.

"You'll be pleasantly surprised, Colonel," was all Mussad had said.

As they approached closer to the compound, Mussad ordered the car stopped. One of the aides, carrying a Geiger counter, leapt out and waved the wand over the surface, moving quickly from one area to another.

"The ground is clear," he called. "The radiation is higher than normal, but nothing of danger. We can go ahead."

The Mercedes moved forward, halting in front of the gate to the compound. Not a soul was visible. The tanks were immobile. At first, Horstmann thought they might be plastic decoys, but as they closed in, he could make out the metal reflecting the sun.

Mussad got out of the Mercedes, motioning for Horstmann and the others to follow. In the stillness, the procession walked through the gates of the compound and into one of the wooden barracks. Some forty beds were occupied, but all the men seemed to be asleep.

An officer carrying a stethoscope, obviously a physician, walked ahead and examined a half dozen men. He listened to their hearts, felt the nodes of their neck, probed their eyes with a light.

"They're all dead, Commander," the physician announced. "The death is by radiation poisoning, as we expected. Their bone marrow has been decimated."

Satisfaction covered Mussad's face. "Excellent. Now we'll check the tanks."

The entourage crossed the sandy barrier outside the barracks, and moved toward the tanks, whose gun turrets were aimed haphazardly across the desert. The hot hatches were soon opened. Inside each tank, three bodies were counted, piled one on top of another, caught in the futile scramble to escape the metal trap.

"They're all dead as well," the doctor reported.

Mussad motioned to Horstmann, and the two walked off alone into the desert.

"You've surely guessed the method," Mussad explained. "We tested just two of your neutron artillery shells with one hundred percent effectiveness. The subjects were my political prisoners—seventy-six of them to be exact. As you saw, most died in the barracks, but three dozen were put into these engineless tanks to see if the radiation would penetrate. It has."

Jubilantly, Mussad kicked the tread of the tank. "Colonel, I want hundreds of these neutron shells. For that, I'm relying on you and Red Swastika. Money's no object. I have all you need to keep the assembly line going."

Mussad's sharp features broke into a satisfied smile as once more he jubilantly kicked the tank tread.

From the desert death compound, Mussad drove Horstmann to another outpost, this one much closer to the city of Al Rashon, his command headquarters.

"Come, Horstmann, now we'll see the magnificent construction work done by your people in Heinschmann. Not even the American Bechtel could have mastered such a job."

Again, they left the Mercedes. Horstmann followed behind Mussad as he walked a hundred feet, then halted. Mussad was standing, it seemed, on desert sand.

"But there's nothing here," the German giant complained.

"Exactly what the Americans will see from their spy satellites or from their RS-71 high-altitude reconnaissance planes," Mussad assured him. "Now, come with me. You'll see what no one except the Heinschmann engineers and my own workers have seen."

Horstmann followed as Mussad walked ahead another hundred feet, then waved his hand in an exaggerated sweep, like a biblical prophet preparing a miracle. Horstmann watched as the desert floor, actually the base of a slow-moving elevator platform, started to descend. He quickly leapt on alongside and the two men traveled down together—Horstmann estimated some 150 feet—until the lift came to a halt and the desert-level door above them closed shut.

"This is the last stop, Horstmann. Come, I'll give you the nickel tour, as the Americans say."

They entered the complex through enormous lead-shielded doors, then traversed steel-shored-up tunnels, bridging off in every direction, leading to first one, then a second large open area.

"We're safe in here against any American air raid, smart or dumb bombs," Mussad explained. "There are three levels, each fifty feet deep, with twenty-five feet of concrete and cross-webbed steel between each level. Heinschmann has designed these bunkers so that any bomb in the American arsenal will die, inert or exploded, in the first layer. Should a bomb penetrate one layer by freak accident and disintegrate a portion of the ceiling, the second layer can hold all the debris of the first layer without collapsing."

Horstmann obediently followed Mussad, who smiled confidently as he continued his peripatetic tour. "In here," he motioned toward the largest of the rooms, perhaps two hundred feet square, "we will store your neutron bombs. Being at the bottom level, it can withstand even an atomic blast, the Heinschmann people tell me. The other rooms will be for housing, for a hospital, for utilities, food and water storage. In all, we can hold two thousand five hundred people here for a year."

Horstmann was impressed. Though German, he had spent most of his years in the Communist eastern sector and was not used to the sophistication of modern German engineering.

"Excellent," he muttered. "But I have a question. What about getting the neutron bombs to the surface in case of an attack?"

"Good thinking, Horstmann. I put that same question to your people. Hans Kreiger, the head of Heinschmann's Brazilian operation, came up with the answer. If all six lifts around the perimeter are put out of commission, we can transport the neutron devices on gas-turbine cars that travel through four radiating steel-supported tunnels. They'll reach the surface about five hundred feet from the bunker."

Mussad grabbed Horstmann by the shoulder with exaggerated warmth.

"You Germans are the wild card in the American plan to run this planet, Horstmann. They play good poker, but I think that by making your own moves—and taking in billions of Deutschemarks along the way—you could eventually become the dealer. I'm counting on people like you and Heinschmann to gain power in Berlin. Soon, I hope."

The North African motioned Horstmann to follow him toward an exit lift.

"And," he added as they rose toward the desert surface, "we won't mind sharing the pot."

15

IN Leesburg, Davidson waited patiently for another signal from Bellamy.

In the interim, he had been studying, probing, sifting through what he knew—and didn't know—to shape an evaluation for the President. Davidson had been summoned to a strategy meeting at the Oval Office the following morning.

He was almost sure the Germans were the key to this maze of information and disinformation. Red Swastika seemed involved and he had taken the measure of their dimensions. Formed in 1990 from the coalition of two German right wing groups—one a fraternal order of former SS troops—it had no open political face. At least not yet. But he had learned that in the next national elections, it was fielding a slate of candidates for the sixteen State elections and the national Bundestag under the banner of "The Fourth Reich."

Their strength was in their anti-Americanism, which had always had a core following in Germany. Now, as the Pax Americana advanced, so did the German "anti-Ami" movement.

Paradoxically, Davidson thought, it was the success of NATO and the American presence in Germany for so many years that had fed these nationalist, pro-Nazi sympathies. When America seemed essential to their security, the GIs were, in the main, admired. Now that Germany had joined with Russia in a mutual security and economic pact, America was considered less important—off on its own tangents, as in the Middle East and Asia. Trying, for example, to keep the Philippines from being swallowed up by a Communist revolution.

Davidson admired the Germans and had worked with them in Berlin after World War II. But he had never fully trusted them. Basically an intelligent and amazingly energetic people, they were also too often selfish and insensitive, he was convinced. After having spent a century trying to conquer first Europe, then the world, they had given up military ambition. As a substitute, contemporary Germans were concentrating on money and influence in Eastern Europe and the Third World, a more subtle form of colonization. Red Swastika was less subtle, hoping to augment that new ambition by expanding politically as well.

Davidson had read both the CIA and the BND reports and knew that Germany had been the silent villain of the Iraqi war, having provided that country with chemical, biological and nuclear war material. The Simon Wiesenthal organization had traced Iraqi chemical gas equipment to over 100 firms in Germany. Even the gas centrifuges for the separation of common Uranium into fissionable U-235 for nuclear weapons were of German origin, as was the hardware and knowledge to expand the range of the Iraqi Scuds, making it possible for them to attack Israel.

The Baptist recalled German Foreign Minister Genscher being shown German markings on Scud debris in Tel Aviv by the Israeli Prime Minister. Even after the embargo, he had learned that twenty German firms continued to resupply Saddam Hussein, but that the damaging information was mainly buried by the American media.

Now, Davidson feared, Heinschmann was working with Cotrell in Brazil to shape a more awesome danger—neutron bombs for the terrorist leader Mussad. He still didn't know who was supplying the triggers and the heavy hydrogen isotopes, especially the radioactive tritium, which could only be produced in a weapons-grade nuclear reactor that normally manufactures plutonium. But he assumed the source was tied to Red Swastika.

The Baptist didn't have to wait long for Mike's signal. The coded, flashing SOS went off while he was at home. Coming prior to six P.M. meant that the meeting was for that evening, this time—he was almost sure—at the movie house in Bethesda.

Davidson drove to the Maryland suburb just on the Washington border, and made the rendezvous, as arranged, on the ticket line. After purchasing the tickets, the two men walked through the parking lot.

"I think I've got something important, John," Bellamy began, the optimism in his eyes visible under the overhead lights. "These files just came in from Ben Latham in Berlin. It's the stuff on the twenty top lieutenants around Mussad. *Ganzfakt* has done a good job. I made a set for you."

Davidson thumbed through the file, halting at one face he recognized.

"Mike, this isn't a Mussad man. This is Izzat Habash, a PLO chief now in Tunis." He rifled quickly through the others. "Yes, and here's Ali Yashir. He's a PLO assassin. The last I heard he was in hiding in Algeria."

Davidson handed the files back to Bellamy. "Mike, this is a fake. Not Mussad's inner circle at all. Someone in BND has padded it with phony profiles. Why, I don't know, but tell Ben to take it back to the BND people in Berlin and raise holy hell."

"Are you sure, Baptist? I hate to embarrass Latham."

Davidson gave Bellamy's shoulder a fatherly hug. "I wouldn't risk my pension on it, Mike, but my smeller tells me it's a plant. If I'm right, it'll tell us if any of the BND people are working for Red Swastika. Give it a college try. OK?"

—— 16 ——

"MY God! Take a look at this videotape. It just came in from Al Rashon."

Mel Shaver, program manager of Central News Service, a Washington-based cable network, waved to his colleagues in the control booth. He had already viewed the first moments of the videotape, then rewound the footage to start it over.

"Look, there's the whole group of teenagers in one of Mussad's barracks," Shaver called out in an agitated, yet excited, voice. "What in the hell is going on?"

They watched transfixed as the tape showed a young Mussad officer and a handful of his troops leading three adult male hostages and a pretty female teenager out of the barracks into a bunkerlike room.

Curiosity shifted to unease as the young woman was forced to disrobe, then to horror as the basketball coach, futilely trying to protect his charge, was shot through the skull. The video camera panned in, focusing on the exploded brain.

"Oh, that bastard," Shaver wailed. Several viewers started to weep quietly, but as the rape began and the sexual terror went on for minutes, the atmosphere in the room changed to a drugged silence.

"Stop the tape!" one woman finally shouted. "I can't take any more!"

Shaver motioned for quiet, determined to run the video's full course. The instant it was over, he was on the phone to the four networks, insisting he'd speak only to the news presidents. One at a time they came to the phone. Yes, they told Shaver, they had received the same tape and viewed it all.

"What the hell are we going to do?" Shaver, still unsteady, asked. "What's our responsibility as a prime media for the public? Can we show the damn thing? Is it obscenity and violence or is it essential news?"

Back and forth, Shaver and the others, now connected in a conference call, debated the point. One network chief insisted he would air the whole thing, if only to prove Mussad's madness. The three others weren't so sure.

"Isn't this a matter of national policy? Doesn't that transcend our own role as news people?" Shaver asked. "I think we should show it to the President first. Not that we have to listen to what he says, but we don't want to start a war just because we're trying to do our job." Shaver paused. "What do you think of that?"

"As long as we agree that the White House is not the final voice on this," said Al Barney, the network chief who had wanted an instant showing. "I suppose a few days' delay won't make any difference."

"Good, then we're agreed." Shaver's voice deadened. "I'll call the President and make the arrangements."

—— 17 ——

BEN Latham was curious why Colonel Lundesberg had insisted that he come personally to Spandau if he wanted the corrected files.

He had relayed Bellamy's message to the BND, complaining loudly that a mistake had been made with the Mussad dossiers. Apparently, Palestinian terrorists had been substituted for Mussad's own men.

This morning, Latham had heard back from Spandau at the American Embassy on Friedrichstrasse in Berlin. No, they couldn't trust such important files to a messenger, either American or even someone from their own HQ.

Actually, Latham didn't mind the visit. Now that Lundesberg had replaced Dieter as head of *Ganzfakt*, he needed to maintain contact with the BND people. Dieter had been very cooperative, but he had died suddenly on the lake boat, they said. Latham tended not to believe handouts, German or otherwise, but this seemed innocent enough. Why would anyone want to kill a *Ganzfakt* chief?

Bellamy had told him of Davidson's suspicions regarding Red Swastika. He had never met Davidson, but had heard he was a compulsively suspicious man. He would meet Lundesberg and judge for himself. Though he had heard scuttlebutt about the pro-Nazi Red Swastika organization, and had passed the rumors on to Bellamy at Langley, he had never seen tangible evidence of its existence.

The old brick of Spandau Citadel loomed as he sought out an easy parking spot on Schönwalder Strasse for his government-issue Ford Escort. Though officially a member of the State Department, Latham assumed that the BND, and most diplomats in Berlin, knew he was Agency.

Tall, Ivy-looking, Latham enjoyed his job. Not quite out of thrillers, it still satisfied his sense of adventure.

In Spandau's reception area, he showed his diplomatic passport to the guard, who directed him to Lundesberg's office on the third floor, overlooking Lake Havel. Latham had barely come out of the elevator when a man with a small beer belly and a broad, if-not-convincing, grin almost bumped into him.

"Ben Latham, is it not?" the man asked in his casual Berlin diction. "I'm Colonel Lundesberg. It's always a pleasure to meet someone from . . . State. Come into my office and I'll show you the *Ganzfakt* operation. It's really the number one computer personnel system in the world."

Still chatting boastfully, the Colonel directed Latham to his office.

"Watch closely, Ben. I'll pull up your own computer chart."

Lundesberg entered Latham's name, adding the system password. In a moment, a 7,300-character profile, including graphics of Latham's face, his wife's, and their home in suburban Fairfax, Virginia, came up on the screen. "Good. *Recht*?" Lundesberg's tone was self-congratulatory.

Latham was surprised. "How in the hell did you learn my nickname at Yale was 'Digger'?"

Lundesberg laughed. "If you read on, you'll see we even have your sex life programmed. What was her name at the Agency? Yes, Atkinson. And while you were married."

Latham's chuckle was self-conscious. "Enough showing off, Colonel. Do you have the new Mussad files? I hope they're more accurate than the last ones."

"Oh, yes." Lundesberg warmly grasped Latham's forearm. "A *dummkopf* made a computer error in that first batch. Trust me. Langley will be pleased."

After a few personal asides, Latham said his goodbyes and exited Spandau, eager to get the material off to Langley by diplomatic pouch. A courier was leaving that afternoon by American Airlines. He checked his watch: he had less than an hour.

He moved out onto Schönwalder Strasse, walking briskly to his parked Ford. Once inside, he turned the ignition, then hesitated. Out of the driver's open side window he could see a short, burly man carrying a Meerschaum pipe approaching.

"*Bitte*," the man said. He stared at Latham's diplomatic plates, then quickly switched to English. "Sorry to bother you, but could I please have a match? Or better still, use your car cigarette lighter. My pipe is cold."

Latham stared up at the white-haired intruder, probably in his mid-fifties. He seemed innocent enough. Latham pressed in the car lighter. Once it had turned a bright orange, he lifted it through the open window toward the pipe smoker. The man leaned over and sucked on the Meerschaum until the elegantly carved bowl was aflame.

"Oh, *mein Gott*, forgive me," the man suddenly said, retracing a step. "I've dropped my pipe into your car! What an *eselkopf* I am!"

Latham reached down and bobbled the hot Meerschaum in his lap. He finally grasped it by the stem and was about to hand it to the smoker when he noticed that the man had turned and left the curb. He was not walking, but running, back toward Spandau.

Latham had just cracked open the car door to check out the strange incident, when he heard it. In a split instant of recognition, he was overwhelmed by the bellowing rumble of an explosion. Rapid and monumental. In seconds, the Ford was a mass of twisted metal. Latham had lost consciousness, his body and the dossier engulfed in flames.

Latham could no longer see him, or anyone, but a block away, the short man halted. He extracted another Meerschaum from his trenchcoat pocket and lit it with a match. Turning, he smiled at the raging fire and moved nonchalantly on.

— 18 —

DAVIDSON turned up the news on the car radio. The airwaves were buzzing with national anger over the hostages in Al Rashon. Mussad was demanding an enormous ransom, in armament or gold, for the return of the thirty teenagers.

Americans had almost become inured to hostage taking by Third World madmen, but this time teenagers, almost children, had been turned into political pawns and the country, en masse, was infuriated. A few were willing to pay the ransom, but most were demanding a strong response from Washington—bomb Mussad, or even go to war.

The hostages would surely be a topic at this morning's meeting at the White House. Davidson had organized as much as he knew. There were still holes in the intelligence picture, but he had developed some reasonable theories.

The Volvo drew up at the North West Gate of the White House on Pennsylvania Avenue, where he was stopped at the blockhouse by a uniformed policeman.

"Who shall I say is calling?"

"Davidson, John Davidson," the old spy answered, displaying his ID. "I'm expected."

The House policeman returned to his small shelter, where he used the phone, then searched through a file holding photos of everyone expected at the White House that morning. He lifted the barrier and waved Davidson on.

Ahead was the Executive West Wing, an appendage to the White House reached from the Mansion by way of a roofed, open portico. He parked and as he entered the wing, Davidson almost walked into the arms of raven-haired Les Fanning, efficient-looking in her jabot blouse and close-fitted sharkskin suit.

"The President is waiting, Mr. Davidson. Follow me."

From the door to the Oval Office, Davidson could see three men gathered in front of the fireplace. With the President was Senator Niles Chase, chairman of the Senate Select Committee on Intelligence, a lanky former rancher from Montana, and a noted dove. Alongside was House Majority Leader Happy Rider—short, slightly rotund fellow Arkansan and a dirt-kicking buddy of the President.

Briggs made introductions all around.

"Well, Baptist, what have you got to report? You can be candid here. It'll go no further than this room. That's right, isn't it, fellows?" When they nodded acknowledgment, Briggs motioned for Davidson to begin.

He unrolled two charts, placing them on an easel Fanning had set up in advance.

"First, as I'm sure you now know, Mr. President, the radiation detected over Al Rashon was caused by Mussad's first

'Enhanced Radiation Device,' a neutron bomb," Davidson began.

"How in the hell did you figure that, Baptist? All I told you was that radiation had been detected."

"It wasn't hard, Mr. President. Had it been an atomic bomb, the whole world would have detected the fall-out. And over the years, I've been talking about the N-Bomb with its inventor, Sam Cohen, who then worked for the Rand Corporation. It's the logical weapon for a non-tech country headed by an aggressive dictator like Mussad. I've also found some additional intelligence. Two foreign companies have been working together to make artillery shells loaded with the neutron devices for Mussad."

"What? I'll be damned," Happy Rider exclaimed, exaggerating his Arkansas drawl. "That's a serious charge, Mr. Davidson. Do you have any proof?"

"Yes, and who are these companies?" Chase of Montana chimed in, skeptically.

"One of them is the Brazilian conglomerate Cotrell, SA. They're running the Project out of a tropical clearing in Recife. But the other company is more important. They're the real brains of the operation. From what I've learned, their top scientists are involved."

"And who's that?" the President asked. His eyes reflected his growing concern.

"A German company called Heinschmann, the high-tech firm out of Dusseldorf."

"Germany? But Chancellor Bessinger's my good friend."

"That may be, Mr. President. But since our troops have almost all left Germany, they're developing a more independent foreign policy, one heavily based on friendship with—and economic exploitation of—Third World countries. I'm afraid they're going everywhere they can to make a buck, or a Deutschemark. Look at their treaty with Russia.

It's a virtual Marshall Plan with giant Russian markets in exchange. Maybe it wasn't meant to freeze us out, but it's doing that job anyway."

"Do you mean Heinschmann's actually building neutron weapons for Mussad?"

"It seems that way, Mr. President. They're bringing the deuterium and tritium into Brazil, plus small nuclear triggers, then assembling them into artillery shells and shipping them to Mussad. The work seems to involve a German right-wing, pro-Nazi group. It's called Red Swastika and it's tied to both Nazi sympathizers and Russian hardliners. Heinschmann's looking for bucks and Red Swastika is looking for political muscle in the Third World. They believe they'll eventually take over Germany, as Hitler did. They're trying to build ties for a future empire."

"They don't have any support in the German government—do they?" asked Majority Leader Rider, intrigued with the firsthand geopolitical briefing.

"Unfortunately, yes," Davidson answered somberly. "Some influential people in the federal government, even in the BND, are sympathizers, if not outright members. They've even started a pro-Nazi political party, the Fourth Reich, as a front group. They'll be running people in the next elections—for state parliaments and the national Bundestag."

Briggs listened intently, bringing the conversation back to Mussad.

"But where is Heinschmann getting the deuterium and tritium?" the President, obviously shocked, asked.

"The Germans can make the deuterium themselves from the electrolysis of heavy water. On the radioactive tritium and small nuclear triggers, I'm not sure, but I'm willing to speculate that they come from Russia. Hundreds of their top nuclear scientists have been fired. All the others are worried about their privileged positions. It makes sense to them to supply the Germans with thermonuclear material in exchange for hard currency. Mussad is their tool."

"What are you saying?" Senator Chase almost shrieked. "That the Russian government is cooperating with this madman in Al Rashon? I can't believe that."

Davidson answered, "No. But some important Russian scientists could be supplying it to Heinschmann. Then from there, to Cotrell in Brazil, then to Mussad."

Turning to his charts, Davidson outlined what he knew about the operation of Mussad's neutron artillery.

"Here, you can see how deuterium and tritium, two forms of heavy hydrogen, are put under great pressure and arranged in a container inside a 155 mm howitzer shell. When detonated with a small nuclear trigger, the light D-T, with atomic weights of only 2 and 3, enter into a fusion reaction, creating a heavier nuclei of harmless Helium and releasing an enormous amount of high-speed neutrons. In an atomic bomb, over eighty percent of the energy is expended in blast and heat. The physical destruction is enormous and the fallout is dirty and lingers, making the ground uninhabitable, as in Chernobyl. The same is true of an H-Bomb, like the one that contaminated the Bikini atoll. In the H-Bomb, fusion of the D-T takes place by using lithium deuteride. It's set off by a nuclear trigger, which creates the extremely hot fusion reaction. That in turn reacts with a large uranium outer shell, making another fission explosion. The whole thing has a horrendous fallout."

Davidson paused, staring at his audience of three to be sure they were absorbing it.

"But in the neutron bomb, which is really a small, controlled, relatively clean fusion device, the nuclei are forced together, not split as in an atomic bomb. Nor is there an outer uranium shell as in the H-Bomb. The result is an energy ratio that's the opposite of an A-Bomb. Here, only twenty percent of the energy goes into blast and heat, and eighty percent into straight, deadly 'clean' radiation. It's clean only because it kills, then dissipates with almost no fallout. It's the perfect mass destruction weapon against infantry and tanks in the field. There is a relatively small explosion and little property is destroyed. Silent death. The high-speed neutrons quickly penetrate iron and steel, paralyzing the tank crews in five minutes, and killing them not long after. A shelter of concrete covered with three feet of dirt would protect anyone in its path, so civilians can easily survive a neutron attack—if they prepare. But from a military point-of-view, the most important thing is that the ground is no longer radioactive after a short time. It can be reoccupied in a few days, sometimes within hours."

With diagrams, Davidson showed how the neutron bomb's effectiveness was based on how it was exploded. Impacting on the ground limited the dispersal of the neutrons. Exploding at very high altitudes dispersed the neutrons over a large area, but made the radiation insufficiently deadly to kill in any one spot. In the ideal scenario, the bomb exploded about 3,000 feet above ground with a proximity fuse, after which it spewed deadly neutrons out over a radius of four-tenths of a mile. The perfect compromise between dispersal and potency.

Davidson looked at the President, who was nodding his head in acknowledgment. But Chase, the dovish Intelligence Committee chair, still looked at Davidson skeptically.

"Very dramatic, Baptist—that is what they call you, isn't it? But are you sure of all this—that Mussad has or is getting neutron weapons? Or is this only a spook's version of history? People tell me you have a reputation as a great spy—in the old days. But weren't you retired from the Agency for excess paranoia?"

"Easy, Niles." The President tried to cool the charged atmosphere. "I can't go into some things for security reasons, but trust me. History has proven Davidson right more than once. And now—I can back his insight with some news. The National Security agency has just given me word that they've spotted a new radiation blast near Al Rashon. About twice as large as the first one."

Briggs turned toward Davidson, his voice plaintive.

"John, what are we going to do about this bastard Mussad? He's taken our kids as hostages, and now he's getting deadly neutron bombs from our supposed friends. He's threatening not only his Arab neighbors but the black countries to the south. All hell could break loose." The President paused. "How long before he'll have a full neutron arsenal?"

"Mr. President, I'd say that in two months he'll have a hundred neutron bombs, enough to do any dirty work he wants."

The President rose from his chair and silently circled the room, his head down. Then he halted, and spoke, his voice charged.

"But how can we stop him? Bombing his headquarters didn't help with Quaddafi, and Mussad's probably got his neutron bombs buried in deep bunkers. And this is no Iraq. There we defended a friend and liberated an invaded country. We had almost total world support. Now, we just don't have those conditions. Mussad's smart enough not to have invaded anybody. He's using surrogate rebel armies for that, like in the United Africa Republic. In any case, neither the nation nor the UN is in any mood for another full-scale war."

The President picked up his pacing. "And we'd need an amphibious operation if we were going in. That could be disastrous. We'd be facing his deeply-submerged 'influence' mines that explode just from the water pressure from a passing boat. It could blow our new Marine hovercraft landing ships to smithereens. Then, once we landed, we could be destroyed by his neutron artillery."

Briggs paused, scanning the historic room in frustration. "Gentlemen, what the hell do we do?"

"There's only one way, Mr. President."

"Yes, John. And what's that?"

"Assassinate Mussad."

"Assassination!" Senator Chase had levitated off his chair, his accusing finger in Davidson's face. "That's back to the jungle. Remember what happened to Kennedy? He used the Mafia to try to kill Castro, then got his instead. And so did his brother. Besides, it violates Executive Order 12333." Chase turned to Briggs. "You signed it yourself—right after you were inaugurated."

The Senator swiveled back toward Davidson. "Baptist, I'm convinced you're as mad as they say."

"Perhaps, Senator Chase. But no matter how you look at it, we have no alternative. As for Kennedy, he was infatuated with the Mafia—you remember they supplied him with his favorite girlfriend. Asking them to kill Castro was amateurish. They're only equipped for the murders of city punks, guarded by hoods. We're dealing with a national leader protected by an army of men. That requires a professional. Someone like Carlos on the other side, and one or two men who've worked for the West."

While Davidson and Chase clashed, Briggs resumed his pensive trail across the thick Oval Office carpet, halting at the head of the woven-in federal eagle.

"John, I think not," Briggs finally said, his head bobbing in quiet decision. "You make good arguments, but Chase is right. Assassination sets a bad precedent, and it's not my cup of tea. We'll have to find another way."

— 19 —

THE Oval Office was not a full house, but aide Les Fanning had moved around some chairs so that nine people could sit in full view of the thirty-six-inch VCR monitor.

She counted the guests as they arrived: Majority Leader Happy Rider; television network executives Shaver, Barney and two others; John Davidson; the President's press chief, Tim Calhoun; and herself.

"OK, I understand you've gotten me prepped for something horrible," the President said, opening the meeting. "Now let the videotape roll." Briggs took the center seat.

The networks had tried to maintain security, but Fanning had heard scuttlebutt in the White House press room that a female hostage had been abused. She gritted her teeth as the tape started to run. When Lonnie Taylor stripped in front of Mussad's soldiers, Les ran her hands tentatively over her own skirt, feeling naked. My God, what humiliation. She cast her eyes around the room to see the male reaction. Despite the horror of it, Les was afraid there was still some sexual titillation.

She let the thought pass. This was a political and human atrocity, not a question of obscenity. But why had Mussad's officer forced the pretty young woman to strip?

Les soon got her answer. A shot rang out on the tape as if it were ricocheting in the Oval Office itself. Fanning shouted "NO! NO!" She jumped out of her chair and raced toward the wall, her back to the monitor.

"OK! Shut the video for a minute," the President called. He approached Fanning's side. "Les, you heard what Mussad's man said. This murder will probably be followed by a rape. It pains us all, but I've got to see it no matter how objectionable. Would you rather leave—maybe see it some other time, without any men in the room?"

Fanning stared at her boss. "No, Mr. President. I'll see it through. If it helps any, Mussad's only building my resolve."

The screening of the rape continued, the cries of Lonnie Taylor haunting the room. The President suddenly rose. "OK, I've seen enough. Shut it off."

He paced around his desk, once, twice, while the others sat waiting. Suddenly, he swiveled toward John Davidson.

"Baptist, I think the nation has to see some of this. Do you agree?"

Davidson nodded. "Absolutely, Mr. President. Mussad condemns himself with this vicious propaganda."

The President nodded toward the expectant network news people.

"Gentlemen, it's not my decision. It's yours. But if you want any guidelines, I think the American people have to view this. Can you cut it to thirty seconds—keep out the worst, but show Borden being murdered and some suggestion of the rape? OK? I want the nation fully on my side when I take on that bastard Mussad."

20

WHEN the meeting with the television executives was over, President Briggs slumped down in a welcoming armchair near the fire and reflected.

His entire life had been annealed in the flames of politics. The battleground of his native Arkansas had burned up many less formidable men than he. Four times he had won the State house in Little Rock, and now he was President.

But no one, in or out of politics, could experience the test of soul that went with the Oval Office. Sitting silently, staring at Davidson, the only remaining guest, Briggs thought that not even the Baptist, friend and counselor of years, could know the drain on his emotions. Or, perhaps, with his gentle insight, he did know it. That was probably the reason he had avoided the political arena. Intelligence, espionage, deception, was war in a way. But in Davidson's chocolate-brown eyes he read that he enjoyed it. Perhaps it even had a more rational base than the vagaries of politics.

The Presidency often seemed like a perpetual war, against his opponents both at home and abroad. Too much, really, for any mortal.

Today he felt truly depleted. The rape of that young woman, the hostage-taking of thirty American teenagers, the ransom demands, Mussad's successful subversive expansion

into the black United African Republic by his puppet rebel
army—and surely more of that to come—had worn thin all
arguments of the National Security Council and its chief,
Otto Kempelmayer. Otto had smarts, but his recommendation of diplomacy, foreign pressures, patience, and resolve
now seemed shopworn.

The chairman of the Joint Chiefs, Marine General Tommy
"Thunder" McAlister, didn't advocate war against Mussad,
but said he was ready if the President ordered it. He did
mention, again, that this would have to be an amphibious
landing, with heavy casualties.

The President also knew, and Davidson had reminded him,
that American military intervention into supposed African
civil wars would be seen by the world not as a moral expedition, but as an evil caricature of the "New World Order."

"What to do?" the President asked himself.

"John, I asked you to stay because I want to hear your
arguments about, you know . . ."

"Assassination, Mr. President?"

"Yes, John. I even find it hard to say the word. But before
you begin, I have to tell you that I went to see my friend
Happy Rider on the Hill. He's a good politician, probably
better than me, and he's got a great smeller. Not just for
public opinion, but for the winds of intrigue in Congress.
In any case, Happy says that assassination is real dangerous
stuff politically. It plays into the fears about the Pax Americana, Big Brother image the world media is trying to wrap
around our neck. Too dangerous for the future, they say."

Briggs paused, staring down at the rug. "Happy also
reminds me that it violates Executive Order 12333—which
Ford, Carter, Reagan and Bush also signed. Happy's a pal
and he wouldn't back any impeachment. But he doesn't
speak for everyone. There are a lot of guys in the House
out to get me—just from the last picture."

"What about the Speaker, Rusty Kembeck?" Davidson asked.

"He's my real problem. Rusty's in line for the Presidency right after my VP, and he hates my guts. If I'm impeached and VP Morse gets the Presidency, then Congress—according to the 25th Amendment on succession—will surely elect Kembeck as VP. That'll put him in a solid position for the White House in the next election.

"Well, to be candid, John," the President continued, "I called Rusty in for a little schmooze yesterday. We talked about Mussad and the hostages and the whole North African geopolitical scene. When I told him one of my advisors—he knows it's you—hinted at assassination, he blew his top. Started to yell and carry on like the Dakota part-Indian he is. Says if I try anything like that, he'll see to it that I'm impeached. Swears he'll crucify me on a Congressional cross." The President stopped to catch his halting breath. "And I tell you, that son-of-a-bitch means it."

Davidson sensed silence was in order. He waited until the President regained his composure. Briggs was obviously distraught at the thought of impeachment.

"Well, John, after that little meeting, I pushed the idea of assassination out of my mind. Just dropped it cold. But today—well, after seeing that rape and killing—I realize I can't push any idea away. There are worse things than impeachment. One of them is seeing a madman with neutron bombs taking over a whole region of the world. So, tell me, Baptist, what do you *really* think I should do? I'm finally angry enough to hear your arguments."

Davidson spoke slowly, forming his words exactly. He wanted to feel no guilt if the worst actually took place.

"Hawley—Mr. President. I can't guarantee you anything on impeachment. Politics is a whirlwind. But that tape we saw is going to be played on national television tomorrow, and the nation will demand some kind of action—even war. But consider this. We didn't take the assassination option on Noriega, even though it was relatively easy. My people tell me President Bush considered it, but the powers on the Hill said 'no way,' just like they told you. Instead we invaded, spent hundreds of millions of dollars, lost thirty American boys and maybe killed three hundred Panamanians, civilians included, in the doing."

The Baptist slowed, to marshal his thoughts. "In Iraq, we faced an outright invasion. We had no choice but war. But with Mussad, we have a choice. Assassination is really the only intelligent solution."

The President listened, his face impassive, displaying no indication, one way or the other.

"John, what will happen even if we wipe out Mussad? Won't someone else just as bad take his place?"

"No, I don't think so. He's a charismatic, somewhat mad, one-man band. He has strong opponents in the country, and a dozen important opposition leaders exiled in nearby Arab countries. One is my friend Hassam Ali, the leader of the Democratic Forum, who's in Cairo. There's also someone right in Al Rashon, General Karadi, a Sandhurst-educated man and retired Commander of the Army. He's well liked by the military, and with a little help could pull off a coup— if Mussad is taken out."

The President started to respond, in a soft, almost inaudible tone, as if talking to himself. "John, do I really have the right to order the execution of any man? Even an evil enemy? I wasn't elected God, was I?"

"No, but the Chief Executive has the duty to protect the nation, come what may." Davidson's voice firmed. "That's the final moral choice."

Briggs rose and began his habitual trek across the thick rug. He stopped and turned.

"Yes, John, you make a good point, but I have to look at this personally as well. If I decide to go ahead as you ask, I could be impeached by the House, then tried in the Senate like a common criminal." Briggs's voice became even more reflective. "If I lose, I'd be the first President in history to be officially removed from office."

"That's true, Mr. President," Davidson said. "So what is your decision?"

There was no response. The President resumed his pacing, then halted, his eyes riveted on Davidson.

"Do it, John. Do it."

"Are you sure, Mr. President? There will be little chance to turn back."

"Yes, John, I'm sure. Do it."

BOOK
—2—

21

DAVIDSON left the Shuttle at LaGuardia Airport and in a rented Chevvie drove into New York City, then headed through the Lincoln Tunnel. He estimated the rest of the trip at ninety minutes. His destination: the small town of Lakewood in Ocean County, New Jersey, once noted for its chicken farms.

New Jersey. Davidson inhaled the air on the Turnpike, confirming what he already knew. At least on its New York fringes, it was the State of refineries and foul atmospheres, with one of the highest cancer rates in the nation. But the State had come a long way since its unpromising beginnings, he admitted.

When the Duke of York became King James II before the American Revolution, he sold the southern part of his New York domain—New Jersey—to two royal friends, Berkley and Carteret. After viewing their property, they returned to England and sold the colony off piecemeal, making a fortune in land speculation. By 1835, when Alexis de Tocqueville visited America in his historic journey, Jersey was already an East coast black sheep, slated to become the subject of bad jokes.

In his classic work, *Democracy in America,* de Tocqueville speaks of Jersey as an eyesore between orderly Pennsylvania and busy New York. But the proximity to New York City developed the State, bringing suburban growth and high taxes. Still, Davidson was skeptical. Hadn't de Tocqueville also said that American civilization halted at the banks of the Hudson?

In any case, he had a destiny date in New Jersey. He took the Turnpike to exit 11, Woodbridge, then picked up State Highway 9, driving west and exiting at Lakewood. His destination was not in town, but in the surrounding rural area. Not at one of its many chicken farms, but at an apiary, where bees were raised for honey and profit. And from what Davidson understood, the profit was good. His friend's honey was marketed only by direct mail through prestigious magazines, at about twice the normal price.

"The Beekeeper," as he was known in the Intelligence community, surely had a real name, but Davidson didn't know it. Nor did anyone else. It changed, from locale to locale. His last had been Marvin Goldschmidt, and his previous residence had been Martha's Vineyard. He regularly moved his operations center to new parts of the country, maintaining only one constant. He raised bees wherever he went. The new location, perhaps two years in use, had been given to Davidson by Proctor, a *nashi* in Agency personnel. Since the Beekeeper never owned a telephone, Davidson decided it was prudent to just drop in on the apiary.

"John the Baptist! I'll be a son-of-a-bitch," the Beekeeper called as Davidson alighted from his rented car on the driveway of the unassuming farmhouse. "It's been years—ever since they sanitized Langley. What's up?"

Davidson smiled. "What do I call you now?"

"Try Alex Knudsen. I like the Scandinavian ring of it. That's how my neighbors know me."

The Beekeeper, a short—perhaps five foot four—heavily balding man of slight frame, spoke in a high-pitched voice that came out slow and hesitant. Almost a stutter.

"Can we talk, Alex?"

"Sure, John, but first you have to see my operation. It's grown since you visited last. Where was that? Oh yes, in Minnesota. Then I was—yes—Giacone, Sal Giacone. I'm afraid I'm going to run out of ethnics. I'll have to become John Smith."

Davidson was given a netted hat and the two men toured the apiary, the Beekeeper providing a running commentary on the life of the species.

"Bees are much better organized than we humans, John," the Beekeeper explained as they walked. "Each one knows exactly what to do. They live by the Protestant work ethic, but there's no unemployment. And like us, they have a class system, but it's much stricter than ours."

Knudsen seemed to enjoy this chance to explain his vocation, which he obviously loved.

"The whole system is based on reproduction, like much of nature," the Beekeeper continued as their tour progressed. "There's only one Queen Bee in a hive and she sits at the top, gets all the glory and attention, lays all the eggs and produces all the offspring. She has an army of gigolos—hundreds of male drones whose only function in life is to screw her, fertilize her eggs, then die. Sounds a bit like modern man. Right, John?"

The Beekeeper laughed. "The drones' tongues are not long enough for them to feed themselves, so they're dependent on the thousands of workers in each hive for food. The workers feed the drones until the fertilizing is done in the early fall, then they kick them out and they die of starvation. The workers do all the labor, while the Queen watches, but they can't fertilize her or have bees themselves. It's a perfect balanced system, except when the humans interfere. We take their honey and make money from it. Even more than reproduction, that seems to be the true way of nature."

Knudsen showed Davidson his prized hives, and as they walked and talked, he stopped occasionally to do some honey sampling.

"So, Baptist, after all these years, why have you come to see me?" the Beekeeper asked.

Straightforwardly, Davidson laid out the hostage situation and the threat from Mussad. Without mentioning the President, he told the Beekeeper of the decision to take out the terrorist leader. "It's a perfect use of your talents, Knudsen. We think that if Mussad's eliminated, the situation will correct itself."

The Beekeeper kept walking, unsmiling, even mute. Finally, he halted.

"Baptist, Mussad's no easy target, but I think I can do the job. But can't you see? I'm retired. I've made all the money I need from the Cold War. And aren't the old days over, anyway? I heard that this is the end of history—that the world is now truly safe for democracy, capitalism and rock and roll. Why does anybody need the likes of me?"

The Beekeeper seemed pleased with his brief analysis.

"Don't be facetious, Alex—if I may call you that. It took thousands of years to civilize Western Europe, and now there are new nationalist villains and empire builders like Mussad popping up all the time in the Third World. I hate to admit it, but as long as arms dealers are willing to supply them, your services will always be needed."

Davidson paused. "And we recognize the dangers not only of dictators, but of inflation. We're prepared to pay five million dollars on successful conclusion. A million should you fail."

"Let's head back to the house." The Beekeeper walked silently, apparently buried in thought, his eyes straight ahead.

"No, John, I won't do it for five million, or even for the booby prize," he finally said, enjoying Davidson's obvious disappointment. "I'm an American citizen same as you. I'll do it just for the pleasure of getting rid of that raping bastard—and for old times' sake. But Baptist, I'm a businessman first and always. To keep my self-respect, you'll have to pay all expenses."

The Beekeeper removed the apiary net from his head. "When do we start, John?"

DAVIDSON pushed back into the comfortable recesses of his large wing chair, circa 1760, and lowered his biography of Churchill. In his mind, he kept turning over the videotape which had already been played on American television. Even in its edited form it had outraged the nation. People were demanding a bombing raid, some—not knowing of Mussad's N-Bombs—were calling for war. Others, Davidson was pleased, were asking for his own formula. One life to save many.

Armed with seed money from Davidson, the Beekeeper had left on his mission, traveling first to Cairo to handle some professional needs. Scrupulously, he had avoided the American Embassy in Cairo. To finance the project, the President, at Davidson's suggestion, had tapped an old fiscal subterfuge. Using emergency foreign aid funds at his disposal, Briggs had taken $5 million—a reserve for Davidson—and assigned it to Panama. President Morales had given Briggs a silent nod that he could use the money for whatever purpose he wanted. The Panamanian books would be cooked accordingly.

Davidson tried to arrange "papers" for the Beekeeper's new identity, but Briggs warned him away. A new federal regulation, encouraged by the Senate Intelligence Committee, blocked the Agency from getting blank passports from State for covert use. That simple, traditional piece of tradecraft, Davidson learned, was now a federal crime.

Instead, the Beekeeper had made his own arrangements. His documents came from an ex-Agency man, a dealer in Atlanta who now papered a less reputable clientele. What Davidson supplied was a contact in Al Rashon—Ibn Feyad, a former history professor who found Mussad and his universities intolerable. Feyad had become a wholesale fish merchant, but was still a leader of the underground Democratic Forum.

Davidson's mind turned back to the videotape. It was not only the shock of the rape and murder that disturbed him. He was unable to pin down a fleeting image on the tape—a man, apparently a European, whom he had briefly spotted. The Baptist was sure he recognized him. But who and from where?

The man had been standing next to Hakim in the barracks just before the girl—now identified as seventeen-year-old Lonnie Taylor—had been taken into the bunker-room and raped. The European was tall, six foot six, Davidson guessed, with the build of a football tackle.

But where had they met? If only he could remember the connection.

Davidson walked to the VCR, inserting a copy of Mussad's video. Using fast forward, he froze the tape exactly at the point where the giant man showed up. In the brief span of no more than two seconds, he was standing alongside and just behind Hakim, obviously unaware that he was in camera range. The man was blond and sharp featured. English? Scandinavian? German?

German! Of course! Before the velvet revolution that toppled the East German communist government, Davidson had seen his photo in an Agency file on the Stasi secret police. His name? Hartmann? Horstfeld? Horstmann! Yes, that was it. Colonel Wolf Horstmann! He had fled East Germany for places unknown, and had now turned up in Al Rashon. He was undoubtedly serving as liaison between Mussad and the German suppliers, as well as Red Swastika.

The BND in Berlin had failed to deliver what he wanted on Mussad, and Latham had been blown apart in the process. He hardly bought Spandau's story that it was an accident caused by a faulty gas tank. Instead, Davidson turned to a lifelong contact, Colonel Moshe Mendelbaum in the Israeli secret service, his CIC counterpart in Jerusalem. He had reached Moshe through the Israeli Embassy in Washington only days before. This morning, a bulky file on Mussad and his council had been left for him at the Cosmos Club on Massachusetts Avenue, secretly hand-delivered from the Israeli Embassy on International Drive, near Connecticut Avenue.

Davidson thumbed through it, stopping short at the Horstmann file. His intuition was right. The Stasi Colonel had come from a strong Nazi family: both his father and grandfather had been SS—his father a Major and his grandfather a Colonel General in the Waffen SS. There had once been money in the aristocratic Bavarian family. The Colonel's full name was Wolfgang von Horstmann, and he would have been heir to the two-hundred-year-old family estate, Raven's Nest, in Bavaria, but it had been lost to creditors after World War II. The family even had a claim to nobility, the great-grandfather having been a Count in the Kaiser Wilhelm era. Despite the abolition of the crown in 1918, under German law titles were still legally part of a person's name. So, Count Colonel Wolfgang von Horstmann.

Davidson's attention now shifted to Berlin, the capital and central point for much of this operation. He needed someone there to hunt out Red Swastika, surely the nucleus of the conspiracy. But who?

Sam Withers's bony Anglo face and prematurely gray crew-cut came to mind. A true soldier of intelligence, Sam was no master of strategy, but he was his best tactician and survivor. The Agency needed a new Chief-of-Station at the Embassy to take over from Ben Latham, who had served in the front role of Second Secretary.

Withers would be perfect for both jobs.

Sam's father, a Warrant Officer helicopter pilot in Vietnam, had been killed in action. Though Sam had never mentioned it, Davidson felt Withers believed he would suffer a similar fate, if in a more civilized environ. Davidson had taken on the role of strategist and mentor, interposing himself between Withers and his fatalism. But he suspected it was still there, digging away at Sam.

Withers was no newcomer to Germany. He had served in West Berlin during the first Cold War days, posing, among other things, as a trade representative. Now that Berlin was the capital of all Germany, he could work out of the American Embassy on Friedrichstrasse, with the contacts and services it offered.

Yes, Withers, the most loyal of the *nashi*, was the man. He would talk to the President about it.

— 23 —

THE sights and sounds of the bazaar of Al Rashon seemed to have been invented on a back lot at Studio City, but they were quite real.

Noise and exotic odors permeated the scene, one of open emotion and a pace so different from that of Western capitals. The feel of the bazaar had changed little in three thousand years, its ethos so strong that the modern backdrop of an occasional neon sign and small cars seemed more out of place than the fervent haggling heard throughout the marketplace.

One of the stands was run by someone who looked and sounded like a European. At a peddler's shop that traded in antique jewelry and trinkets, from fake zircons to nineteenth-century gold-plated pocket watches, was a short, slender, balding man with a high-pitched voice. Under his clothes, he hid a money belt stocked with 100-franc Swiss bills.

Like the German Deutschemark, the Swiss franc was a popular hard currency in North Africa and had served the proprietor well. It had provided the means to buy out the previous owner, who had agreed to flee to Egypt after receiving 60,000 Swiss francs, five times the value of his struggling enterprise. It also dispelled any notion that the new owner of "Khalid's Jewels" was an American.

The new proprietor was the Beekeeper, now "Paul Lager,"

a semi-alcoholic, untidy Zurich expatriate carrying a Swiss passport, supplied not by Langley but by his own contact in the Swiss police.

Wearing long khaki shorts and a stained bush jacket that had seen better decades, the Beekeeper, who was fluent in German, moved quickly to the end of his stand. A non-commissioned officer in Mussad's army was examining some mother-of-pearl brooches.

"*Gut, gut.* Do you speak English?" Lager asked the Sergeant in a studied German-Swiss accent.

"English, a little. How much for this pin—the one with the place for a picture?"

"Usually, five-hundred dinars. But that's too much for someone who serves Mussad. You can have it for three hundred."

"I'll give you a hundred and fifty."

Lager stared at the young Sergeant, who was fully mustached in North African style. "For a soldier, all right. Take it."

As the Beekeeper wrapped the trinket in an old newspaper, he whispered confidentially to the soldier.

"Would you like to make some extra money?"

"How?" The Sergeant's tone was suspicious.

"Soldiers are good customers for my trinkets. I'll pay you twenty percent of everything I take in if you can bring me to your friends at the army base. I'll stay only a short time and show them a fine assortment at bargain prices—like the one I just gave you."

The Sergeant seemed to be appraising Lager and the deal. "OK. Sounds good. But you must stay close to me. Otherwise the security people will get angry."

"When can we do this?"

"Come with your goods at eight in the morning. I'll be waiting at the main gate."

• • •

"He's OK," the Sergeant assured the security MP at the army base outside Al Rashon, where Mussad was reportedly last seen. Davidson also believed it was the holding point for the thirty American teenagers.

Balancing four black velvet trays of trinkets, "Lager" smiled at the MP, then pushed a Swiss 50-franc note into his hand, doing the same with the Sergeant. "*Salaam alacheem*," the MP responded appreciatively. "Peace be with you."

Inside the gate, the Beekeeper was quickly surrounded by soldiers drawn to the glittering gold-plated items. "Only fifty dinars for anything on this tray," Lager said, making sale after sale. The accommodating NCO seemed to be tallying up the commissions in his head.

"What's going on here?" A booming voice interrupted the brisk trade. The Beekeeper looked up to see a giant of a man, maybe six foot six, standing over him.

My God, Lager thought, it's Colonel Wolf Horstmann—the former East German whose picture he had seen in Davidson's dossier. Mussad and the hostages had to be close by.

"Just peddling my trinkets, *mein Herr*. I am Paul Lager, Swiss. I own Khalid's stand in the bazaar."

The Beekeeper took a large sapphire and gold ring off the tray. "I see you're European. I have something special for you."

He brought the ring up to Horstmann's eye level, then handed the German a jeweler's eyeglass. "Look in here. It's perfect quality. A true star sapphire."

"How much?" The bear of a man bent to hear Lager's whispered response.

"For you, only four thousand dinars, or in Deutsche-marks—I presume you're German—only four-hundred. A bargain, but only for a soldier of Mussad."

Horstmann smiled. From a roll of 1,000-dinar notes, he peeled off four. "*Abgemacht*. A deal, Herr Lager. I like the ring and the price is good. Now finish up your business and get back to the bazaar."

That night, the Beekeeper shut the decorative iron grillwork on his stand. He placed the better jewelry in the small safe left by Khalid, and added his cache of Swiss francs. At a desk in the rear living quarters, he made coded notes on the progress of his assignment. He hadn't yet seen his target, but he had made contact with Horstmann, who was close to the dictator. Ingratiating himself with the giant was the first order of business.

From his molded Samsonite suitcase the Beekeeper removed the precision tool of his trade, an Austrian-made Steyr long-range sharpshooter rifle, 7.62 mm caliber, Model SSG P2, reconformed into three interlocking pieces. Quietly, he sat at a small kerosene light and dismantled, then greased the weapon with a synthetic oil.

He was startled by a rattling noise outside. Was someone trying to break open the stand's protective metal mesh? Lager rushed out to investigate and was met by an Arabic-accented voice, calling out in English.

"Let me in, Lager. This is important."

The Beekeeper put the rifle back into the Samsonite case. The Mauser was shoved into his rear waistband under the bush jacket.

"Coming," he called.

At the gate was a junior officer in Mussad's army, surely from the base. As the young soldier smiled and displayed his identification, Lager opened the mesh gate.

"Thank you. May I come in?" the Lieutenant asked, crossing the threshold before the Beekeeper could answer. "I'm from security. I understand you were selling your trinkets at the camp today. Could I ask a few questions?"

"Surely. Come in and have a seat."

In rapid order, the officer, who gave his name as Mustafa, plied the Beekeeper with queries about his passport, his nationality, and the rest of his fictitious background—all of which had been screened with both Davidson and his Swiss police contacts.

"Why all the questions, Herr Lieutenant?"

"Just routine, Mr. Lager. There are many threats from the enemies of the Great Mussad, so we are careful. I'm sure you understand."

The Beekeeper nodded. When the questioning was complete, he led the officer to the door.

"Just one more, Mr. Lager."

"Yes?"

"I forgot to ask for your passport. Swiss, isn't it?"

"Yes, it's in the rear. I'll be right back."

"No, that's not necessary. I'll come with you."

As Lager opened the drawer that held his documents, he noticed Mustafa's eyes focused on his Samsonite case.

"Is that your entire luggage, Mr. Lager?"

"No, I have a second one that holds my clothes. This one just has some trinkets I bought for my inventory."

The young officer kept staring at the suitcase. The Beekeeper moved slowly toward the other side of the room to divert his attention. Finally, Lager offered the red-covered Swiss passport in his hand.

Mustafa opened it, examining the photograph and visa markings.

"I see the passport is new. You have only one entrance visa, to Al Rashon. Didn't you travel before?"

"Yes, but not on this passport. The old one had expired."

"Oh." Mustafa's response was indifferent. He kept edging toward the suitcase which held the Steyr 7.62.

"So, I suppose that's all, Lieutenant. Shall we bid each other goodnight?" The Beekeeper moved toward the door, waving for the officer to follow.

"I hate to seem over-curious, Herr Lager. But before I leave, I'd like to see some of the trinkets you've bought. Could you please open the suitcase? Or is it unlocked?"

"Oh, it's quite unlocked, but you'll be disappointed."

"Fine, I'll look anyway." As Mustafa leaned to lift the suitcase lid, the Beekeeper circled silently behind him. His hand stretched for the Mauser in his waistband.

Mustafa opened the suitcase. His head jerked upward in surprise at the sight of the dismantled rifle. He turned aggressively, facing the Beekeeper.

"Mr. Lager, this rifle . . ."

The sentence was never finished. In a swift, sweeping movement, the Beekeeper pulled the gun from his waistband and fired a single, muted shot. The bullet embedded itself in the center of the skull, over the bridge of the young officer's nose. Without even a gasp, Mustafa fell, his face frozen into an expression of surprise.

The Beekeeper picked up the phone and dialed a number in Al Rashon.

"Ibn, this is Paul Lager. I have a package of dead fish waiting for you. Could you bring your truck right away and transport it? I know it's late, but it's starting to smell up the place."

— 24 —

"GOOD evening, Frau Knabel, don't you worry about your back. Just do the exercises I gave you—flat on a hard floor. Eat more green vegetables and take the vitamins. If it really hurts, use the Motrin."

Dr. Koller escorted his last patient of the day to the door, then moved enthusiastically to his true vocation, the regeneration of the power of Hitler's prewar Germany.

To the intense chiropractor, his nation—despite its miraculous economic power—was still repressed by the defeat of fifty years' standing, a pall of humiliation that hung over the national psyche. It was seldom spoken of in public, but underneath it was more corrosive than what Americans called their "Vietnam Syndrome." Just as the "Amis" victory in Iraq had helped soothe that, so Germany needed its own healing, Koller was convinced.

He feared that modern Germany cared too much about money, as if *Geld* could erase shame. But he also knew that many Germans, like him, were still searching for ways to give expression to their injured Teuton pride. All they needed was a cause, and he would give it to them. Hitler's was born out of despair. His would come out of an affluent nation's secret frustration.

The phone in his office rang.

"Yes, this is Dr. Koller. Who's calling? Oh, Beimeister. Good. What's up in the States?"

He welcomed these calls from the German Embassy on Reservoir Road in Washington. Covertly a BND man and a friend of the cause, Beimeister was cautious, placing his calls from a busy public pay phone at DuPont Circle, or sending his messages in coded telex through *Ganzfakt*.

"Dr. Koller, we've been watching the Baptist coming and going to the White House over the last weeks," Beimeister began. "That troubles me. Barenchenko's people at Langley tell us that Davidson has been pushing for information on our Mussad connection. We tried some preventive action, but so far it's failed. And yes, we understand a protégé of Davidson's—Sam Withers—is being sent to Berlin to replace Latham. Keep a careful eye on him."

Koller relaxed at the news, pouring himself a schnapps.

"Excellent work, Beimeister. I'll do more than that, rest assured."

"HELLO, who's this?"

Sam Withers stretched back into the uncomfortable government-issue chair and stared out the brass-trimmed window of the baroque mansion. Once the home of a Hohenzollern prince, it had escaped World War II bomb destruction and was now the American Embassy on Friedrichstrasse. Withers's own office in the rear of the left wing was considerably less impressive: an 8 x 10 foot former pantry that now served the Agency Chief-of-Station, in disguise as a modest bureaucrat—the Second Secretary.

This was only his third day in Berlin. After a decade of disuse, his German was rusty. But the caller, a woman, was speaking in English, slightly accented but quite serviceable.

"Mr. Withers, this is the Merrill Lynch branch on the Ku-Damm. I have your investment account from the Washington office, transferred to me in Berlin. Could we get together and talk? I have some wonderful investments in Eastern Europe, and several in Germany tied to our economic expansion into Russia."

"Who is this and how in the hell did you know I was here?" Withers half-shouted, startled by the caller's overly direct approach.

"Oh, forgive me. I forgot to introduce myself. I'm Marieanne Luft, an account executive at Merrill. I handle a lot of American accounts. Now, I suppose, yours included."

"But you still haven't told me how you knew I was here."

"Oh—again. It's difficult for me to say exactly, Mr. Withers, but we do have our connections at the Embassy. Let's say a birdie whispered it. In any case, I called our Washington office and arranged everything." The woman's voice, dulcet and feminine, became more so. "I hope you're not angry, or even annoyed. I have a lot of good investments. And, modestly, I have a reputation for picking winners."

Withers was intrigued. He needed to get acclimated to Berlin and all German contacts were important. Candidly, he liked her voice. And less important—but what the hell— he might make some money. Living on Agency pay, even with overseas allowances, was belt tightening in the inflated modern world.

"Your name again?"

"Luft, Marieanne Luft. What would you say, Mr. Withers, to drinks after work, say at the Bristol Kempinski. It's one of our best hotels."

Withers leaned on his instincts.

"OK. Meet you at the bar at six. You'll know me by my hair. Crew cut and gray. And I'm a little guy—about five foot six. But don't let that fool you. I'm as tough as nails."

A cascade of laughter came from the other end. Lilting and charming, he thought.

"I doubt that very much, Mr. Withers. I'm looking forward to this meeting."

Over drinks at the Bristol Kempinski bar, Withers found himself only half-listening to her jabbering about this German firm or the other and about local anti-pollution companies whose stocks had tripled and would double again as they started to clean up the environmental disaster of Czechoslovakia, Hungary and Poland—especially the coal area of Silesia. There was even the promise of a deal with the Russians to resurrect their ruined environment. She talked and talked, but what he mostly watched was her face and demeanor.

Marieanne Luft had sharp features, but somehow they blended into a beautiful whole. Something like Marlene Dietrich, he guessed. But the bones were softer and the dark blonde hair longer. Though swept up, he could imagine it down and light on her shoulders. Her speech was what really got him: articulate, half-whispered, and despite the fact that English was not native to her, a fine, precise diction.

If he had to choose one facial feature, it would be her mouth. Less sharply defined and Germanic than the rest of her features, it was full, sensual, and inviting. Sam caught himself, then remembered that he was entitled. As a widower of five years, he had first suffered and then been celibate. But he was now out of his mourning stage. And, he had to admit, taken with the woman.

"Sam—may I call you that? I know I'm telling you too much too soon, and it's impossible to understand our German finances. Sometimes the corporate interlocking is too much even for me. But they do make money. They love making money and they are very good at it. I know Americans like money too—but maybe not as much as we do. So I want you to know that I'll help you, maybe even double your portfolio. What do you have there now? Oh, yes, I remember, thirteen thousand dollars or so." She paused for only a second. "Good. Now . . ."

"Slow down, Marieanne. I'm impressed, but I'm too busy to get involved in Wall Street or even the Frankfurt DAKS. Send over a piece of paper tomorrow and I'll give you discretionary power to make me a lot of money. This way

I can concentrate on my job—and you."

Marieanne laughed. "Mr. Withers, I don't know if you intend to be, but I find you very amusing. Light spirited and young, but . . ."

"Yes, but what?"

"But underneath, very serious and dedicated to whatever you do. Whether business—or in your case, the American government. Or even love? *Recht*?"

Her use of the German word reminded Withers that she was not an American. He had to use Marieanne, as he did all foreigners, for his Intelligence labors. But in her case, the exploitation, if that's what it was, was sure to be pleasurable.

Withers stared again at Marieanne, dressed in a smart fitted navy-blue suit with a beige silk blouse. Inexplicably, he felt a strange surge of emotion. He had known the woman for only an hour, but felt like a teenager in pubescent heat.

"I enjoyed so much meeting you," Sam said as it turned 7:30 and she peered down at her watch. "I suppose you have a dinner date and have to be going."

Marieanne again let out her laugh, a high, tremulous one. "No, dear Sam, or should I say 'dear boy'—though you have at least ten years on me. No, I have nowhere to go, except where you want to take me."

"*Wunderbar!*" Withers shouted in stage German. "Then it's off to dinner. What about the Klimpt and Wagner, a traditional place—used to be a winehouse—close to here. I went there in the old Cold War days."

"Right you are, Sam. Let's be off. And, thank God, we have no more Cold War!"

Withers turned fitfully in the bed, under a luxurious, padded down cover, a German and Swiss specialty. He had just woken to a bright slit of sun coming through the blinds of the modest Embassy-arranged apartment in the Wannsee suburb in southwest Berlin near Lake Havel.

Glancing down at Marieanne, still asleep at 7:30, he wondered whether he should wake her. It may have been a monumental night for both of them, but it was another business day at Merrill Lynch, and at the Embassy as well.

After dinner, he had maneuvered her to his apartment, or vice versa. He couldn't recall the exact initiative, but it made little difference. The kissing, then the more serious lovemaking could only be described as wonderfully reminiscent, a twenty-year *déjà vu*, as if he were making love again, for the first time, to his late, beloved Katherine.

Why? He had no answer. The woman's name was Luft, German for "air," and that's the way she made him feel. Like the GI who attaches himself to a woman who offers a house, sex and homecooking on his first leave from a miserable army base, Withers was sure he had fallen in. Still, he had preserved enough perspective to see Marieanne as an "asset," someone who could connect him to other Germans, especially in the financial community. Never would he give his assignment short shrift. He had been sent here by Davidson—and he presumed the President—to find and root out Red Swastika. Though Marieanne didn't yet know it, she might help him accomplish it.

That didn't change the fact that he had fallen in.

"Marieanne, wake up. It's 7:30." Withers gave her a gentle nudge on a bare arm. "We've both got to go to work."

She opened her eyes, wrapped two arms around Withers and kissed him, her fullness pressed against him. His mind drifted to the chalky purity of her naked body. Almost compulsively, he fondled her breasts, then her thighs, before he exercised control.

"Sam, you're right. You'd better go to work. I don't have to be there until later."

Withers dressed, and by 8:00 A.M. was on his way out of the apartment.

"Don't forget to call me later," he said in farewell. "It was great. Really great."

Marieanne laughed. "Better even than that for me."

Within twenty minutes, Marieanne was dressed, and had left the apartment. From a pay phone on the corner, she anxiously dialed a number in central Berlin, not far from the Ku-Damm.

"Dr. Koller?"

"Yes, I recognize your voice. How did things go?"

"Wonderfully. I made contact. Very good contact, if you know what I mean."

"I can imagine. Good work and keep it up."

"I'll tell him you said that."

Koller laughed, really for the first time, Marieanne thought.

—— 26 ——

THE Beekeeper examined the trays of jewels he had bought from Khalid. The star sapphire had been the queen of his inventory and he feared that none other would entice Horstmann, who was his entry to Mussad.

He'd have to use some of Davidson's Swiss francs, as many as 3,000, to buy a new lure—perhaps a tasteful gold and diamond pinky ring. Its masculine feel would appeal to Horstmann, and be worthy, as he knew from Davidson, of a German nobleman.

As "Paul Lager" put on his bush jacket, he thought of the Mussad lieutenant he had dispatched the night before. He hoped no one at the base knew about the nocturnal visit. The Beekeeper had conditioned himself to convert worry into action, and was about to do that when he heard the sound of a car engine.

Peering through the curtains, he saw an old Mercedes taxi come to a stop. He moved quickly outside.

"Paul Lager?" the cabbie asked. In his hand was a letter, posted from Cairo by express courier. The Beekeeper smiled at the contents, an order for a dozen zircons without settings. Inside the stand, he deciphered the coded message from Davidson. It was cryptic but vital:

BREAK CAMP AND PROCEED TO BERLIN. ISRAELI INTEL-
LIGENCE SAYS MUSSAD IS LEAVING FOR A VISIT TO
GERMANY. GOOD HUNTING. BAPTIST.

The Beekeeper reread the message, wondering if he had
enough zircons to fill Davidson's order.

—— 27 ——

BND Major Paul Niemann was elated. He never thought
of himself as part of the upper echelon, but he had been
invited to the mansion of Klaus von Stimmel, the chairman
of Heinschmann, GmbH, the covert financial backer of Red
Swastika.

With Dr. Koller seated alongside him, the chauffered
Mercedes 560SEL made its way through the lacy iron gates
of *Nachtgefluster*—Night Whisper—the 105-acre estate in
Potsdam, the western suburb of Berlin that had been the
setting for the Truman-Churchill-Stalin summit that had
carved up Europe. Niemann wondered if a new world order
might someday be born here as well.

The entry posts, topped by enormous stone imperial German eagles, stirred his patriotism. Not only had they been
used by the Kaiser, but when merged with the Swastika—
actually an ancient American Indian sign—had become
Adolf Hitler's symbol as well.

The car turned up a continuously curving driveway lined

with naturally perfumed linden trees, until it approached the house at the crest of the shallow hill. Niemann stared in admiration. A French mansion in stone and brick, touched with baroque German detail, it dominated acres of ancient lawns. Carved stone pots filled with topiary trees graced the Palladian entrance, fronted by a circular fountain whose water spouted from a ten-foot-long stone fish. Old Daimlers and new Mercedes limousines graced the large gravel courtyard.

Niemann, son of an SS Übersturmfuehrer born into poverty in a Hamburg slum, breathed in the aristocratic scene. He felt gratified by Germany's special strength—the marriage of money and political power. Even under the so-called National Socialism of Hitler, capitalism and the strongest of class distinctions had flourished until the very end.

He knew that von Stimmel's own father had been a supporter of Hitler as far back as 1923, when the failed Munich beer hall putsch landed the Fuehrer in jail, where he wrote *Mein Kampf*, My Struggle. As head of Heinschmann, Stimmel's father—like his colleagues at Daimler-Benz, the Mercedes car manufacturer who built the Panzer tanks—was one of the Nazi industrialists who mass-produced Hitler's extraordinary war machine.

The limousine halted at the base of the twenty-two broad stone steps leading up to the house. The overweight chiropractor-politician puffed his way up, while Niemann, laughing to himself, took the steps like a boy in a gymnasium. He was young and fit and a logical successor to the older generation that led Red Swastika. Koller would pave the way for those like himself, who would some day rule Germany.

Two butlers, dressed in eighteenth-century livery, with satin knee breeches, took their coats, then led them into the main salon.

"Dr. Koller! Major Niemann!"

Klaus von Stimmel, an especially thin, ascetic-looking man, about six feet tall with over-refined features, approached. He extended a long arm and shook hands, barely touching each man's fingers, as if the exercise was too demanding, perhaps even distasteful.

Niemann studied von Stimmel, who superficially looked like a weak effete son of a wealthy family. But from what he had learned of the Heinschmann chief, the impression was false. More likely, his whole manner of a pale aristocrat was a pose meant to lull his enemies into underestimating him. Niemann decided he would never be guilty of that.

"You know everyone here, except for a new guest, Hans Krieger, manager of my Brazilian operations," von Stimmel said. "He's in Berlin for a week, supposedly to meet Mussad, but really checking up on me. Yes, Krieger?" von Stimmel laughed.

Krieger looked more German than Latin. Only his Portuguese-tinged accent was Brazilian—surely a descendant of the Germans who had immigrated to Brazil in heavy numbers, both before and after World War II.

Niemann scanned the room. Aside from Krieger, he recognized everyone there: General Menck; Dollop of the Foreign Office; Helmut Zolb from the Bundestag; Heinrich Wilhelm, Werner's assistant in Heinschmann, and Dr. Frederick Olmst of the Federal Nuclear Agency.

Von Stimmel made the introductions and at his signal, everyone sat.

"I'll not take much of your time," he began in a soft voice. The others leaned precariously forward to hear him. "But I have some good news to report. The Great Mussad will be in Berlin in a few days to attend a Fourth Reich rally. I have spoken to my good friend Chancellor Bessinger—who only last weekend was a house guest at Night Whisper—about greeting Mussad during his visit. He has agreed to welcome him on behalf of the State. A great victory for Red Swastika."

The reed of a man seemed enervated. He sat and nodded toward the chiropractor.

"Now I'll turn the chair over to Dr. Koller."

Physically the obverse of von Stimmel, Koller rose from his Louis XVI armchair.

"Gentlemen, things are going well in Recife and in Al Rashon. The Americans are totally confused. They have no idea what to do about their hostage situation. We understand they know something about the neutron weapons we're delivering to Mussad, which is good. It will abort any ideas of an invasion. But we don't believe they know the source of the heavy hydrogens or that Heinschmann has built bombproof caverns in the desert to hold the N-Bombs."

Koller motioned for a butler and whispered into his ear. Seconds later, a glass of schnapps was handed him. Quickly, it disappeared.

"Here in Germany," Koller continued, "we must use this time to make our mark, to gain attention from the press and legislators. Everyone must learn that we're a force to reckon with, both as an underground, and at the polls—through the Fourth Reich Party. We'll remind the world that Germany is no longer a vassal of the Americans."

Koller's voice suddenly turned more confidential.

"I've decided that Red Swastika will complete what the Fuehrer started in 1933. Gentlemen, we are going to destroy the rebuilt Reichstag, the symbol of democratic Germany and the site of the Bundestag parliament. We'll not just burn it as Hitler did. We shall blow it into nothingness."

The room stilled.

"The Reichstag? Brilliant, Herr Koller. But who will do the job?" Dollop asked. "Do we already have a terrorist wing?"

"Not yet. But we have friends. General Barenchenko, our Moscow chief, has volunteered. And it will not be done by Russians. That would be a political faux pas. Some of the Marxist Baader-Meinhof gang have taken refuge in Moscow along with former Stasi people—all Germans. They will do the job without any visible ties to Swastika."

"Marxists?" General Menck, garbed in a gray uniform little changed since Hitler's time, seemed skeptical.

"Yes, General. No reason we can't use them, just as Hitler used Ernst Roehm of the SA and other former leftists and workers' groups . . ." Koller answered, his short figure turning in a half circle. " . . . Until it was time to do away with them. If you remember, on the Night of the Long Knives, in June 1934, the Fuehrer eliminated 10,000 of his useless followers."

"I agree with Dr. Koller on both points," von Stimmel said, now up and balanced delicately on his heels. "We can always deal with unwanted allies and bombing the Reichstag now will alert all Germany to our presence. But have you cleared it with the Fuehrer?"

"Yes, 'Frederich' knows of the plan and has agreed. Many of you are curious who leads us, but he wishes to be anonymous. At least for now."

Koller rose, indicating the meeting's conclusion.

"Good," General Menck said as they milled to leave. "I never thought I'd be so pleased to cooperate with Marxists."

— 28 —

SAM Withers still couldn't believe his luck.

Marieanne had virtually moved in with him, bringing some order to his bachelor existence. She refurbished his closets, even cooked him a good German breakfast of hot rolls, butter, eggs and *gekochten Schinken*, boiled ham, before racing off to the office. He took stock of his sex life. Never since the death of Katherine—or even before, he confessed—had it been so good, evolving toward perfection. Not only was Marieanne beautiful, an aphrodisiac in itself, but she was adroit in her movements during love-play, yet never at the expense of tenderness. Even, he feared to say, love.

Was he in love? He wasn't sure. He had had only one such experience in his life, but this was a reasonable substitute, if not the real thing. His mind wandered into near fantasy. Could he convince Langley to let him stay as Chief-of-Station in Berlin once this assignment—of which they were ignorant—was over? Then he could face up to the seriousness of his affection for Marieanne.

This morning, at the breakfast table, he'd broach the general subject, even bring up another idea that had been gnawing at him.

"Marieanne, I've been meaning to ask you something."

"Yes, Sammie, what is it?"

"It's about my job at the Embassy. You know I'm Second

Secretary, a not very exalted slot. But I hear there's a chance I may be promoted—perhaps even to Chargé d'Affaires. What I mean is that Berlin would then be attractive to me career-wise, and . . ."

"And what? Come out with it, lover."

"Well, if I did stay here, would you be interested in a more . . . let's say serious . . . relationship?"

"Oh, you Americans are always so direct, and so impetuous. And besides, Sam, everybody at Merrill Lynch says you are really CIA, and not State at all. Then you couldn't stay here so long. Am I right?" Marieanne bent over and squeezed his chest, laughing uproariously.

"No, that's all spy story stuff. I'm a straight State Department button-down type." He paused. "No, Marieanne, sorry to disappoint you, but I'm no spook. Don't even like them or their work."

He stared into Marieanne's quizzical blue eyes, but couldn't tell whether she believed him. In any case, he needed to broach what he'd once have considered foolhardy, even dangerous. He had cleared the idea with Davidson, who, though unsure, thought it worth a try.

In probing Marieanne, the Baptist had learned that her grandfather, Colonel Fritz Luft, had not only been a top SS officer in World War II, but had voluntarily taken his life alongside Hitler in the Reichchancellery bunker on April 30, 1945. "Keep that in mind," the Baptist advised. "It could work for or against us."

"Marieanne, you've got me wrong if you think I'm Agency. But as Second Secretary, I could use any Berlin scuttlebutt I can get my hands on," Withers said as he dove enthusiastically into his boiled ham. "At Merrill Lynch, I know you have good access to a lot of people, and a lot of gossip. Would you mind sharing some of it with me? It'll make my job a lot easier." Sam hesitated. "I'd like to offer you money, but your salary of 9,000 Deutschemarks a month is about twice mine."

Marieanne moved away from the sink and kissed Withers heartily.

"Idiot. Sure I'll help you, without money. But about what?"

Withers felt suffused with embarrassment.

"Marieanne, first I've got to confess to one thing. My government likes to know who I'm hanging out with, so the security people at the Embassy did a check on you. I swear it wasn't my idea."

Marieanne arched back. "So, and what did they learn?"

"Nothing much . . . except about your grandfather. I understand he was a top Nazi, and that he died with Hitler."

"Yes." Marieanne's manner turned cool. "That's true, but of course, I never knew him. And isn't that what you people call 'McCarthyism,' guilt-by-association?"

"Marieanne, I didn't mention it as an incriminating fact." Sam drew back, convinced he was putting his outsize shoe for a little guy—an 11D—into his mouth.

"Then why?" she asked. Withers sensed a chill dampening what had been ardor.

"Because it could be useful for me, and it needn't hurt you. Through your family or work, maybe you could meet some people with right-wing connections. I understand there's a new political party called the Fourth Reich, started by some older SS veterans and others who feel the same way. You know, a kind of Nazi Germany Redux."

Withers was now worried about her reaction, fearful that his duty was interfering with his pleasure. Or actually, vice versa. He studied her face for the smallest clue.

"Sam, I know all that. I may not be a professional diplomat, but I'm not stupid. What exactly do you want me to do?"

"Not much, darling. Just get to know some of these

people. They'll accept you once they know about your grandfather."

"Oh, come out and say it, Sam. You want me to be a spy for America. To find out the secrets of Germans, then tell them to you. That's it, isn't it?" Her manner seemed almost acrimonious. "But I thought our two countries were allies."

Withers was sure he had made an enormous mistake. Confident at intelligence labors, he was a fish on dry land when it came to women. And, apparently when he mixed the two, he was, as the Germans said, a pure *Trottel*, a fool. He waited for the verbal crucifixion.

Marieanne removed her apron, slowly and deliberately. She walked three paces and now stood over Withers. Her features were tight, even menacing, Withers thought, as she bent over.

With a sudden movement she kissed his face, forehead, finally his surprised near-open mouth.

"Sam, darling. Of course I'll be your Nazi-hunting Mata Hari. But I want to get paid—under the sheets. Beginning right now."

That evening, Withers could hardly be more exuberant. After a day's work they had met for dinner at the Kempinksi Grill, and were now walking down the Ku-Damm, window shopping and exchanging soft pleasantries in the warm spring evening, refreshed by an almost imperceptible drizzle.

Marieanne had hired on as an agent, of sorts, and Withers had heard from Davidson that Mussad was coming to Berlin for a three-day visit. That meant the Beekeeper would soon be following. He'd be called on to make arrangements, which meant his work was advancing nicely. But Withers still worried whether he was devoting too much time to his magnificent social life. Rationalizing, he strained to believe that Marieanne would soon bring him intelligence leads to Red Swastika.

"Darling, do you like that man's watch?" Marieanne asked as they stared into the glareproof window of Steinhaus und Sohn, a glittering jewelry shop on the Ku-Damm. "It's a copy of a gold Rolex, but I think even better looking."

"Yes, it's attractive, but beyond my pocketbook. I'm more in the Timex class."

"Don't be foolish. Your birthday is next week. No?"

"Yes, but don't get any ideas."

"My pocketbook is a lot bigger than yours, little Sam. I just sold 3,300 shares of Heinschmann at 67 Deutschemarks, with a profit of about $15,000. And maybe you know that for the first forty years after the war, we had no capital gains tax in Germany. Some people say that's what made us so rich. What do you think?"

Withers was about to offer an uninformed answer when he felt a light tap on his shoulder. He swiveled to see a man, about his height, but bulky, even flabby. Dressed in a parka, he held out a Meerschaum pipe with large carved gargoyles on its side.

What in the world, Withers thought.

"*Bitte*. A light for my pipe?"

Sam stared at the face, half lit in the glow of a street lamp. The man's features were pudgy, almost amorphous, with an expression that gave away little. Withers had never fully shaken the nicotine disease and he scrounged through his coat pockets for matches.

"Sorry, sir, but I'm all out. Maybe my *Fräulein* has some."

Withers turned toward Marieanne. He was startled by her expression. She had frozen in place, her pink, lineless face now gray, twisted in fear.

"Something wrong, darling?" Withers asked, ignoring the man with the pipe.

"Sam, watch out!" Marieanne screamed. He swiveled in time to see the glint of a knife emerge from the man's parka, the hand moving swiftly toward him.

"YEHHH!" Withers gave out a high-decibel karate cry. His right hand grasped the man's wrist, while his left pummeled the soft solar plexus. The knife was twisted away from the short man, but not before it had sliced into Withers's hand, drawing blood between his forefinger and thumb.

As Sam pulled back in pain, the man grabbed the knife off the pavement and raced into an alley thirty feet away. He had left behind only one spoil—a white, heavily-carved Meerschaum pipe.

"Sam, you're bleeding." Marieanne quickly wrapped his hand in her handkerchief. "Should we call the police? Maybe they can catch the mugger."

Withers examined his wound. The knife had cut a quarter inch deep into his skin, but it looked less serious than he first feared.

"No, Marieanne. He's gone. Let's get a cab. I'll go over to the Embassy doctor. Probably need a stitch or two." Sam stared at Marieanne, who hadn't stopped quivering.

"Thanks for saving my life. If you hadn't called out, that knife would have ended in my gut. What makes you think it was a mugger, anyway?"

"What else, darling? Who would want to kill an Embassy Second Secretary?"

Her question needed no response. He leaned over and kissed Marieanne's cheek, his lips tasting a small tear.

"OK, let's go. This thing is starting to hurt. But do me a favor. Pick the Meerschaum off the floor. It'll make a nice souvenir of my second tour in Germany."

⸻ 29 ⸻

"YES, this will do fine," the Beekeeper assured the real estate agent showing him the sparsely furnished two-room apartment in an old red brick building that had escaped Allied bombardment during World War II. The ancient lift had ceased to work, and the apartment's only access was by six flights of winding stairs separated from the stairwell by a precarious iron banister.

The apartment's main asset was its proximity to his target.

The Beekeeper was now only two blocks off the Budapester Strasse, the home of several hotels including the Schweizerhof and the new Berlin Hilton, the tallest building in the city. The penthouse floor, some forty-two stories skyward, Davidson had told him, would probably be the site of the three-day encampment of Mussad and his entourage—at a cost of $21,000 a day, without meals.

His own surroundings were plebian, but he was close enough to easily reconnoiter the hotel and the area, and to help plan a strategy for *Der Tag*. He seldom underestimated the rival security, and this would be no exception.

"I hope you don't mind cash," the Beekeeper was saying. "Here's two thousand Deutschemarks for a month's rent and a month's security."

"Will you be bringing in much furniture?" The rental agent skeptically surveyed his client. "The old tenant left a box spring and mattress, over there in the corner, and one moth-eaten armchair."

"No, it's good enough. I'm only taking it because hotel elevators give me claustrophobia. I'll be here for less than a month anyway."

"Well, I hope it'll do. There's no sense trying to say it's a palace, because it's not."

The rental agent finally departed, leaving the Beekeeper in the center of a large room with cheap paper curtains in a floral design, stained wallpaper and two small windows facing the street. Out of the corner of one, he could make out the towering Hilton. He walked into the next room, not much larger than a closet, where there was another chair, a lamp and a television set. Beyond that was an ancient kitchen of cracked white tile and what looked like a neglected Victorian bathroom. He laughed when he thought how strongly they were coming back into vogue.

He unstrapped his "luggage," a duffel bag slung over his shoulder. His exit from Al Rashon had been less than graceful. Khalid's stand had been sold to a neighboring merchant for just 10,000 dinars, less than $1,000, with a promise that the buyer would keep the price confidential. Though a loss to the federal exchequer on 14th and Pennsylvania, it was the only way the Beekeeper could make a hasty exit from the country without seeming to desert his shop, and arousing suspicion.

From Al Rashon, he had flown first to Cairo, then to Berlin on Egypt Air, through Frankfurt.

The Beekeeper lifted the duffel bag off his shoulder, handling it more gingerly than he had any of Khalid's sapphires. Laying it on the mahogany parquet floor, the apartment's only vestige of elegance, he sat down cross-legged and extracted the paraphernalia of his trade. First a large, folded Baedeker map of Berlin, followed by a pair of Mead 11 X 80 binoculars that could bring a man's profile to eye-filling proportions from 100 yards away.

His tenderness became almost theatrical as he removed a flat, leather-covered box—the "toolkit" that had filled his numbered account at Banque Swiss in Zurich with more than $22,000,000 over the past two decades. For an instant, he regretted turning down Davidson's $5 million offer, but there was a thing called patriotism. If ever he'd have a chance to exercise it, this was it.

From the opened box, he removed his Austrian Steyr rifle and practice-mounted the sniperscope, the fixed ten-power Swarovski ZFM that was the favorite of the trade. At the left end of the box was a leather-lined compartment housing his hand-selected 7.62 mm cartridges, each packaged in a small felt bag.

Like all good professionals, the Beekeeper trusted no gun maker or arms merchants. He hand-loaded his bullets. Extracting one blank two-and-a-half-inch brass cartridge at a time, he began the exacting job of creating his own ordnance. After placing a primer at the base of the cartridge, he carefully funneled in the powder. Finally, the ensemble was tipped with a lead, copper-jacketed, NATO-equivalent 190-grain Sierra Match King bullet, accurate up to 800 yards, approximately half a mile. He worked slowly, painstakingly, until he had loaded twelve cartridges.

With a jeweler's glass, he examined each finished unit, searching for scales or defects. In a trade where the window of opportunity might last only seconds, a slightly marred bullet could make the difference of inches at the target, the margin of success or failure. When he finished, the Beekeeper returned each loaded cartridge to its felt bag.

From the bottom of the duffel bag came the more prosaic accoutrements. First his toilet articles, then a cheap 35mm Kodak camera, followed by a gaudy Hawaiian sports shirt, a pair of beige polyester doubleknit slacks, and a pork pie hat—the caricature makings of an American tourist. Tomorrow morning, at 8 A.M., he would don the costume and start his tour of the area and the Berlin Hilton.

With the camera slung over his shoulder, the Beekeeper anticipated perfect mobility within the city. No one would take him seriously, the best possible disguise for someone like himself—with the deadliest of intentions.

30

IN Washington, Mel Gordon sat at his GI-issue walnut veneer desk, which he swore was a veteran of the Harding administration, and ate his paperbag lunch of roast beef on seeded rye, topped with an OJ. The usual $4 special was bought at a local deli on his way to work at the General Accounting Office's Office of Special Investigation on 5th Street in an unfashionable part of the capital.

Mel was one of twenty-five "Special Agents" of the GAO, legislative detectives assigned to oversee the entire executive branch, from the President on down, for any excesses, ranging from bribery to submitting imaginative expense accounts. The GAO, solely an arm of Congress, was a giant executive in itself—like a shadow government—with over 5,000 employees and a budget of half a billion dollars. Like his fellow white-collar gumshoes, Mel was ever hopeful of uncovering another Watergate, or Iran-Contra, that would embarrass the President and propel him to stardom.

Gordon fit no image of a cop. He was New York incarnate. A law graduate of street-smart Brooklyn Law School, with an accounting degree from CCNY's Baruch School on 23rd Street, he loved the slower pace of Washington and the chance to poke his nose into big government spending. Unlike most of his friends and relatives, Gordon was a political conservative, or at least a neo-conservative, the distinction being that the "neos" tended to be shorter, balder, and ex-liberals.

Gordon fit all those categories, with a special twist as well. He absolutely loved the law. Not the practice of law, which bored him stiff, but the very existence of laws, which he considered the only true distinction between man and animal. It made little difference what the law was. It had to be enforced, whether jaywalking or paying the last penny in taxes. If not, he saw the entire Judeo-Christian ethic tumbling to Hell in a supermarket basket, to mix a few metaphors.

But language didn't interest Mel. His interests were (1) being a cop, of sorts (2) the law (3) supporting his mother in style in Silver Spring, and (4) searching for a bride who'd be acceptable to both himself and mater, which so far had been a futile activity.

Tonight, he'd been burning the midnight fluorescents in his dreary ten-foot-square office. Gordon had a streak of the wry in him. To complement the somber environment, he wore an old celluloid green eye shade when he worked, a subject of tittering office conversation.

He was about five foot six, barely 135 pounds, with a receding hairline. Frankly, he admitted to looking ten years older than his own thirty-three. Gordon might be considered Woody Allenish, especially since he walked and sat in a perpetual slouch, except that Mel was handsome, or at least female admirers told him so. To husband hunters, his pay grade of $55,000 was not insignificant, but his "potential" as a lawyer-accountant outside government, he had heard many times, was "enormous."

Gordon eschewed firearms. Most of his colleagues had a more conventional background for the job—FBI men, city detectives, labor racketeer busters from the Department of Justice. But Mel had his own weapons: a computer-level mind and a mouth. At first polite, sometimes almost obsequious, his voice rallied when confronted. When faced with law-breakers, it became a virtual artillery piece.

He dealt mainly in obsessions, but fortunately one at a time. In the process, he had built a reputation at the GAO as a demonic investigator who could argue a single, seemingly isolated, point into what used to be called "a federal case." His latest obsession was the White House. Specifically, how much money they spent, whether on decorating, or limousines, or the lunches of the White House staff. Eating his $4 special, it burned his New York ass to review $60 lunch tabs of the executive branch.

Constantly, he plotted some form of accounting vengeance against the White House. He even went to the extreme of lobbying Congressmen friends to legislate half the President's staff out of business. They listened, but when Gordon turned the conversation to the wasteful army of 25,000 employees of the House and Senate, the Congressmen turned deaf ears. To many on the Hill, Gordon was "that little New York guy who thinks we should go back to the 1940s when Representatives had four assistants instead of eighteen."

This evening, nearing 9 P.M., he was scrutinizing vouchers, checks, bills, and budgets of the White House, which now ran over $350 million a year.

Gordon was plainly frustrated. He had been working for six days, including Saturday night, searching, without success, for a clue to any errant White House employee, President Briggs included. The size of the checks turned his Baruch School stomach, but the expenditures jibed with the budget supplied by the OMB, the Office of Management and Budget.

Only one item, too minor to be troubling, was not accounted for. Normally, he'd ignore it as a bookkeeping oversight, but his compulsion was going unfed. It was a White House expense check for $1,273, comically small by federal standards. Surely, it involved a "consultant," a band of Washington freebooters who lived magnificently on the government's need-to-know-nothing.

Then again, the smallest clue could presage bigger things. His mind immediately slipped into Watergate gear, his daydream picturing him as a thinner Carl Bernstein with a bestselling book, a bank account and girls to match.

The pale light coming through his green eyeshade dragged him back to reality. The check was a White House item made out to one Alex Knudsen, with no address imprinted on it. It was not the amount, but the endorsement on the back that sparked his obsession. Dutifully signed by "Alex Knudsen," it had been deposited in a Swiss bank, Banque Suisse, in Zurich. Below the endorsement was a notation that it was for a numbered account: 97675.

A secret Swiss bank account for a lousy $1,273? Why would anybody rich enough, or sneaky enough, to have one, be dealing in such petty numbers? Whatever, Knudsen was no regular White House consultant, Gordon's instincts warned him.

Tomorrow morning, first thing, he'd call Merlin Atkins, the Comptroller at the White House.

"Knudsen, you say. Alex Knudsen? Hold on, Mel. I'll check it right out."

Gordon held the phone, worried there would be a conventional explanation. His instinct would be refuted and the chase ended. An unworthy finish to such a nice daydream.

"Mel, I have it here. Knudsen. Yes, the appropriation shows it was for air travel for a consultant."

"To where, and who authorized the expenditure?" Gordon's mind quickly shifted to foreign climes. He could feel his daydream being revived.

"One second . . ." Atkins's response was followed by a mute pause.

"So, what's the story, Atkins? It's been more than a second."

"Mel, I can't give out this information. It's confidential . . ."

"Confidential? Merlin, you're talking to someone who feeds on such ideas." Gordon could feel a compulsive rush of blood. "How can anything be confidential to the GAO? Congress controls your budget. You people work for us."

"That's all very good in theory, Mel. But this voucher is signed by the President himself. If you want more information, why don't you call him? You know the White House number. So long, pal."

With that the phone went dead.

Gordon smiled the grin of a hungry shark faced with a drunk scuba diver. And besides, he had just won himself a free, and quite legal, trip to Zurich, Switzerland.

—— 31 ——

SHE had not seen the rape, but Lonnie, sulking in shame in her bunk, had told her about it one night after she woke in a sweat from a nightmare.

Julie Paichek was Lonnie's best friend and she couldn't get the rape, or the murder of coach Borden, out of her mind. The girls, who had now been separated from the boy hostages, had wanted to band together to fight the menace of Mussad. But the rape had split them. There were those who still wanted to resist in union, and those who had become isolated, nursing their fears in private. Julie was ashamed of it, but she had become a loner in captivity. Would she be raped too? Nothing she could imagine could be as horrible.

She hoped America would do something dramatic to save them. But what? Bombing would probably kill all the hostages, or give Mussad an excuse to do the same. Could they expect a war? Even so, would they survive? Or more likely, would they be the first casualties?

Julie decided she'd have to escape on her own, using her own resources. Instead of submitting to rape, she would use sex as a weapon for survival—not defeat.

His name was Abu, and he was not without charm. He was one of the guards outside her barracks. Whenever she went to and from mess, they exchanged glances, his more than casual. Their first rendezvous was at midnight, when Julie sneaked out the barracks door. As he was about to detain her, she gave him an impulsive kiss, allowing his hands to wander, swift and surprisingly tender she thought, over her breasts and body. The second night they met in the desert patch at the back, the furthest point from the guarded cyclone fence. Julie stripped in the warm night and made love with abandon, hoping for some emotional respite for herself and to secure him as a friend, bound, if necessary, by sex.

They made love every night for a week, each time in a different place to avoid detection. Then one night, after the festivities, Julie looked at him imploringly.

"Abu, I have little chance here. I must get away. I have an idea."

"Yes, Julie?"

"Why don't we leave Al Rashon together—across the border where we'll be safe. I couldn't make it on my own, but maybe you know a way. Once we're out of Mussad's grasp, well . . . then . . ."

"Julie." He spoke in hesitant English, but with no indecision. "Tomorrow morning, after breakfast, pretend to trip on a stone, and sprain your ankle. I'll help you into the barracks and tell you the plan."

She did as instructed, and now, a day later at 7 A.M., Julie waited for its execution. Abu would be arriving in a Red Crescent ambulance with his cousin as driver. The pretense would be to go to the local hospital for an Xray. In reality they would dash to the border, some thirty kilometers away, where other refugees had regularly been allowed through. For insurance, Abu was prepared to bribe the border guard.

"Lean on my shoulder, Julie, as if you can't walk," he whispered, leading her down the barracks aisle under a guard's watchful eye. Then louder: "Don't worry, we'll have you in the hospital in no time."

The ambulance traveled at normal speed down the road to the Al Rashon Hospital. Just before entering the gate, it made a casual right turn away from the hospital and onto the road leading to the border. A half hour later, the ambulance arrived at the checkpoint.

"Morning, good soldier," the driver purred. "I have a sick patient that must get to the nearest hospital. The emergency room in Al Rashon is full." Unobtrusively, he pressed a 1,000-dinar note into the border guard's palm.

The soldier smiled, waving to the blockhouse to raise the barrier. "Go ahead, the hospital is just five kilometers down the road. Allah be with you."

In the back of the ambulance, Julie listened, anticipating freedom.

"One minute, what's going on here?" The harsh tone of a young Lieutenant preceded him. After a heated discussion with the border guard, the officer approached the ambulance driver.

"All right, you and that other soldier. Out."

The officer entered the ambulance from the rear and bent over Julie. "How are you feeling, young American? Surely you didn't think such a crude plan would work? Come out of the ambulance. You'll want to see this."

At the blockhouse, the Lieutenant waited until Julie was

standing alongside. "On your knees!" he commanded Abu and his cousin.

Deliberately, the young officer strode behind them for a moment. He halted, then lifted his service revolver out of its holster.

"Allah Akbar!" His shout drowned out the gun retorts. First one, then a second bullet drilled into the skulls of the hapless men.

"No, I won't shoot you, little American lady. We have a better reception waiting back at camp."

The desert encroached on Julie's mind as ferociously as it attacked her body. Stripped and placed in a six-foot-deep hole in the sand outside her barrack-prison, she quivered in the night air, starved and denied water. The hole served as a latrine as well as living quarters. The next morning, Julie stared, half-maddened, up at a soldier videotaping her suffering.

That tape was soon on its way to New York, to the major networks, with an extra copy to President Briggs.

"In one week," said Mussad, his menacing presence dominating the tape, "we shall expect the ransom. If not, we will execute one teenager each day, until none are left."

— 32 —

PRESIDENT Briggs was outraged and heartsick. Sick over the videotaped sight of the young American girl, unclothed, freezing and starving in the desert hole. He was outraged by Mussad and his continued persecution of the young hostages, and only the thought of Davidson's operation—now as much vengeance as policy—sustained him.

He expected inhumanity from a leader like the North African dictator. What he hadn't anticipated was being sabotaged by a friend.

President Briggs shuffled the incriminating memo from side to side across the turtle-green leather desktop, trying unsuccessfully to restrain his temper. The news had come to him, through Davidson, from the Israeli intelligence service. In itself that annoyed him. Langley always seemed the last to know.

His anger was directed at Chancellor Kurt Bessinger of Germany, ostensibly a close ally. "Les, have the operators gotten Bessinger on the horn yet?" Briggs called out, his Arkansas twang exaggerated by frustration.

Garbed in her usual tight suit and jabot blouse, Fanning strode closer to Briggs's desk, smiling at his barking.

"Mr. President, they're six hours later there. It's past midnight in Berlin. Please be patient."

"I don't give a damn what time it is! Wake up that German

son-of-a-bitch. This is intolerable! And after all we've done for his country."

Fanning's smile disappeared. "I'll press the point with the White House operators. I'm sure we'll rouse him."

Fanning disappeared. Only ninety seconds later, she returned to the Oval Office, out of breath, her bosom heaving.

"Chancellor Bessinger's on the phone, Mr. President."

Briggs grinned with reassurance, but the scowl returned as he picked up the phone.

"Bessinger?"

"Yes, Mr. President. What can I do for you in the middle of the night? You've woken not just me, but my whole official household. And most important, my wife. What in the world could be so important?"

"What's wrong you say? I have a report in front of me that Mussad, that terrorist son-of-a-bitch who's holding our hostages for ransom and raping our girls, is being invited to Berlin—by you, who's supposed to be my ally. What do you have to say to that?"

"Where did you get that information, Mr. President?"

"Where? Not from your damn BND, and surely not from my CIA. No, this is from an authentic source—the Israeli intelligence people. Now 'fess up, Bessinger. Is it true?"

Only a cough came through the line.

"Mr. President. I did *not* invite Mussad to Berlin," Bessinger finally responded. "His embassy here just informed me he's coming to address some right-wingers, a new neo-Nazi political party called the 'Fourth Reich.' Germany *is* a democracy, and I could hardly stop the conference, or Mussad, for that matter."

Briggs felt only slightly mollified.

"Then you'll not receive him officially? And not at all at the Chancellery? You'll ignore his presence in Berlin. Am I right?"

Silence.

"Yes, Bessinger, I'm waiting."

The Chancellor coughed again, this time with a raspy edge.

"You have to excuse me, Mr. President. It is the middle of the night here."

"What the hell does that have to do with it? What's your answer?"

"Well, I don't believe you understand Germany's position, Mr. President. Of course we're against terrorism and we've supported you in the United Nations in condemning Mussad's action." A short pause was followed by another cough. "But we are a sovereign nation with our own concerns. You must understand that our relations with the Arab world are very precious to us."

"So?"

"Well, we Germans are not 270 million strong like you. We have one-fourth of your population and must live off our exports. We simply cannot offend 200 million Arab customers. In pure dollars and cents, Mr. President, we can no longer seem to be pro-Israel, holocaust or no holocaust. That was a long time ago. Why, I wasn't even born at the time."

"Bessinger, I'm going to ask you one more time. Are you going to receive Mussad in Berlin?"

"Again you don't understand. I am trying to play good broker between you and Mussad, to settle this horrible situation amicably. Also he's threatened to break diplomatic relations with Germany and to block all our exports—not only to his country but to nations friendly with him. Mr.

President, with the help we're giving Russia and Poland and
Hungary, and now the Baltic states as well, we really can't
afford to . . ."

"Damn you, Bessinger. I think you're all goddam Nazis
at heart!" Briggs shouted, hanging up before the Chancellor
could get off one more transatlantic cough.

── 33 ──

JOHN "The Baptist" Davidson leaned back into the First
Class lounger of the Airbus on the Lufthansa ("Air Com-
merce") non-stop night flight from Washington to Berlin.
The eight-hour trip, which he hadn't even contemplated until
yesterday morning, now seemed essential.

Berlin had become the confluence of everything—the
planned assassination of Mussad, the uncovering of Red
Swastika and its support of terrorism and neutron weapons.
Fond memories of Berlin going back to the Airlift of 1949,
when he was a young counterintelligence agent working
out of the Allied High Command under General Lucius
Clay, filled his mind. It had been a time of intrigue and
exhilaration, and coming back to the city gave him the
unrivaled pleasure of nostalgia.

The plane landed at Berlin's Tegel Airport at 9:05 A.M.
without incident. Davidson quickly made a taxi beeline to
the American Embassy, where he had been hurriedly signed
on as Cultural Attaché. If he hadn't been an Intelligence

man, he confessed, he would have enjoyed a cultural career. It was eons ago, but he thought warmly back to his Princeton days when he had edited the literary journal, *Papyri.*

With the Beekeeper surely in Berlin, and Mussad scheduled to arrive, Davidson felt pressed by time. Borrowing Ambassador Belkin's sumptuous bath, once the marble lavatory of a prince of the Hohenzollern line, he made ready for his first appointment. It was with Manfred Lichtenstein at BND headquarters at Spandau Citadel. A fellow young Allied agent during the Airlift days, Lichtenstein was now BND's Chief of Counterintelligence, Davidson's former job at Langley.

"Baptist, I had no idea Germany was in the midst of an espionage crisis," Lichtenstein warmly greeted his fellow Cold Warrior. "Your being here confirms it. No?"

Lichtenstein was a German with English pretensions. After two years at Oxford, he spoke perfect English but with a strange mixture of a clipped Prussian accent and the casualness of the British upper class. Tall, thin, almost hawk-faced, he looked more like a seasoned division commander in the Afrika Corps than a counterspy.

The conversation ranged over the years, of evenings spent in the rain at Glienicker Bridge at the Spree River in then-divided Berlin, waiting for Allied compatriots to be returned in prisoner exchanges. Davidson especially remembered the night KGB Colonel Rudolf Abel, who had been the senior undercover "illegal" in New York, was handed over to the Russians in exchange for Gary Powers, the downed American U-2 reconnaissance pilot.

"So, colleague Davidson, what can we insignificant, but grateful, Germans do for America today?"

"Manfred, I've come over here to learn anything I can about Red Swastika," Davidson began. He felt no need to divulge anything about the German/neutron bomb connection.

Lichtenstein placed his chin in his hands.

"Red Swastika, eh? News travels fast. We've had rumbles that the fascists—I suppose you could say the Nazis—are becoming active." Lichtenstein stared at Davidson. "John, I'm afraid that fifty years after his death, there are still more Hitler admirers in Germany than people are willing to admit. But information on them is short, unfortunately. I'm even afraid they have sympathizers in the BND, which doesn't help our investigation."

"Do you know who?"

"No, that would make life easy. But whoever they are, they are sharp professionals, and keep us guessing."

"But why, Manfred? Germany is united and successful. Isn't that enough?" Davidson enjoyed asking questions for which he already had the answers.

"Oh, yes, for most of us. But there are many who dream of lost glory, of new nationalism, even of a new empire, a new Reich, the Fourth. I despise it all, but I understand it. After Hitler, Germans carried the memories of conquest, then defeat, one on each shoulder. Now that they are whole and sovereign, some of them want to get even. First they brag that they are number one economically. I suppose that's OK, as long as it's only bluster—you know, the Ugly German instead of the Ugly American. But when they talk about violence, or coups, that's not so kosher, as you say."

Davidson sensed that Lichtenstein would again be a major source in Berlin.

"What about talk that Russia is somehow tied to Red Swastika?" the Baptist asked.

"I've heard that too, and I suppose it makes sense. The hardliners in the Kremlin could use an ally in the West. Who better than neo-Nazis? It encourages their dreams and inflames their political passions. Both governments, in Berlin and Moscow, talk against the right-wing fringes, but believe me, Baptist, underneath, they have a lot of support— in and out of the bureaucracy."

Lichtenstein smiled, as if he were playing a strong poker hand.

"And, John, of course it's a mere coincidence that you've come to Berlin just before the visit of the Great Mussad?"

"It's purely a coincidence, Manfred. But now that I'm here, I suppose I'll send a report back to the President. And maybe while Mussad's here, someone can convince the madman to change his course."

"John, I guarantee you—the German government is totally behind your President. I personally don't approve of Mussad's coming to Berlin, but nobody asked me. Still, Germany does have a special relationship with the Third World, especially the Arabs." He laughed. "They're a wonderful market for our goods."

"Where's Mussad going to stay in Berlin?" Davidson's manner was as offhanded as he could make it.

"At the Hilton, in the penthouse suite, protected, I might add, by a slew of bodyguards. Plus a few of my people, and the Berlin *polizei*." Lichtenstein's response was delivered in the same monotone.

Davidson smiled at the news about the Hilton. He had already guessed that would be Mussad's home during the visit, and had clued in the Beekeeper.

"And the public reception?" he asked.

"At the Reichstag building, on the Platz der Republik. Where else, John?"

The BND counterintelligence man leaned over his desk, his face now within inches of Davidson's. His sharp features were stretched into a broad smile.

"Tell me, Baptist. Why all this curiosity? You're not

planning to assassinate Mussad in Berlin, are you?"

With that, Lichtenstein broke into a raucous laugh and heartily slapped Davidson on the back of his herringbone.

"That's a good one, isn't it, John? Assassinate Mussad right here in Berlin!"

Lichtenstein led the old spy toward the elevator, shaking his head in farewell, still laughing uproariously over his joke.

—— 34 ——

DAVIDSON stayed close to his telephone at the American Embassy on Friedrichstrasse, where he was ensconced, without a secretary, as the Cultural Attaché—waiting for his contact message from the Beekeeper.

He had spent the morning with a group of American students studying advanced German at the Free University of Berlin, apologizing for his less-than-fluent command of the language. This evening, he was to host a conference of the Johann Wolfgang von Goethe Society, made up of emigré Americans and Germans intent on practicing their English. A longtime fan of Goethe, especially his "Dr. Faustus," Davidson admired not only the writer but the man who had climbed the tall Cologne cathedral spire to cure his acrophobia, the fear of heights, and had methodically cut his own skin to conquer his loathing of blood.

Davidson had his own fears: of exposing his President to political danger should the Beekeeper fail. Perhaps doing much the same if he succeeded.

Around lunch time, while he was sipping a cup of packaged soup at his desk, the phone rang.

"Hello," an American voice asked. "Is this the Cultural Attaché?"

"Yes, this is John Davidson."

"Good. I'm an American, just moved here by my firm, Taylor Chemical. I'm looking for a music teacher who speaks English. Can you recommend anyone?"

Davidson relaxed. Contact had been made with the Beekeeper.

"Why yes, there's a Herr Gontz. His studio is on Budapester Strasse, close to the Tiergarten, you know, near Bellevue, that English-style park. Perhaps twenty minutes from here by foot."

"Thank you, Mr. Davidson, you've been very kind."

The Baptist told the receptionist he'd be out most of the afternoon. He'd return for the evening Goethe meeting.

Leaving the Embassy, Davidson entered the U-Bahn subway, the *Untergrundbahn*, prominently marked with a large "U" in white on a blue background, and the first move in shaking any tails. At the Zoologischer Garten, the Zoo stop, he left the U-Bahn and moved out on foot, ready to learn if he was being followed. It was soon a question of who, not whether.

He had found that window shopping was the quickest way to spot persistent tails. Heading down to the Ku-Damm, Berlin's Fifth Avenue, Davidson walked along the busy boulevard, stopping at every fourth shop to ogle the merchandise. By the time he had covered sixteen, *two* tails had made themselves obvious by choosing the same store windows and skipping those Davidson did.

One shadow was a caricature of the burly private eye raiding lovers' motels. The second was a lady of a certain comely appearance, conspicuously dressed in a worsted suit and a tall feathered hat, the whole outfit reminiscent of the Thirties.

Davidson assumed that three groups were interested in his movements: the BND, Mussad's people, and Red Swastika. The PI was probably BND, but he couldn't guess who the woman worked for, or which of the three groups were absent.

He parked himself in front of a jewelry shop window next to a bus stop, ostensibly staring at the gems, but actually watching the plate glass reflection for the right moment. The bus arrived. He counted the seconds. At the fifteenth, he swiveled about and raced for the open bus door. Mounting the steps just before it closed, Davidson offered a friendly wave to the two tails, who stood helplessly on the sidewalk, looking at each other in bewilderment.

The bus ride was brief, after which he hailed a Mercedes taxi. "Englischer Park in the Tiergarten," Davidson told the cabbie, then relaxed in the rear.

At the park, he decided on prudence. He'd pick out and observe the Beekeeper before making contact. Standing by a cluster of linden trees at the edge of an open area, he spotted Knudsen sitting on a bench. Davidson laughed. The Beekeeper was outlandishly dressed in a gaudy sport shirt, with two cameras slung around his neck. Davidson made no move, nor did he give any sign of recognition. One hundred feet away and half-hidden by the trees, he wasn't sure if Knudsen had seen him.

Ten minutes. That's the time the Baptist waited in the green shadows, watching the Beekeeper while holding his own position. Time was his insurance policy. If anyone had managed to follow him and was waiting for a premature contact, they might be flushed out by their own impatience.

Davidson checked his watch. He had been cautious enough. Only the finest professional would have maintained his incognito that long. He made his first, tentative, steps in the direction of the Beekeeper, when his progress was halted—abruptly.

A fattened, oversized hand sprung from behind a tree and encircled his neck, pulling him against the trunk. A gun pressed into his lower back radiated pain from his kidney up to his brain. Davidson groaned.

"All right, Baptist," a powerful Germanic voice commanded. "Which one is your contact?"

Davidson twisted his head just enough to see the Beekeeper. Knudsen had spotted the scene and was casually leaving the bench, mixing quickly into a gaggle of tourists. The Baptist relaxed a touch. Now only he was at risk.

"Which one, Baptist?" the voice again demanded.

"You're late. My contact is gone."

"Really? Well, my people want you out of this busy Berlin scene anyway." The gun dug deeper into his kidney. "Follow me into that clump of trees. The silencer will muffle any noise."

As Davidson turned, he caught a glimpse of his captor. It was the giant ex-Stasi man and German blueblood, Colonel Count Wolfgang von Horstmann, the Mussad aide he had briefly spotted in the hostage tape from Al Rashon.

"We've never met," Horstmann said as Davidson picked his way through, the gun prodding him on. "It's a shame our acquaintance will be so short." Horstmann paused for breath. "All right, we'll stop here. As good a spot as any. Commune with your Maker, old spy."

Davidson was walking, Horstmann behind him, when the unearthly silence was broken by a sudden crash. Followed by a thud.

The Baptist turned quickly, as if dancing. Facing him

was the impish smile of a short, gray crew-cutted man—
Sam Withers. On the ground, almost twice the size of the
victor, was Goliath. Horstmann's eyes were blinking in pain,
the dull wound on his temple bleeding a slow leak. Withers
held his .45 in hand, gun barrel backwards, the blunt end
still in its menacing position.

"What the hell, Sam? What are you doing here?"

"Is that my thanks, Baptist? You know I don't approve
of your playing lone wolf. When you scrammed out of the
Embassy, I followed along with your three tails. When
Horstmann grabbed you, I was afraid to shoot him without
a silencer. So I waited and clobbered the big bastard with
the butt end of my .45. It took all my strength."

Withers bent over the moaning giant. "I think he's coming to."

Davidson knelt on the ground and picked up the Beretta.
Slapping Horstmann across both sides of his face, he finally
roused the semi-conscious German.

"Horstmann, can you hear me?"

A series of moans was followed by a grunt. "Yes, is that
you, Baptist? You're not dead?"

"No, but you almost were. Now listen carefully. I know
all about your family estate, Raven's Nest in Bavaria. If
you want it back, call me at the Embassy."

Davidson rose and motioned to Withers to follow. As
they walked toward the open area, the Baptist lowered his
arm over Withers's shoulder.

"Thanks, Sam. But forget that old spy stuff. There's plenty
of pizzazz left in these herringbones."

"WHERE in the hell were you? I was worried. It's almost midnight," Withers said, his anxiety showing.

He had answered the buzzer, then opened the apartment door. Before him stood Marieanne, soaked to the skin from a quick flash rain that had begun just twenty minutes before.

"Darling, I can't kiss you. I'm all wet." Marieanne shook out her soaked overcoat. "But don't be angry. I was out spying—for you."

Inside, disrobed except for a towel covering the lower half of her body, Marieanne moved closer to a fire Withers had started, and told of her night adventure.

"I was working until about eight, then a friend at the office—Beatrice Fleiss, I don't think you know her—asked me to go to a political meeting. It was at the townhouse of an old Prussian blueblood, Ludwig von Kleber. I swear it was like being at a Nazi meeting, a lot of socializing with right wingers, all talking about the glory days. I stayed late because I wanted to learn as much as I could—for you, darling." Marieanne leaned her bare bosom against Withers. "I got all wet waiting for a cab." She looked at him imploringly. "Dry me off, Sam."

Adjourning to bed, Sam found the lovemaking as stimulating as ever, only stopping to caution his German lover.

"Marieanne, could you do me one favor?"

"What's that, Sam?"

"Stop talking about my work when we're in bed. I think I've created a geopolitical monster."

She laughed and leaned back, her eyes inviting. "I promise I won't say another word until morning."

Withers brought Marieanne's information on von Kleber to Davidson, who immediately rushed it to Lichtenstein at the BND.

The next morning, Davidson received a call at the Embassy.

"John, this is Manfred. I've gotten the *Ganzfakt* material you asked for. It reads like Shirer's *Rise and Fall of the Third Reich*. Kleber joined the Hitler Jugend when he was twelve, was decorated by Hitler at sixteen in the defense of Berlin. His father, an Übersturmfuehrer in the SS, and a member of the Party since 1924, was convicted of war crimes at Nuremberg and died in Spandau prison. Since then, von Kleber's used his considerable inherited fortune to help support—quite legally—every right-wing fanatic in Germany."

Davidson whistled silently into the phone. "Thanks, Manfred."

Leaning back with slight satisfaction, he wondered: could Sam's new lover have found the route to Red Swastika? Or was it all too convenient?

— 36 —

AT three in the morning, the Reichstag, proud and isolated at Platz der Republik, was bathed in two bright spotlights, illuminating the triangular classical pediment atop the overscale entrance, and the simple German flag of three stripes—red, yellow, and black.

In the corner shadows, two Berlin *polizei*, only lightly armed with non-automatic pistols, carried out their routine tours of the building and its grounds. The Bundestag parliament, which had moved to the Reichstag, was not in session. Its members were back in their sixteen constituent States drumming up votes for the coming national elections.

The Greens—a liberal, environmental group—had lost all their Bundestag members in the last contest by failing to get the required five percent of the total vote. Under Chancellor Bessinger, the Christian Democrats still held a majority, but pundits were predicting that the new "Fourth Reich" party of right-wingers and neo-Nazis would take the Greens' place in the Bundestag.

Lloyd's of London were laying even money that the Fourth Reich—the "Fourth Empire"—whose parades featured posters with just the suggestive word "HEIL" in giant red and black letters, would take more than ten percent of the vote, about the same percentage Hitler had gotten in the early 1930s.

At the flank of the Reichstag in the darkness were three vans, each with a team of demolition experts. One was from the Red Army faction, a German far-left terrorist guerrilla organization that had grown out of the Baader-Meinhof gang. The second was made up of ex-Stasi men. Both groups had taken shelter in Moscow after the East German revolution. The third team were Red Swastika men training with the veteran terrorists. The group was equipped with both the tools of modern demolition and the simpler instruments of murder.

Their chief, Helmut Girden, had been trained in Czechoslovakia by the Russians in the 1980s, and had been freelancing since. Tonight, he was receiving $100,000 for his job, with $50,000 for each of the others, the money supplied by Red Swastika. Girden understood that it was a well-financed organization.

Like his men, Girden had half covered his face with a ski mask and blackened the rest. In each three-man team, two carried a total of twenty-four packs of German-made plastique, with time fuses imbedded securely within. The detonator-clocks were set for from five to ten minutes, the trigger time to begin once the plastique had been placed in designated spots in the Reichstag—just as they had rehearsed in a large barn in the Berlin countryside.

The two outside men, carrying Israeli UZI automatics, moved in a long arc, approaching the building to the rear of each *polizei* guard. Girden checked his watch, then blew into a dog whistle. The high-pitched signal, inaudible to human ears, silently pierced the night, then was received by the flankers through a small device clipped to their black sweaters. At the call, they pounced like leopards, their sharpened bowie knives cutting the vocal cords of the surprised policemen.

With their own dog whistles, they signaled that the way was clear for the sappers. Four demolition men raced to the back of the Reichstag, where a rear door was blown open by a Mauser with silencer. Fanning out, the deadly quartet ran through the building, the architectural layout engraved in their minds. A plastique bomb was spotted every forty feet, on each floor, with six spaced around the modern meeting hall. Those with the longest trigger time were laid first.

As each one was dropped, the release timer was set. Within five minutes, the work was completed. The men retreated to their vans, but not before making a quick bypass to the front of the building. In a flourish devised by Dr. Koller, they left behind a pre-loaded record player with a powerful 1,000-watt Hafler amplifier.

They started the van engines but waited for the tape to blare out their message: "Deutschland Uber Alles," the national anthem.

When the rousing song was over, a new chorus began. Twenty-four plastique bombs exploded in simultaneous concert, raising the Reichstag building into the night with one groaning, brilliant firework.

— 37 —

IN his single room in the Berlin Hilton—at a daily tariff of
400 Deutschemarks, or $300—Davidson opened his copy
of the Washington paper, flown in each day. He searched
for a column he had worked on before he hurriedly left for
Berlin.

The story was actually a "plant," although Davidson hated
to use the word, as if he were feeding false information to the
press, which was not his way. He had met with Washington
columnist, Jake Connors, the Darth Vader of syndicated
journalism, whose sometimes depressing, but usually accurate, revelations ran in 310 newspapers coast-to-coast.

He and Connors had met at a corner lunch table at
the Cosmos Club—an elegant stone French mansion on
Massachusetts Avenue once owned by FDR's socialite
Assistant Secretary of State Sumner Welles—and chat-
ted about the morality, and feasibility, of assassination
as an instrument of American foreign policy. Davidson
was careful not to push the idea, but he did outline the
obstacles the President had in handling the Mussad affair,
either peaceably, or with war.

Nothing was settled, but Connors said he would think
about the subject. Maybe he would even do a piece on it.

"But do me a favor, Baptist," Connors asked.

"What's that?"

"Don't get anybody assassinated until my column comes out."

In his hotel room, Davidson scanned the paper. There it was, on page five, headlined right under Connor's bulldog profile: "SHOULD THE PRESIDENT CONSIDER THE ALTERNATIVE—ONE LIFE FOR THOUSANDS?"

The columnist carefully laid out the dilemma: the dog-eat-dog nature of assassinating a foreign leader, along with the problem of finding a reasonable solution to the North African mess.

"This reporter hears that Mussad has his shoreline mined with modern 'influence' mines, submerged where we can't get them, and which could cripple any amphibious landing. There're also whispers that he's trying to get his hands on nuclear weapons. Meanwhile, he's fomenting rebellions in sub-Sahara Africa to grab up a handful of satellites, all with seeming impunity. This time, it's courtesy of the UN's hesitance to interfere in so-called 'domestic' squabbles.

"What's left to do?" Connors asked his readers. "Kill the bastard. That's what. The President may yet have to do that, if he has the Arkansas guts he came into office with. It's a tough call, but it looks like he has little other choice if he wants our kids back and hopes to stop that North African country from dominating his area, both white and black."

Davidson read the piece, then the paper's sidebar item with satisfaction. They had interviewed several people on the subject, including those in the hinterland and a few on the Hill. One interviewee, House Speaker Rusty Kembeck, was outraged at the idea. "I hope Connors is not talking for the President," Kembeck said, "because it sounds like some crazy CIA spookery."

But other citizens, further from the Beltway, disagreed. "A quick telephone survey of a hundred readers of the Connors column," reported the Washington paper, "sided with Connors. Seventy-one out of a hundred said, in effect: 'Kill the bastard!' "

Davidson hated to arouse such primitive emotions, but he needed to advance his cause: protection of the nation as he, and Briggs, saw it. Now that all four protagonists in the drama—he, Sam Withers, Mussad, and the Beekeeper— had arrived in Berlin, it was time to make Jake Connors happy.

— 38 —

"OUT of my way, girlie, or I'm going to push you over, the way my people took Custer."

Rusty Kembeck, part South Dakota Sioux and mostly intemperate Speaker of the House of Representatives, waved away Les Fanning's objection that he couldn't see the President without an appointment.

"What's all that noise out there?" Briggs called from his desk.

"It's me, Hawley, your goddam conscience."

Kembeck roared into the Oval Office, copies of Connor's column and the newspaper's public opinion poll in hand. His tanned complexion was reddened and his oversize cowboy boots thudded resonantly on the rug.

"What in the hell are you talking about, Rusty?" the President shouted back. "Sometimes I think you take too much firewater."

"Don't give me your patronizing Indian bullshit. What's this talk about assassination? Smells to me like hanky panky from your old spook, John the Baptist. Whose country is he messing up now?"

Silence was the best tranquilizer, Briggs decided. He said nothing for twenty seconds, then motioned the Speaker over to a chair near the warm fireplace.

"Now tell me slow, Rusty. What's got you all inflamed?"

"Hawley, I don't think that Connors loony is spouting off on his own. I have no proof, but my smeller tells me something lousy is afoot. Could it be that one of your people, maybe the Baptist, put Connors up to this to get the public riled up? Maybe even to set up an excuse in case you tried something as crazy as assassination?"

The lie was not usually part of Briggs's political inventory, but he thought about the hostages, about possible neutron war in North Africa, about the territorial designs of a leader a lot smarter than Saddam Hussein.

"Rusty, you know the President is not supposed to go around talking about his war, or non-war, policies. But I will tell you that I had nothing to do with Connors's column."

Kembeck stood up, his face now fully reddened. Again, he stamped his cowboy boots against the rug.

"What kind of Arkansas cowshit is that, Hawley? I ask you if you've authorized the killing of another national leader and you tell me you didn't talk to some shitass columnist. I warn you, Mr. President, if you violate Executive Order 12333, which you signed on yourself, and start a personal shooting match between heads of government, I'm not only going to impeach your ass, but I'll permanently hang your political hide on the Taft Campanile higher than a wild tornado."

Kembeck strode toward the doorway, where Les Fanning

stood, her pale complexion now ghostly white.

"And you can get that scared look off your face, pretty lady. Cause the next time you see me, I may just have had a drink and I'm really going to get my Indian up."

39

DAVIDSON heard from the Beekeeper again. Obviously he was frustrated by the failure to make contact at the Tiergarten.

It came in a call to the Embassy, made from a public phone. Cryptic in style, the message assumed Davidson's official phone had unofficial listeners.

"I'm sorry, Mr. Davidson," Knudsen said, "but your music teacher who speaks English is no longer practicing. Can you recommend another? Perhaps I could come over to the Embassy right away and you could help me."

Davidson knew the last thought was a diversion. The Beekeeper was really seeking a lead to a secure, private rendezvous.

"No, I'm sorry I can't see you today. I have a Goethe meeting until 7:30 P.M. But you can get the information at the main library—the Staatsbibliothek, the Stabi. It's near the Opera House. They have a list of music teachers, including those who speak foreign languages. I wish you luck."

Davidson was sure the rendezvous arrangement had been

properly transmitted: 7:30 P.M. at the main library. It was now 6, and Davidson gave himself some time before his trip, which he hoped would be unencumbered by intrusions from any of his shadows. But he couldn't be sure.

He feared that secure travel through Berlin would be even more difficult now that Mussad had arrived in the city. The US Embassy had received formal notice from the Foreign Ministry from a man named Paul Dollop, along with Mussad's supposed itinerary. The visit was to begin with a diplomatic reception in the Adenauer Grand Ballroom at the Hilton, followed by a tour of the city highlights, culminating with a joint address by both Mussad and Chancellor Bessinger before the Bundestag parliament. Since the destruction of the Reichstag, which Davidson was sure was the work of Red Swastika, they would meet at a former Kaiser's palace in Potsdam.

At exactly 6:20 P.M., Davidson left the Embassy and walked to the U-Bahn entrance nearby. He boarded a No. 7 train going west, then after traveling almost to the end of the line to Bismarck Strasse, he switched to the No. 1 line going east, then to the No. 9 headed due south—in the opposite direction to the library—all the way past Friedrich Wilhelm Platz. At the end of the line, near the district of Steglitz, he crossed over to begin the journey back to the main junction at the Ku-Damm. Carefully, he scanned anyone who might be crossing over with him. Either they were correcting a misdirection—or following him. There were four such people and he recognized none of them. All appeared innocent, at least at first glance.

The train back to the Ku-Damm would take about twenty minutes. Then he would change to the No. 1 line, riding it one stop to the Wittenberg station. From there, he'd feel free to surface and continue by taxi to the library.

The return to the Ku-Damm stop was uneventful. People on the train were occupied, as in all large cities, in minding their own business. Some were snatching a nap, others reading. Copies of the daily *Berliner Morgenpost* and the weekly *Die Zeit* were all over the train. Davidson, who avoided carrying any English-language publications, pulled a copy of *Der Spiegel*, the popular newsmagazine, from his pocket. He read, roughly translating as he went, trying not to move his lips. When in public, his incognito required that he pass himself off as a Berliner.

At the Ku-Damm station, he waited for a No. 1 car, glancing down the platform for an approaching train. Several people were doing the same. For an instant, his claustrophobia overtook him. He started to turn back, away from the track, when, seemingly from nowhere, his eyes made contact with someone he recognized—the burly shadow from the other day, the man with the bearing of a private eye.

The eye contact lasted only a split second. Suddenly, Davidson felt himself being pushed toward the platform edge, the sound of an incoming train coming simultaneously with the attack. The two mixed into confusion. He quickly moved one, then two, steps backwards, trying to resist the aggressor, whose face had become a sardonic mask. But it was futile. The arms kept pressing against his chest until his heels felt the slippery edge of the platform. His voice rose from inside his larynx, poised to scream for help.

"*Vorsicht!*" Watch out! a man shouted.

Davidson felt a hand clutch at his suited forearm, then twist him to one side. He fell onto the platform and rotated wildly, his body rolling to the edge. Desperately, his hands grasped for a hold. One clutched at the metal border of the platform. His other arm was tight in the grip of the Samaritan, whose fingers tenaciously held on.

Davidson glanced up at his attacker, whose forward motion was now unblocked.

"*HILFE!*" HELP! he heard the voice scream as the burly aggressor tottered, then was hurled onto the track.

The train whistle wailed as the engineer tried to brake the train to a stop. It halted, but not until it had crossed over the unconscious body.

"*Danke, Danke,*" Davidson muttered as the Samaritan, dressed in blue workclothes, helped him to his feet. A crowd started to form, looking at, even touching, Davidson. Everyone seemed to be waiting for some sign of authority to sort out the confusion.

"*Danke,*" Davidson repeated, walking half-backwards toward the station exit. This was no time to become ensnarled in a bureaucratic police morass. He turned forward and started quickly up the stairs to the street, passing two Berlin *polizei* on their way down.

On the Ku-Damm, where the shoppers were unaware of the murder attempt or the track death below, Davidson hailed a cab.

"Staatsbibliothek, *bitte,*" he said, his breath still coming in gasps.

"Baptist, you look a little pale."

The Beekeeper, dressed more appropriately in slacks and a windbreaker, was waiting alongside the stacks. They walked down the aisle to an empty desk used for reference work at the rear.

"Yes, someone's trying to make things difficult for me. I guess I'll have to become even more circumspect." Davidson smiled at his operative. "And how are you doing? Now that Mussad's here, I suspect you'll soon be quite busy."

"I'm already too busy, John. That's why I called you. Since Mussad came in, this town's become an armed camp. I've been all over it, and it's swarming with security people—both the local gendarmes and Mussad's men. I need to change my thinking."

Davidson was surprised. The Beekeeper seldom held doubts about his missions. "Why, is anything wrong?"

"Well, I originally planned to take him out anonymously, using my Steyr and catching him outside. I could still do that if he kept to his schedule, visiting places and really making that joint appearance with Bessinger at the Bundestag. But . . ." The Beekeeper had moved into contemplation.

"But what?" Davidson asked.

"But, I don't believe it for a minute. Too risky for Mussad. My guess is that he's going to stay put at the Hilton. The people are going to come to him, including the Chancellor. For that my sharpshooter is no good. I need a different weapon, small, personal, automatic. Can you get one for me?"

Davidson grinned in relief. He turned his head in both directions. "We seem to be alone, Alex." He reached into his jacket and removed a gun from his shoulder holster. "It's an M-9 Beretta, 9 mm, a 15-shot semiautomatic with a full clip. I took it off Colonel Horstmann the other day in the Tiergarten. I was saving it for myself, but here, it's yours."

The Beekeeper stroked the gun, as lovingly as if it were a family puppy.

"This is very nice. Thanks, Baptist. I have a feeling I'm going to earn my plane fare real close up."

— 40 —

MEL Gordon gratefully stretched his legs as he left the Swissair 747 at the Kloten International Airport in Zurich after a seven-and-a-half-hour trip from JFK. On the train to town, located with Swiss efficiency right at the airport, he traveled eleven kilometers in some ten minutes, and arrived at the Bahnhofstrasse, or Train Station Street, the main drag of this metropolitan area of almost a million inhabitants at the north end of Lake Zurich.

He calculated the cost of his trip so far. It had set the GAO back $1,322 for his round-trip economy ticket, almost $100 more than the White House check he was tracing. But he sensed there was a larger payoff, greater than money, somewhere down the line. Gordon's problem was that he had no idea what, or where.

Checking into the St. Gotthard hotel, just a few blocks from the station, he marked his itinerary into a pocketsize leather notebook, the chronicler of his routine. Every move, from his dental appointment to the number of shirts he had left with the cleaners in Chevy Chase, were duly marked by date. Simply by studying his daily diary, he could assess the state of his life.

Gordon left nothing to chance, and surely nothing to anyone else. He had the obsessive thought that everyone in the world, except himself, was somewhat dull mentally. If that weren't enough, he also harbored the suspicion—some said it was paranoid—that they were after his mind. And nothing he had seen in his thirty-three years had led him to change that opinion.

The next morning, his first stop was the Banque Suisse office about five minutes by cab from his hotel.

"*Guten Morgen*, Herr Gordon. We were awaiting you."

Karl Stauffer, the slim, fastidious-looking bank manager, escorted Gordon to the conference room, where they sat some fifteen feet apart at ends of a highly-polished birch table.

"Now that you've arrived, we're curious what the General Accounting Office of the United States Congress would want of a banker in Switzerland. Has someone stolen billions from the US Treasury—other than your own S&Ls?" Stauffer laughed. "Oh, excuse me, I forgot to ask for your credentials."

Gordon passed over a black leather wallet, on which was pinned his gold-plated badge of office, with the legend "SPECIAL AGENT" clearly emblazoned on it. Inside was his ID and photo from the GAO.

"Good, then we're dealing with the right man. Now, again, how can I help you?"

From his inner pocket, Mel extracted a Xerox copy of both sides of the White House check, and crossing to the other side of the conference table, handed it to the bank manager.

"This?" Stauffer asked, his eyebrows arched in disdain. "This check for $1,273 is why you flew from Washington to Switzerland? Come now, Mr. Gordon, this is some kind of a joke. No?"

"If you turn it over, Mr. Stauffer, you'll see that it was deposited into a numbered account in your bank."

"Yes, and so? It is still a pitiful amount of money to be

concerned with. Whoever it is, did he steal more money through another bank?"

Gordon could see the Swiss mentality at work. If big money was not involved, how could there be a crime afoot?

"As far as I know he hasn't stolen a damn thing, Mr. Stauffer. That's not why I'm trying to find this man."

"I don't understand. But anyway, what can I do for you?"

"It's simple. I just want to know who opened this numbered account. His name and how to reach him."

Stauffer rose and straightened up, seeming to come to military attention. "Oh, no, Mr. Gordon. We can't do that. Secrecy of deposits is our specialty, the reason people come to Zurich to sequester their funds."

Gordon decided to mimick his adversary. He, too, jumped up and came to attention, almost clicking his heels.

"No, Mr. Stauffer. I represent the United States government, and we *must*, I repeat, *must* get this information."

Mel's decibel level rose as he spoke, the singsong New York inflection rising with it. "Chapter and Verse, Mr. Bank Manager—US Treasury Mutual Legal Assistance Treaty, signed with the government of Switzerland in July 1986, giving us access to your secret numbered accounts if one of our citizens is involved and we have probable cause that a felony has been committed. Well, we're *sure* a crime, some horrendous one, has or is about to take place."

Gordon hesitated for an instant, gauging his sedate surroundings. A sharp lesson in urgency was needed.

"IS THAT CLEAR, MR. SWISS BANKER?" he shouted, the echo bouncing off the heavily-paneled wooden walls. Within seconds, a half dozen bank workers and officers had rushed into the conference room.

Stauffer had turned ashen, quickly resuming his seat at the table.

"You needn't shout, Mr. Gordon. If the United States government is so insistent, I suppose I can show you this one account. If you'll wait here, I'll bring you the details."

Gordon waited, his foot tapping, his adrenaline still racing from his legal-intimidation performance. One of the most effective of his career, if he had to say so. Especially since he had invoked the Swiss-American banking treaty without evidence, of any kind, that a crime had been committed.

"Ah, here we are, Mr. Gordon. The depositor's name, at least the one he gave us, is Alex Knudsen. He has a balance of eight dollars, twelve cents."

"What?" Gordon's voice was filled with disappointment. "Is that all?"

"Yes, but he has made a recent transfer of $3.7 *million* to a bank in the Cayman Islands, specifically, the First Caribbean Trust. I'm afraid that's all I can help you with."

"That's enough, Mr. Stauffer," Gordon said as he exited.

Knudsen was obviously a rich man, and on some mission for the White House. But if had committed a crime, or was about to, what in the hell was it?

— 41 —

DAVIDSON couldn't sleep. At 3 A.M., he reached over and put on the bedside lamp in the Berlin Hilton, his home since arriving in that city. Instead of resting, he had been tallying up his intelligence assets and liabilities. Now, he needed to put them on paper, to design his next move.

Aside from Mussad, he had come five thousand miles to find and isolate Red Swastika, the link between the North African terrorist and the technological and political sophistication of the West. That movement was a threat not only to the relatively new democratic institutions of Germany, but to the world.

He listed one point after another, stopping when he came to the name of Marieanne Luft, Sam's new *amour*. She had branched into right-wing territory for Withers, and had come back with news that Ludwig von Kleber, an aged wealthy Nazi sympathizer, might be the covert leader of Red Swastika. The BND's c.v. on the aristocrat at least confirmed his past.

Where, Davidson asked, could he check out the truth? He had found that the middle of the night was his best time for reckoning. This 3 A.M. break confirmed it.

Jessie Leinsdorf! It had been thirty years, but this daughter of a democratic Berlin attorney who had survived two years in Hitler's Bergen-Belsen concentration camp, might have the answer. Would she remember those salad days of the Cold War, of shared intelligence work against the Russians and a tender, if brief, love affair?

Davidson checked the digital clock: 4:05 A.M. In four hours, he would call Jessie and find out.

"John, you don't know how wonderful it is to see you again. My father sends his fondest."

Davidson was seated alongside Jessie Leinsdorf in the back of her chauffeured Mercedes, marveling how gentle time had been. Her face showed only a few mature lines appropriate for a woman of fifty-four or five, and she had added ten pounds, which had nicely filled out her lithe figure. Jessie's hair was shorter, but still long for someone her age, and naturally blonde. Perhaps now a shade darker. She had been attractive then, he remembered. But today, unless it was an illusion of his own age, she had become beautiful.

"Jessie, it's great seeing you too, a shot of instant youth. But I feel awkward asking you to help out, as if you still worked for the Agency."

"Nonsense, John, this time it's for me. I've heard the same talk about Red Swastika. And look at the sick popular support for their Fourth Reich political party. No, I'm the one who's grateful."

Davidson touched her hand, noticing the third finger choked by an enormous diamond. "I see you're married. Children?"

"Oh, yes, four, all grown. But my husband is gone. An early heart attack. And your wife? You were thinking of marriage at the time. When was it, 1960?"

"Yes, she passed away a few years ago. I'm just an ancient widower."

The two veterans spent a moment in silence. Not anguished, but reminiscent.

"John, on the phone you asked about Ludwig von Kleber and a connection to Red Swastika. No, it can't be. He's a silly old dolt, playing with his collection of antique weapons and dreaming of German military glory. He's a pathetic jingoist who thinks Hitler's only mistake was that he didn't appreciate Prussian aristocrats like himself. No, all the right-wing groups flatter him and take his money—which is considerable. But he leads nothing, except his fantasies. If you're looking for Red Swastika, I think you have to search elsewhere. They're much smarter than von Kleber." Jessie smiled impishly. "That's why I had you invited to this dinner tonight. I think this is closer to pay dirt."

If Jessie was right, then Marieanne Luft was either an amateur, or—it crossed his mind again—no friend of Sam Withers. He had once raised the idea with Sam, as pure speculation, but it had only riled his quarter-Irish.

Jessie was the heir to an old Prussian fortune and had a reputation for being intelligent but non-political, giving her access everywhere. It had proven an invaluable asset in Cold War days. Now she had come out of "retirement" for Davidson, and he was pleased.

"John, this man you're going to meet—your host—is important. You mentioned the Heinschmann connection to Mussad. Well, that's where we're going tonight, to *Nachtgefluster*, Night Whisper, the estate of Klaus von Stimmel, the principal owner of the conglomerate. An extraordinary person, as you'll see. And not without charm."

"How did you pass me off as a proper dinner guest?"

"Oh, no problem. They think I'm an old eccentric so I just told them the truth. They were thrilled that you were coming. I explained that you were the former counterintelligence chief for the CIA and the great hero of the Cold War. You know, they don't like Communism either—although you tell me they're in some kind of partnership with the secret hardline Russians right now."

Jessie stared at Davidson's thick black eyebrows, which always seemed quizzically raised. "That's not the first time that's happened, is it, John?"

"Hardly."

Davidson lived simply and usually avoided the lifestyle of the vainglorious. Occasionally, his path crossed those of the over-privileged, but never had he seen the likes of Night Whisper. Once their coats had been taken, he and Jesse were shepherded into the Stimmel banquet hall. The enormous table, walnut with inlaid gold, was set for twelve, but could easily seat three dozen. The place settings were obvious museum pieces, also of gold and hand-enameled.

Introductions were made all around and Davidson was impressed with the political stature of the guests: a high official from the Ministry of Export Trade; a deputy of the Foreign Office; a section chief from the BND; and Helmut Escher, a nuclear expert from Heinschmann.

The dinner went well, a most civilized experience. That characterized the Germans, he decided. In some ways, they expressed the height of Western culture. Yet beneath the cultivated exterior, they often suffered from an insensitivity that permitted the gas chambers, and now their penchant for surreptitiously selling nuclear, chemical, and bacteriological warfare for Deutschemarks.

He found Klaus von Stimmel interesting. Though frail and soft spoken, he seemed to have an inner fire. His appearance of other-worldliness was probably a magnificent pose, Davidson divined.

Von Stimmel's conversation, echoed by all the guests,

centered on German resurgence, reflecting a pride that was beginning to addict the nation. With an occasional apology to Davidson, the only foreigner present, they found ways to mercilessly belittle America, Britain, France, and Russia.

He had only read about them, but this seemed like a classic repetition of the wealthy salons of the 1930s, when German industrialists gave money, and spirit, to build the power of Adolf Hitler. Then, the reason was military conquest. The excuse was anti-Communism. Now, Davidson sensed, the rationale was anti-Americanism. The resurgence of Germany was no longer just a matter of national pride. It was also the expression of a new competitive spirit—to beat America at the world game.

"Mr. Davidson," von Stimmel asked over dessert and cigars, his voice barely crossing the table. "As an American, aren't you troubled by your country's constant economic flip-flops—prosperity, recession, and always, it seems, debt and more debt? Your people are badly profligate. Am I right?"

Davidson was caught a bit off guard, but he quickly recovered.

"Herr von Stimmel, from the outside we're often misunderstood, in peace as well as in war. We're a very optimistic society. The debt is an expression of our unlimited faith in the future—and it also pays for a lot of German exports. But the most important thing to know about America is that we violate the European idea of human nature. A great deal of what we do, including helping to rebuild your country, comes from an unselfishness other people can't understand. In some ways, I suppose, it is naive. But it has shaped the modern world."

Stimmel became silent, apparently digesting Davidson's words.

"Who do you think won World War II, Herr Stimmel?" Davidson suddenly asked, partially to amuse himself.

The German industrialist laughed. "Oh, that's an easy one, Mr. Davidson. I believe they call you 'the Baptist.' Appropriate, I would think. In any case, we're the real winners. War or no war, you cannot stop determination and work. And geographically, we are the fulcrum of Europe. Russia and Britain? They're the real losers. Both had large empires that wanted out. France? I would say that's a draw. Their ethnocentric paranoia keeps them from losing entirely. America? The jury is still out. As history teaches us, in the long run, only money talks. And the books are still being balanced in your country."

Stimmel's voice suddenly gained strength. "You must know, Mr. Davidson, that political power eventually follows the dollar, or in our case, the Deutschemark."

The table laughed, somewhat self-consciously.

"Mr. Baptist, it will happen one way or another, but we're not beneath giving it a shove." The speaker was Hans Brecht, the Export Trade official. "You know this is not 1960, or even the 80s. It is almost the end of the century, and Germany will, one way or another, find its rightful place in the world."

The group of ten, excluding himself and Jessie, smiled smugly. Nothing was said for a moment, until Brecht spoke up again. This time his voice was tinged with bitterness.

"You Anglo-Saxons have never wanted us to achieve our destiny." His eyes singled out Davidson. "But now that the European military wars are over, the Monopoly Game—as you Americans say—is the real contest. And there I believe we hold both Boardwalk and Park Place."

"Yes, but never forget the Third World, Mr. Brecht," Davidson interjected. "They outnumber us all—Germans, Russians and Americans combined."

"Absolutely right, Mr. Davidson," Stimmel called from across the table. "That's where the action will be from now on. It's the largest market on the globe, and that's where the future wars will be fought, and where the new power will be gained. I assure you, Mr. Davidson, Germany has no intention of being left out."

42

"WHAT did you think of the dinner?"

Davidson didn't have to reflect.

"Jessie, not only was the food great, if a little heavy, but the evening was invaluable. Not just in meeting those aristocrats and jingoists, but in getting to know how they think. I have no proof yet, but I think most, if not all, of them are involved in Red Swastika and the Fourth Reich."

"I think they were most impressed with you, John." She touched his hand, softly.

The Mercedes was humming along on the no-limit autobahn at 125 kilometers—or 80 mph—an hour, while other cars were speeding effortlessly past. As Jessie spoke of the dinner, offering comments on the guests, Davidson's eyes focused on a red Porsche sportscar on the next lane. It had not passed them like the others. It was hanging right alongside, not ahead, or behind.

"Johann," Davidson called to the chauffeur. "Do me a favor. Speed up to a hundred and fifty kilometers for about thirty seconds, then pull quickly back below a hundred."

The chauffeur raced the engine, then softened his foot pressure, jolting the Mercedes. Davidson watched out the side window. The red Porsche was mimicking their moves, always ending up in the same place, right alongside the Mercedes.

A warning suddenly flashed through Davidson's mind.

"Down, Jessie!" the Baptist shrieked, throwing his body over hers, pressing their profiles below the window level.

The call had been intuitive, but it was answered by deadly reality. A rain of automatic fire, from an UZI or Kalashnikov, shattered both windows on Davidson's side. Up front, the chauffeur had bent to his right and was driving with his left hand, with almost no forward vision. Hoping to avoid a crash, he slowed the car.

Davidson listened to the gunfire, then drew the Mauser from his shoulder holster. The instant the raucous automatic chatter stopped, he jumped off the rear floor. He leaned out the shattered side window, his eyes trailing the speedily departing Porsche.

A volley of five shots left his pistol, each aimed at the screeching tires ahead of him. At least one bullet found its mark. The Porsche screamed in agony, then left the autobahn and bounced off the center divide. Instead of stopping, the 100 mph acceleration twisted the vehicle into a small, irregular arc, bringing it to rest only after the Porsche had crashed, front grill on, into a large tree.

Davidson surveyed the scene as the Mercedes slowed, then stopped on the shoulder. From the Porsche, came the noise of a ruptured radiator, like steam escaping a kettle. Then a large orange puff, followed by a raging fire. As the Porsche was being consumed, Davidson stared but couldn't make out anyone leaving the inferno.

He leaned back, holding a quivering Jessie in his arms.

"I don't think they liked my American table manners," he said, smiling in relief.

— 43 —

"JOHN, what's going on in Berlin? Has the Beekeeper finished the job?"

The President's voice was coming in to the Embassy through a secure phone scrambler set up at both ends. To Davidson, Briggs sounded more agitated than he had ever heard him.

"No, not yet, but Mussad's in town, as you know, Mr. President. Our man is making his preparations and I'm working with him to be sure it comes off as planned."

"John, you've got to hurry. That bastard has killed one of our boys and put a teenage girl into a desert hole. Meanwhile his guerrilla army is already in Harashi, the capital of the United African Republic. I'm complaining like a bastard but the UN has me blocked. The Chinese are threatening a veto, saying we're not supposed to interfere in a 'civil war.'

"But the American people are demanding action," Briggs continued, his voice breathful. "They want an invasion, any damn thing. But they don't know about his neutron shells or the real danger of an amphibious landing. The whole thing spells trouble."

Davidson listened sympathetically. He privately knew the

reason the Marines didn't make an amphibious landing in Kuwait during the Iraq war. It was not, as the Central Command claimed, because it was only a feint meant to deceive. The true reason, Davidson's sources told him, was that we had no way of clearing the "influence" mines submerged in front of the landing beaches.

The President paused. When he came back on, his voice was a decibel higher.

"John, a lot of people here want me to nuke his whole damn country. The Joint Chiefs are suggesting a laser-smart raid with B-2 Stealth bombers. But that won't do any good with that scumbag in Berlin. Besides, we think he's already got fifty neutron shells stored in bombproof underground caverns. And the first casualties in any action will be our hostage kids."

"What about the domestic political situation? Is that any better?"

"Hell no, John. Rusty Kembeck's warning that he'll impeach my ass if I break Executive Order 12333. To be honest, I don't give a damn anymore. I'm convinced that what you're doing is the right thing—the only thing that has a chance of working. Please get on with it."

Davidson understood the President's pressure.

"Mr. President. My deadline is forty-eight hours. That's how much longer Mussad will be in Berlin."

"What are our chances?"

"I'm not a betting man, Mr. President."

"But what if you were? What would the damn odds be?"

Davidson knew a lot rested on his answer. Perhaps even military action. "I'd say fifty-fifty, if that'll do you any good."

"Not a hell of a lot, Baptist. But I know you're a conservative poker player, so I'll stay with you—for forty-eight hours anyway—before I do anything else."

The phone was silent for almost a half minute. "Please do it, John," the President said.

The next sound Davidson heard was the click of the receiver.

—— 44 ——

MEL Gordon prepped himself for another encounter with a stubborn bank manager.

This one was Clarence Martine, the smoothly dressed head of the First Caribbean Trust, who was seated in his office—an indoor tropical garden sheltered by a large glass atrium. Two enormous ceiling fans, more for atmosphere than cooling in this air-conditioned space, gave the jalousied room the tranquil air of a nineteenth-century British colonial scene.

The Cayman Islands, one of the few remaining British Crown colonies in an era of independence, were three specks of 100 square miles and only 24,000 souls in the middle of the Caribbean. Their principal export was once turtle products, but they had more recently gone into the profitable business of banking and finance, hoping to become the "Delaware" of off-shore corporations and the "little Switzerland" of silent cash.

No nation, if that's what one could call this miniature way station, had done more in the last decade to make itself the refuge for money, mysterious and otherwise.

"Mr. Martine," Gordon said after displaying his credentials. "You've taken some business away from the Swiss, so I've flown here to ask your cooperation. I need to trace a slightly sneaky personal bank account."

Martine adjusted his panama-white double breasted suit with large pearl buttons and smiled as insincerely as the expert banker he was.

"Investigator Gordon, if I may call you that," he answered in precise, lilting West Indian tones. "We absolutely *love* the American government and its people, and we are happy to handle their deposits—as many as they want. But you must know that under the Mutual Legal Assistance Treaty, which we only signed in 1990, you must show us *probable cause* of a crime before we divulge secret banking information." He smiled again. "Do you have such proof on your person? Otherwise, we can't cooperate with you in any way. We do have our reputation to uphold."

Mel returned the smile, then gingerly bounced his small body on the armchair, as if practicing for some miraculous levitation. He stopped, and leaned forward, his face half across Martine's desk.

"Let me tell you something, small-time banker. I represent the United States government, the U.S. Congress to be exact. My bosses pass all the legislation that runs America, and in many ways, ends up on your sandy beaches. That includes banking regulations, control of all air traffic, in and out of the country, excise taxes, tourist regulations, etc. In addition, my buddy investigators in the Drug Enforcement Agency have been watching your little islands, and would welcome any leads I can give them to banks that process and launder drug funds."

Gordon leaned even further forward, threatening to end up on Martine's desk.

"You don't know me, and I'm only a little guy from New York. But I tell you this—you don't want to tangle with me, for any reason. Our President sent an army into Panama to straighten things out there. I can handle this little dump all by myself. Get me?"

With that Gordon relaxed back into his chair, adjusted his tie, and smiled the grin of a satisfied Cheshire.

Martine's suntanned complexion seemed to fade.

"Well, what exactly do you want to know?"

"Just one little item. Banque Suisse in Zurich transferred 3.7 million dollars here a while ago. Name of the depositor was Alex Knudsen. I just want to know how I can reach the gentleman. It's a matter of national security."

Martine rose, his expression dour. He walked to an adjacent room, where the computer records were kept. In three minutes he had returned, a small printout in hand.

"Yes, Investigator Gordon. I have it here. Knudsen lives in a small town in New Jersey—Lakewood to be exact. His address is RFD No. 6, The Beehive."

"The Beehive?"

"Yes, that's what it says. I understand Mr. Knudsen raises bees for a living."

"And he has 3.7 million dollars on deposit?" Gordon asked rhetorically. "Some honey."

The bank manager shrugged. Gordon rose to leave, forgetting to shake Martine's hand. As he moved toward the exit, he called out, almost over his shoulder.

"Very cooperative, Mr. Martine. I'll tell my people back in the States. A very cooperative bank," Gordon said, exiting the friendly tropical paradise.

— 45 —

"Oh, Sam," Marieanne muttered passionately, her body yielding to his, her breasts firm and inviting. The sexual festivities had begun early that evening at her apartment in central Berlin, and now, still only 8:00 P.M., were continuing apace.

Withers feared he was losing something. Not his mind, but his steel discipline, one that had never allowed outside influences, or people, to come between himself and duty. That duty was sacred, a trust inculcated in him by his late Warrant Officer father and nurtured by his work of the last twenty years.

It was never the Agency right or wrong. He had even found Langley sometimes negligent, vacillating in determination from Director to Director, even President to President. He had suffered their faults and failures, some of which he was sure were purposeful. But he had stayed on, hoping for better days, which had sometimes come unexpectedly. But of his country, there was never any doubt. He had been brought up to salute the flag, and he did it daily. If not physically, in his mind. USA.

Now he had come to Berlin on a vital mission for Davidson and the President. He hadn't slacked on that duty, but he wondered if there wasn't some unconscious conflict between his obsession with Marieanne and his obligations.

He thought about it often these days. But pleasure—or was it love?—seemed to hold its own.

"Darling, would you look over at the clock?" Marieanne asked from an awkward position under Withers. "I can't see it from here. What time is it?"

"Not late. Just five after eight."

Marieanne suddenly pulled her body away, rolling on the bed as if frightened. "Oh, my God! I completely forgot. I'm supposed to be at a seminar at Merrill Lynch at eight forty-five tonight. Please, Sam, excuse me!"

She jumped out of bed, and like a figure in a fast-motion film, dressed in minutes, from underclothes to a quick application of makeup.

"I've got to go, Sam. I'll take the U-Bahn both ways and be home by eleven. Love you."

Withers sat on the bed, desolate. He rose and stared at himself in the bathroom mirror. In his expression, he saw an uncharacteristic loneliness, a weakness he thought he had conquered after Katherine's death.

"Oh, what the hell," he finally confessed. "I miss the woman already. Might as well learn something about German stocks anyway."

In minutes, Withers had dressed. Chasing down the stairs, he headed toward the U-Bahn station, expecting to meet up with Marieanne at Merrill Lynch. He hadn't gone more than fifty feet from the apartment when he saw her. Marieanne wasn't at the subway stop, but was hailing a cab. As she pulled away, Withers frantically called another.

"Like in the movies," he told the confused cabbie in English, then switched to German. "Follow that cab. Here's an extra ten marks."

Both taxis took the same route toward Merrill Lynch, located catty-corner from the Decayed Tooth, the bombed-out church on the Ku-Damm. As they approached the ruin, his cab slowed and Sam got ready to make a quick exit. But Marieanne's taxi was not stopping. Had she made a mistake?

"Keep going, and stay with that other cab," Sam ordered. Soon after the church, Marieanne's taxi made a left and Withers followed. About a mile in, at a small cul-de-sac facing an alley, her cab stopped. She alighted, walking briskly. But to where?

Withers held his taxi back half a block. On foot, guided only by slivers of light from the apartments above, he moved toward the alley. Perhaps a hundred yards in, the pavement ended at an old limestone townhouse. Withers approached the door and bent to read the inscription, engraved on a small, well-polished brass plaque: "HANS KOLLER, CHIROPRAKTIKER."

Could anyone see him? Drifts of light from above only occasionally illuminated the alley, but he decided on caution. Dropping to his knees, he half-crawled on a concrete walk alongside the house so as not to be seen from the windows above. At the back, he spotted a single small window and peered through into a large space, apparently the doctor's examining room.

A group of people, some eight or nine, were seated in folding chairs facing a lectern. All were men, with the exception of one woman. The glass was grimy and his vision partially obstructed. Slowly, Sam rubbed the pane with his jacket sleeve. Yes, now he could make out more. A man was standing at the lectern speaking to the group. Above him was a color portrait. My God, it was of Adolf Hitler!

Withers scanned the room again, trying to fix the faces in his mind. Most were looking away, with only the backs of their heads visible. Then the woman sneezed and reached for her pocketbook, turning her face as she did. It was Marieanne!

Withers's mind whirled in confusion, even denial. He had stumbled on a meeting of some rabid right-wing group, probably Red Swastika. And Marieanne was there.

Had his beloved amateur sleuth infiltrated them on his behalf? Or—a thought overtook him that ached more than loneliness—had he been taken in by a clever, and so lovely, Nazi agent?

BOOK
—3—

— 46 —

UNLIKE Sam, whose reaction was confused, Davidson was pleased by what Withers had learned. His night excursion to the limestone townhouse had probably uncovered the operational center of Red Swastika. A chiropractor behind a resurgent Nazism? It struck him as strange, almost humorous, at first, but wasn't Hitler—who was responsible for the death of 50 million people of all nationalities, not just 6 million Jews—a frustrated architect and sometime house painter?

As to Marieanne's motives, he would leave that to Sam to divine. He wouldn't press him. Even though Sam had an Agency reputation for stoicism, Davidson knew that in this case, great emotional danger was involved.

The next step was to look for confirmation. Though he trusted Lichtenstein, he wouldn't share the information on Dr. Koller's group with the BND, which was obviously riddled with Swastika sympathizers. No, this had to be a covert field exercise for himself and Withers.

"Ready, Sam?" Davidson asked as the two men met in the service garage of the Embassy, equipped with what passed for the yellow van of the Berlin utility company— the *Berliner Elektrizitatsversorgungsunternehman*—which the locals naturally called just BEWAG.

The truck was a duplicate of the original, except for one feature. On its roof was a small, parabolic listening device capable of picking up fifteen decibels of noise or conversation through a plate glass target at a distance of 100 feet. The sound vibrations off the glass, like voice transmissions into a telephone receiver, were detected, then retranslated into voice and recorded.

The two-man team, dressed in the work clothes of BEWAG, drove the truck to the Decayed Tooth on the Ku-Damm, made their left, and traveled another mile to the small alley that led to the chiropractor's townhouse. Up ahead, Davidson could see four cars parked in the tight cobblestone yard. He stopped the van a safe distance away while Withers placed a collapsible aluminum ladder up against an adjacent building. Sam climbed up, ostensibly to repair a city light fixture, which had actually been shattered the night before by an Agency clerk.

Davidson noticed Withers's morose mood, but decided not to interfere. Sam had to work this out himself. Marieanne had called the Embassy earlier that evening canceling their dinner date. She was sorry, she said, but she had to work late. This possible ploy only deepened Sam's self-absorbed mood, but he tried to brush it off nonchalantly.

From inside the van, Davidson aimed the parabolic dish at a ground-level window near the front door. Dr. Koller's meeting-examining room, Sam had explained, was a few steps below the main floor, itself raised the same height off the ground. Davidson put on his earphones, motioning for Sam to do the same with his small listening plug.

As they tuned in, it appeared that the meeting had already begun, mostly with housekeeping reports from each member of the cabal. Davidson heard several voices, all male, come on. If Marieanne was there, she hadn't spoken. Davidson looked up at Withers, whose face had broken into a smile.

Perhaps a vindication of his beautiful amour.

After the preliminaries, the first speaker was a man who identified himself only as "Fox." Each person obviously had a code name, but one—"Friedrich," or "Frederick the Great"—was bandied about frequently. From the conversation, Davidson deduced that the person was not present in Koller's examining room, and that "Friedrich" was the code name for the absent Red Swastika "Fuehrer," whose authority exceeded even that of Dr. Koller.

Davidson concentrated on "Fox." His tones were surprisingly familiar, low and sonorous. Yes, he had heard that same voice at *Nachtgefluster* just the other night. Almost surely it was Paul Dollop, the Foreign Ministry official.

"If we want to advance the new Germany, we have no choice but boldness," he could hear Fox say. "We all know the pros and cons. We've discussed it for weeks. Now it's time to vote." The pause was only momentary. "How many nays?"

In response there was only silence.

"Good. Then we're all agreed. Now that the Reichstag has been fire-bombed, the real challenge lies ahead. At exactly the moment of Mussad's visit, we'll assassinate Chancellor Karl Bessinger. The job will be handled by the one with the pipe. With Bessinger gone, the deputy head of his party— Otto Kemp, one of us—will surely be named the next Chancellor. A vision of the 1930s will return to Germany."

Davidson had heard enough. They had to break away before the meeting was over. At his signal, Withers scampered down the ladder and loaded the equipment on the truck.

As they drove back toward the Embassy, Davidson realized his assignment had suddenly multiplied. He now had two assassinations on his hand. One to execute, the other to block.

47

"I can't believe you're telling me this, Manfred. I threw caution away and raced the tape over here because the contents were explosive. I figured you had to know real quick about an attempt on Bessinger's life."

"Baptist, you were right to do that and I believe you. Why would you invent such a thing? But I tell you again, the crucial portions of the tape are indistinct. Absolutely useless," Lichtenstein was explaining to Davidson in an embarrassed voice. "We've had our digital computer enhancement people work on it, but no luck. Technically it's either the fault of your equipment or someone in Spandau's recording lab screwed up. Or . . ."

"Or what, Manfred?"

"Or someone at Spandau is playing tricks on us, which I've suspected for a long time. The Red Swastika BND clique seem to have their own agenda."

"But aren't you going to do something about this threat on Bessinger's life?" Davidson's frustration was near the break-point.

"Of course, Baptist. I've already given orders to beef up security on the Chancellor, at his home and at the Chancellery. But I'm in no position to make any arrests. There are no names in the recording, not even Dr. Koller's, although I've had my eye on him for some time. But I still have no proof."

"What about Dollop?"

"I'll watch him too, Baptist, but only because you say so. On the tape you gave me, his voice—if it is his—is absolutely indistinguishable from that of a million other Germans. Our *Ganzfakt* file on him is as pure as Adenauer's memory, but I'll look into him myself. OK, John?"

It was not "OK" with Davidson, but there was little he could do with German officialdom. Once again, the BND had been useless. Surely, it made little sense to give them another chance.

The lone wolf strategies of the Cold War had once stood Davidson well. Berlin today seemed the right place, and the right time, to reaffirm that proven route.

—— 48 ——

MEL Gordon could smell the honey from the road.

He had come almost full circle—Washington to Zurich, now to a bee farm in New Jersey—all in search of a $1,273 White House check no one could, or would, explain.

He drove down the driveway, unpaved and unattended, until he came to an old farmhouse. Not only was it without pretension, but the structure, which he guessed was a turn-of-the-century wooden shingle, was in abysmal repair. The outside "Tobacco Road" porch was off its perpendicular, both horizontally and vertically, and hardly seemed the home of a millionaire, bee farmer or otherwise.

He rang the bell and waited, with no idea what to expect. After five minutes of intermittent buzzing, a slatternly woman, about sixty, answered the door. Her apron was stained, her hair uncombed.

"Yeh, whatdeya want?"

Gordon was taken aback. "I'm looking for Mr. Knudsen. Is this his house?"

"Was last time I looked. But he ain't here."

As the door started to slam in his face, Gordon jammed his Florsheim wing-tips into the space, taking a hard hit.

"Why'd you do that, lady?"

"I ain't no lady and you did it yourself. Can't you see I'm busy?"

Mel was afraid to push the woman, the female sex being the only mortals who intimidated him. But he needed information. Leaning persistently against the door, he smiled his best. "I see Mr. Knudsen's not here. But can you tell me where he is?"

"Don't know," the housekeeper—that's what he assumed she was—said, then delivered a swift kick to Gordon's shin, closing the door as he retreated in pain.

Defeat didn't come easily to Mel Gordon. He got back into his car and headed toward the center of this bustling Jersey town, once famous for migrated New Yorkers and its chickens and eggs.

"Mr. Wilson, is that your name?" Gordon asked as he entered the Wilson-Lakewood Travel Agency on the main street.

"No, old man Wilson's been dead thirty years. I'm Feldman, Josh Feldman, proprietor. Where would you like to go?"

"Don't really know. Depends on what you tell me," Gordon answered the confused travel agent. Only after he had shown his GAO credentials were things clearer.

"I'm trying to locate a Mr. Alex Knudsen, a local bee farmer," Gordon explained. "Can you help me?"

"Has he committed a crime?"

"Not that we know. It's more a procedural matter involving the expense account of a top federal employee. Sort of hush-hush. I have to reach Knudsen right away."

Feldman motioned Gordon inside to a computer station, where he typed in Knudsen's name.

"Yes, just as I remembered. He said he was going on a vacation for a few weeks, so we got him tickets."

"To where?"

"Cairo. Egypt. Yes, he was going to visit the pyramids."

Finally, he had some solid information. He was tempted to have Feldman write up plane tickets to Cairo, but the GAO had its own central booking people.

"Well, thanks, Mr. Feldman. That's what I needed to know." Gordon turned and headed for the door.

"Not really, Mr. Gordon." Feldman's smile held a secretive touch.

"Why is that?"

"Because Knudsen's not in Cairo anymore. Left there a few days ago. Sent me a telex to book him a flight on Egypt Air out of Cairo."

Gordon halted, soldierlike.

"To where, Mr. Feldman?"

"To Germany. Berlin to be exact."

— 49 —

"SAM, we need to take another look at the chiropractor's place, all by our lonesome. Some *ex-officio* breaking and entering, if you know what I mean."

From Withers's grin, Davidson sensed that he missed those tradecraft tactics, outlawed by the Agency after pressure from the Congressional committees on Intelligence oversight.

They left the Embassy together, concentrating for signs of omnipresent tails. Since the near-miss on the autobahn with Jessie Leinsdorf, Davidson had become convinced that Red Swastika's intentions were serious. He and Withers casually walked a full square block around the Embassy building, then back again. Davidson spotted one obvious tail: the lady of 1930s fashion, wearing a new hat and still reminiscent of early films.

The U-Bahn, the Berlin subway. That was their best avenue of deception, Davidson decided. The efficient Berlin system, whose nine lines covered 113 miles below and above ground in the metropolis of four millions, offered a number of escape possibilities. The trick, if there was one, was to constantly change lines and trains, expecting—or at least hoping—that their shadows would be held back by crowds, or fail to enter the right car before the impatient electric doors closed shut.

Davidson found her somewhat attractive. Taller than most women, she appeared even more imposing because of her hats. Each was a high, colorful pyramid-like piece that was fashionable in the days of Garbo. The woman was resolute, dogging their every move. But after changes of four trains on three different lines—the north and south No. 9, and the east-west No. 7 and No. 1, they lost her at the Fehrbelliner Strasse station, where No. 7 meets U-Bahn No. 2. Now more secure, they got back on the train and ended up at the Kurfurstendamm—the Ku-Damm—stop on line No. 9.

The safest tactic was to walk the rest of the way. Twenty minutes later, the two men entered the alley, picking their way in the semi-darkness until they reached Koller's place. It was only 9:00 P.M., but the house was totally dark, not a light in evidence.

"Put your flashlight here," Davidson told Withers, his own hand occupied with a Mauser 7.65 semi-automatic. "Can you read it?"

"Dr. Koller is on vacation," Sam translated the German script sign. "Will return August 1."

"Let's go around back, John." Sam led them along the concrete side path to the back door, which Withers jimmied open with an all-purpose tool. In front of them was the examining-meeting room which Sam had seen, and which had been the site of Davidson's recording only days before.

It was deserted, as if it hadn't been used in months. No chiropractic examining tables, no charts, no lectern or chairs. The only furnishing remaining in the large room was the nineteenth-century German landscape. They tried the light switch, but the current had been disconnected. Flashlight in hand, Withers moved quickly across to the painting and expectantly turned it over. No Adolf Hitler. Just a dusty old wood frame.

"What in the hell, John?" Withers's face was twisted in

frustration. "They've taken off, as if they were never here."

They moved on together, the flashlight panning peripatetically, their hands following on, searching for files, or any further lead to Red Swastika.

"I believe we've been foxed," Withers said. "They haven't left a single lead or follow-up. Somehow they learned we'd been eavesdropping—I suppose their people at Spandau. John, we're in the middle of an intra-government conspiracy, and I haven't been trained to fight both sides at the same time."

Davidson gave the setting a last glance, motioning for Withers to pan again with the flashlight. "OK, we've done what we can," the Baptist said in resignation. "Let's get out of here."

They picked their way across the room and were opening the back door when the room was suddenly lit for an instant, as if a strobe had rushed through the air. With the flash came a loud sound—a short burst of automatic fire from out of the corner, shattering the dark silence.

With trained instincts, both men instantly dropped to the floor, guns out and firing a burst of rebuttal, all within seconds. Their aim was concentrated on the site of the flash, Withers sending four bullets, two to the point of the light, two more twenty inches above.

There was no return fire. Only silence. Cautiously, they rose from the floor and approached the source. Withers's flashlight preceded them, Davidson's Mauser at the ready.

The light scanned the general area, then came in for a close-up. In the corner was a body, twisted on its back, obviously turned as the gunman fell into a heap. Withers held the torch in one hand and used the other to grasp the body, clothed in a raincoat with a ski cap pulled down over the forehead.

With a rough pull, he flipped the corpse over onto its front.

Davidson closed his eyes, but not before he had seen both the face and Sam clutching at his heart. In front of them was Marieanne Luft. Two bullets had pierced her chest, another charting a hole, like a tracheotomy, through the neck. The last bullet had entered at the perfect divide of her chalky forehead.

"MARIEANNE!"

Sam's scream was unearthly. He had given out an unanswered cry for help, even pity.

Withers raced out into the front cobblestoned court, running as if the motion could shake off the truth.

"MARIEANNE!" he cried again, running, then walking, then finally falling to his knees.

Davidson approached. He said nothing, only placed a soft consoling hand on Withers's shoulder.

━━ 50 ━━

DAVIDSON liked the looks of the Berlin city detective. At first glance, he could be taken for the archetypical Aryan—flaxen-haired, light azure eyes, regular if angular features. But Davidson saw that the smile of the young man—he figured him to be about thirty—was not mechanical. Rather human, even warm.

"Our investigation seems to check out your story, Mr.

Davidson," Detective Sergeant Kurt Langer of the Berlin
City Police was saying. "The bullets in the body all came
from Sam Withers's gun, all four of them, but we've concluded that it was self-defense. Ms. Luft's automatic fire
was all over the room, and it was good you left her weapon,
an UZI, just where it was. You had been set up for a double
killing." Langer's smile became knowing. "But of course
that still leaves the charge of breaking and entering. Could
I ask why?"

The Baptist hesitated. Frankness was not usually rewarded
in his business. But something about Langer seemed
simpatico. Still, he'd reveal only enough to see if he
could enlist an ally.

"You know we're both employees of the U.S. Embassy.
State Department career officers. Naturally, we're interested in knowing about any anti-democratic forces in friendly
nations. In this case, incipient Nazi groups that could hurt
our alliance."

"You mean like Red Swastika?" Langer shot back to a
surprised Baptist.

"You know about them?"

"Sure, we've had Koller under surveillance for some
time. And we've been watching you watch Koller. But we
have no real evidence against them, nothing to tie them to
terrorism. Especially the Reichstag bombing, which I think
they did. You know, Mr. Davidson, we have no RICO laws
in Germany, so conspiracy without action is not a crime.
Besides Koller is gone, and we can't find him—yet."

"Any evidence against any other people in his cell, besides
Ms. Luft?" Davidson asked.

"Like you, we've watched some important people come
and go. But the one we're after doesn't attend meetings.
He's the elusive 'Friedrich'—or 'Frederick the Great'—the
unseen head of the movement. We think Koller knows who

he is. He's obviously a paranoid Nazi who's determined to have Germany reconquer the world. But we have no idea who he is. As for the others, we were disappointed in the most important piece of evidence—the damaged tape you gave to Lichtenstein."

"You know about the assassination plot against Chancellor Bessinger?"

"Oh, sure. Lichtenstein called us from the BND right away. He seemed sorry your proof was destroyed, maybe in his own lab. Anyway, we've tripled our protection on the Chancellor. In fact, I'm in charge of security for his meeting with Mussad, when it takes place."

Davidson sensed the beginnings of a profitable relationship. Langer seemed like a cop free of political bias, and not subject to easy intimidation. Someone who dealt only in good and bad guys.

"Try to keep out of any more trouble, Mr. Davidson, even if you have diplomatic immunity. I'd hate to expel a friendly American from Berlin."

"I'll try," Davidson answered by rote, knowing he was about to enter the most troubled hours of his Berlin stay.

— 51 —

LONNIE Taylor had thought the worst was over after her rape. But one morning her fears were revived when a guard came into the barracks and roused the girl prisoners before six A.M.

"All right, everyone up and outside," the guard yelled.

The dawn was only a glimmer and the dark multiplied her anxiety. The worst part of it was the news blackout from America. They were not allowed radios or newspapers, and the thirty isolated teenagers feared they had been forgotten at home. To Lonnie, that sense of nothingness was almost as bad as the rape itself.

"Lonnie Taylor, Alice Krofiss and Pearl Gibbons. Fall out," the guard shouted. "The commandant wants to see you."

In minutes, they were brought before "Horny," as the girls called the young Captain, whose expression was one of a continuous leer. He enjoyed having the stewardship of the American girls and although he wasn't as brutal as the Lieutenant who had ordered the rape, he was constantly walking unannounced into their barracks, straining to see the young women in stages of undress.

"What do you want from us, Captain?" Lonnie asked, acting as spokesperson. "Don't you know that our government is going to take vengeance on you once they free us.

Your raping Lieutenant is as good as dead. Do you want to join him?"

The Captain may have been cowed, but he hid it.

"Brave talk, Miss Taylor. But the truth is you've been forgotten in America. No one speaks of you back home. Your President has done nothing to free you. There is no bombing of our country, no invasion. Not even a ransom payment. No, I'm afraid your government has written you all off."

Lonnie felt stabbed by his comments, afraid there was some truth in what he said. If it weren't true, why hadn't Washington done something?

"We don't believe that for a second. But is that why you called us out here so early?" she asked, screwing up her courage.

"I've called you here because we've decided on a more harmonious course with our prisoners. To celebrate that, all I want you to do is make a videotape telling your people back home how well you're treated."

"WELL TREATED!" Pearl Gibbons, a black teenager shouted back. "We're wearing the same clothes we came with, without any water to wash them in. We're given only a thousand calories of food a day, and we haven't had any medical attention. Most of us have lost thirty pounds. I don't know what you're always sneaking around looking at. There's not much left to us. Well treated, baloney!"

The Captain rose and circled his desk.

"There's always worse treatment you know," he shot back. "I warn you. If you don't do what I ask, the three of you are going into the desert—into the same kind of hole Julia was in. But not for a day or two. For a full week. Do you understand now?"

Lonnie exchanged glances with her friends. She knew they couldn't survive the hole. Julia still suffered nightmares, almost every night. She decided the best way was to bargain—limited cooperation for survival.

"If we do this, don't expect us to say anything bad about our country. Because we won't do it," Lonnie said with false bravado.

"Why would we ask that? We're trying to show your countrymen that we aren't the evil people they've been told. You have my promise on that."

"Then we'll do it, but only if you really improve our treatment. Give us water to wash our clothes, more food, and—more privacy."

The Captain contemplated for only seconds. "No, all your requests are denied. Now go to your barracks and get ready for the video. We're returning one set of clean clothes from your suitcases. You'll have one good meal this morning, and we'll give you some makeup. We want you to look as pretty as the day you arrived in Al Rashon. Now that's all."

The Captain waved his hand, dismissing them.

"Bastard," Lonnie said under her breath.

"What did you say, young woman?"

"I just said 'thanks.' We so appreciate your kindness."

══ 52 ══

MEL Gordon was not crazy about Germany or the Germans, but he did like Berlin as a city. He even found some saving grace in the Berliner humor, which was wry, satirical and, if he remembered, had given birth to a post–World War I cultural renaissance in the 1920s under the Weimar Republic.

But now that it was so affluent, could Germany recreate such a mood? He doubted it. They had become too full of themselves. Ridicule of self seemed to be the core of humor, even creativity. No, he assumed the Germans would be the stiffest stiffs of the twenty-first century. They were more likely to become Nazis again than become funny, he figured. But oh, so rich.

Gordon had come here to find another rich one, but this time an American who was off on some mysterious mission for the White House, one that had so far dragged him to his fourth destination: Berlin.

His first stop, sort of obligatory, was the U.S. Embassy on Friedrichstrasse, an elegant piece of architecture. He made a note to investigate the State Department costs in this city. Did they really need a mansion in the middle of expensive downtown real estate? He'd talk to some penny-pinching Congressmen about it when he got back.

At the Embassy, he was sent to two men, one at a time. First the Second Secretary, a little gray crew-cutted guy named Sam Withers. More like a Marine than a diplomat, Gordon thought. After introducing himself, he asked a few questions. Since this was State Department territory, he tried to be polite.

"Mr. Withers. Could you look at this picture? It's only a newspaper shot and the guy's tending to his bees, but maybe you've seen him in Berlin. Has he come to the Embassy for information—or anything?"

Withers seemed curious about the photo, even a little upset by it, Gordon sensed. But after a moment of contemplation, he dismissed it. "No, never seen the guy. What's he done? Rob Congress?" Withers laughed. Sort of a smartass, Gordon thought.

The next Embassy person, the Cultural Attaché, was quite the opposite. John Davidson was courtly, even aristocratic. The name Davidson struck him: hadn't there been a CIA bigshot by that name years ago? Davidson seemed old enough, and perhaps this is how they pensioned off their veterans. But he didn't raise the question, even though he'd heard rumors from other embassy personnel that Davidson and Withers were actually a covert CIA team using the Embassy as a cover.

"Have you ever seen this man, Mr. Davidson?" Gordon finally asked the Cultural Attaché. "He's leading me a merry chase."

Davidson didn't even seem to reflect on the subject. Instead he tried to turn the interrogation around.

"I understand you're a Special Investigator from the General Accounting Office," Davidson said. "Why in the world would you want to chase a beekeeper?"

Gordon had no intention of tipping his hand, especially if he was *the* Davidson he had heard about.

"That's kind of confidential, Mr. Davidson. But I can tell you it's part of our executive overview, which covers the

White House and goes all the way up to the President."

"That's fine, Mr. Gordon. And I'd like to help out, but I'm afraid I've never seen this man before. What did you say his name was?"

"I didn't. But it's on the newspaper clip. Alex Knudsen of Lakewood, New Jersey."

Davidson smiled, raising his black bushy eyebrows. "Well, the best of luck to you, Mr. Gordon, and to your employers, the U.S. Congress," he said, then turned and walked away.

Gordon had come a long way but he didn't feel much closer to his target. Except for one thing. He had no idea why, but his Bronx intuition was working overtime. There was something about these two Embassy, or Agency, employees that rang less than true.

"Beekeeper." That's what Davidson had called Knudsen. He had never used the word himself and it was not that unusual. But somehow the way Davidson said it had the ring of familiarity. As if Davidson really *knew* the beekeeper.

He'd just hang around Berlin a while and watch this odd couple. In any case, it was the only clue he had to the damn puzzle.

══ 53 ══

"HAWLEY, we gotta do something, which really means *you* gotta do something."

Happy Rider, fellow Arkansan and Majority Leader of the House, was sharing a lunch of barbequed chicken on wooden trays in front of the fireplace in the Oval Office.

"People are beginning to say you're a bag of wind, railing at the monster Mussad, but doing nothing. No bombing, no war, just talk in the U.N. which is getting you nowhere speedier than a scared raccoon." The craggy southerner leaned over his tray, his slightly pocked face almost up against that of his crony of years. "He's taken thirty of our kids as hostages and now grabbed the United African Republic by subversion, with eyes on another neighbor. What in the hell are you going to do, Hawley? Your poll figures are scraping mud bottom."

The President couldn't argue with Happy. The sage pol had put his finger on his dilemma. He *was* doing something, probably the only thing he could do, but he couldn't share it with the nation. One reason was political. The other was that he'd alert that Mussad son-of-a-bitch before Davidson could carry out his assignment. But the more he stared at Happy, the more he realized that if he didn't confide in someone, he'd go crazy. He might even find his last ounce of confidence sapped.

"Happy, what if I told you I am doing something?"

Rider sat up sharply. He put down the chicken and started to lick his fingers, then found a napkin.

"Whatdeye mean—doing something? The army's going nowhere, and the U.N.'s sitting on its ass. Doing what, Hawley?"

"Remember John Davidson?"

"Sure. That old spook. He was in here the day Mussad took our kids."

"Remember his advice to me, what he thought I ought to do?"

Rider's faced paled. "Jesus, I remember. He told you to kill the son-of-a-bitch. But you turned him down." The Majority Leader halted, seeming to reframe that crucial meeting in his mind. "In fact, I told you assassination was a bad idea, that it broke the Executive Order. And . . ."

"Yes, Happy, and what?"

"And that you'd get your political ass in a sling. That your enemies on the Hill—especially Speaker Rusty Kembeck—would impeach you as fast as a jackrabbit looking to make babies." He paused. "Do you mean . . ."

"Yes, Happy. Any day now, I expect, or at least hope, that that Mussad bastard will be blown off the face of the earth. By order of me, the Commander-in-Chief."

Rider stood up sharply. "Well, I'll be a son-of-a-rattler." He extended his hand. "Hawley, I was wrong in my advice. There's no other way to deal with that bastard. It's a hell of a lot better than losing our whole amphibious Marine contingent, and maybe getting our army killed by neutron bombs. I congratulate you, Mr. President. It took balls, but I always knew you had 'em."

Rider halted, smiling warmly at his friend. "But how about the impeachment, Hawley? They won't get my vote but a lot of those wind-blowing lowlifes will try to make you look like a villain."

"I don't like the idea of impeachment, Happy, and I'll fight them all the way—right up to a Senate trial. But VP Morse won't make a bad President if I lose."

"But then Kembeck will get the VP nod from Congress under the 25th amendment," Rider objected. "That bothers the hell out of me."

"Well, we'll have to wait until it plays out, Happy. Meanwhile, I should be hearing something soon."

"Is Davidson doing the job himself?"

"I don't think so. He hasn't told me, but I suspect he has his own 'Carlos,' sort of a leftover from the old Cold War."

As the President rose, the Majority Leader, still shaking his head in incredulity, moved toward the door of the Oval Office.

"Well, good luck to the U.S.A., Mr. President."

"Happy, one last thing. You're the only person who knows what I've told you. I expect you'll . . ."

Rider placed his arm around his Arkansan buddy, now a vulnerable politician.

"Mr. President, don't you a-worry. The secret's locked in my alcoholic bosom. Not even a Barbara Walters could worm it out."

54

"HELLO, may I speak to Count Horstmann," Davidson asked, having decided on direct confrontation.

"Who's calling?" asked the Berlin Hilton operator.

"Just tell him it's Mr. Tiergarten."

As Davidson waited, he catalogued his strategy. Mussad had settled into the same hotel, taking the entire 42nd penthouse floor for his entourage, including Horstmann. In the next forty-eight hours the terrorist chief would be fulfilling his Berlin diplomatic obligations, especially a meeting with Bessinger, before returning to Al Rashon. The Beekeeper needed the security details of the penthouse if he was to get in "at close range," as he called it.

Horstmann was the key.

"Baptist, my head still has a bald swatch where they put in three stitches from our last meeting," Horstmann said as he picked up the phone. "Are you or that midget henchman planning another mugging?"

Davidson ignored the quip. "Remember Raven's Nest. Your family must be desolate without it." Horstmann was mute for an instant. "So, let's talk. You know where. Alone." With that, Davidson hung up, assuming he had set a rendezvous, of sorts, for ASAP.

On the way to the Bellevue section of the Tiergarten, Davidson reviewed his assets. At his suggestion, the real estate people in Munich had approached the current owner of the Bavarian estate, a German rock star. He had tired of the country squire role and was willing to sell for $1.85 million. That was about a third of the money the President had approved for the project, and Davidson had only drawn down a few thousand in expenses. He had readily agreed to the real estate broker's asking price.

The Baptist and Horstmann met at the Bellevue, in an open area. Davidson's head swiveled about by instinct, searching for uninvited guests.

"Don't worry, Mr. Davidson. Nobody's here except me. What do you want?" Horstmann spoke rudely, as if he had a more important appointment elsewhere.

"If you're not interested, we can call this off right now," Davidson bluffed.

"No, I'm ready to listen."

"Good. I've spoken to the people in Munich about your family estate, all 300 acres. It's available for 1.85 million."

"Marks or dollars?"

"Dollars. 2.5 million Deutschemarks by my translation."

The giant German sat on a park bench and started to roar, drawing some spectator attention.

"Davidson, that's 2.4 million more than I've got. Forget it."

"Don't be hasty, Wolf. I've got the money and it's deposited right here in the Dresdner Bank. In fact, I've already signed a binder on the place, stables, horses, main mansion, out-buildings and all—just as it was when your father lost it after the war. I can transfer to you, mortgage-free, any time you say."

The German, now standing, was no longer laughing. "You're serious, aren't you, Baptist. You would do this?"

"Under the right circumstances, Wolf. In exchange for a favor."

"Tell me. What do I have to do—kill Mussad?" With that the giant German began to laugh uproariously again. He halted only when he caught Davidson's mien, the chocolate-brown eyes seriously focused.

"No, Wolf. You don't have to kill Mussad."

"What then?"

"Just help us do it."

— 55 —

"FRIEDRICH" dialed the extension number at the BND for Major Helmut Niemann.

He was sure he had chosen the right man. Niemann was a confident young officer who had the mettle to carry out the most distasteful orders. Only this understanding of rigid hierarchy, so well entrenched in their history, would regenerate German power in the twenty-first century, now a bare few years away.

Dr. Koller had done a creditable job, but had outlived his usefulness, Friedrich had decided after much lonely wrestling. The ambitious chiropractor might even now be an obstacle to Red Swastika's future. The public was warming to their nationalistic message, as witness the support given the Fourth Reich in the polls for the upcoming Bundestag elections.

In the midst of this, Koller's failure of security—especially the senseless attempt to kill the Americans in his own townhouse—had backfired. The chiropractor had even brought Red Swastika to the premature attention of the non-political Berlin *polizei*, an unwanted player. As the Fuehrer, he, Friedrich, had to take extreme measures to safeguard the movement.

"Hello, Niemann."

"Yes? Who is this?"

"This is Friedrich. Please meet with Fox. He will have an urgent assignment for you."

With that, he hung up. Aside from Koller, only Dollop and General Barenchenko knew his identity. It was best not to extend the circle of recognition any further.

Niemann took the BND-issue small Mercedes 190E and drove out of Berlin, into the pastoral hinterland toward the town of Angemunde, once part of East Germany and about fifty kilometers from Berlin.

After forty minutes on Autobahn 2, he exited and drove through the village to a pastoral landscape beyond, a farm area where corn and garden vegetables were raised. Koller had told him that he couldn't be reached by phone, or even post. Only those who knew his redoubt—Friedrich and Paul Dollop—could contact him. Now Niemann also knew.

At the stucco farmhouse, painted a pale yellow and neat, but not as tidy as prosperous farms in the Western sector, he pulled up into a dirt driveway where two Dobermans howled their displeasure. As Niemann tried to leave the car, the dogs lunged, almost reaching their mark before he slammed the door shut. Locked in the Mercedes, Niemann leaned on the horn.

"What in the hell is going on?" a man shouted, his short

arms flailing as he emerged from the farmhouse.

Niemann opened the window a crack. "Koller, it's me. Niemann. Get those damn dogs away from here."

The chiropractor, dressed in a farmer's blue jacket, laughed.

"All right, Schätze and Eva. Down. Nice dogs, down."

Once the Dobermans had retreated, Niemann got out of the car and approached Koller.

"What's happening in Berlin? And how did you know how to reach me?" Koller's questions came like automatic fire, his voice betraying anxiety.

"One at a time, doctor. Perhaps some hospitality? I could use a schnapps after this trip. I had no idea there was such a provincial setting so close to Berlin."

"Yes, come in. The farm is my sister's. I sent her away for a few weeks to her mother's home in Leipzig. Please come in."

The farmhouse was a nineteenth-century place of simplicity with a pump handle sink, tile floors and stucco walls. The two men sat at the kitchen table, a set of planks that would fetch a great price in the Berlin flea markets, Niemann thought.

"So, again, how did you know I was here?" Koller asked.

"Dollop told me. He thought it was important for someone to contact you. Being in a federal ministry, he didn't think it wise to come himself."

"So what is new?"

Niemann told him of Marieanne's death, of the visit of Mussad to Berlin, and of the preparation of the man with the pipe to take out Chancellor Bessinger.

"Bismarck has been training like an athlete for the Olympics. He won't show anyone his plan, but he says it has been perfected to the last decimal of time."

"Good. Once Bessinger is gone, Kemp will surely be

elected Chancellor. Then we shall be on our way." Koller mused for a moment. "Somewhat like Hitler taking over from General von Schleicher, who only had the job for fifty-seven days when he was pushed out by our Fuehrer."

While Koller was speaking, Niemann rose from the table and walked to the sink for a glass of water. He primed the primitive pump, then turned. But instead of water, he held a Mauser in his hand.

"It's a shame, Herr Chiropraktiker, that you won't live to see that glorious day."

"But . . ." Koller started to say, then gasped as the first of a rapid volley of shots pierced his neck, then punctuated his entire body, from skull to stomach.

Niemann's smile of accomplishment was quickly replaced by a grimace. He had forgotten about the dogs. The instant his shots left the automatic, the two Dobermans raced into the kitchen, their eyes bloody with hatred. The first leapt almost from a standing start, lunging for Niemann's neck. The Mauser exploded its shell into the brain of the dog, who fell with a whimper, lifelessly to the tile floor.

But the second Doberman continued its charge as Niemann's next Mauser shot only grazed the agile dog.

"*Hilfe!* Help! Koller! Anyone!" Niemann cried into the emptiness of the farm house. It was the Major's last syllable before an involuntary grunt left his mouth.

The second dog had found his mark in Niemann's throat. Bleeding from a sprung artery, the once-meticulous BND officer fell to the tile floor alongside Koller and the first Doberman, awash in a pool of his own lifeblood.

—— 56 ——

MEL Gordon had never felt more intrepid.

Accounting and law were the tools of his usual investigations, but in Berlin he had turned into a literal gumshoe—lurking, stalking the tracks of John Davidson, whose travels across Berlin were the strangest he had ever seen.

Davidson took the U-Bahn a lot, but not in an ordinary way. Instead of going in a straight line, he crisscrossed the town, changed trains, changed lines, sometimes even moved from one car to another on the same train. If not for his New York subway experience, Gordon was sure he'd have lost Davidson many times over. As is, he barely kept up with the man, who he guessed was twice his age. But to his own credit, Gordon thought he managed the entire maneuver without being spotted by Davidson.

As they traveled, he did notice one other unusual thing. Aside from himself, someone else was making these same, seemingly asinine, U-Bahn switches. It was a woman, about forty-five, wearing a distinguished woolen suit and an easily-spotted tall, pointed hat. There was something about her that looked World War IIish, he guessed, although he hadn't even been born in that era.

That morning, Davidson finally reached what Gordon assumed was his destination—a park. He continued to fol-

low him on foot, proud of a newly acquired skill he hadn't
learned in the GAO.

Davidson moved briskly through the park until he suddenly stopped and sat on a wooden bench. He assumed
the Baptist—he had learned that was his nickname—was
waiting for a rendezvous. Some discreet inquiries around the
Embassy had verified what he suspected. Davidson was the
ex-Agency big shot, the former head of counterintelligence.
It was unlikely he had been farmed out to such a minor
position in Berlin. Surely, it was a cover for a more interesting project. Perhaps one that involved Knudsen, the bee
farmer.

Gordon watched Davidson from a small wooded knoll
overlooking the bench. He had to wait only minutes, when
someone approached and sat down alongside the ex-CIA
official.

The man, slender and short—meaning shorter than himself—was ridiculously dressed in a Hawaiian sports shirt,
incongruous in Berlin. Quickly, Gordon pulled out the
Lakewood newspaper clipping and compared it with what
he could see of Davidson's companion. Unfortunately, the
man was showing only his profile, and Gordon was afraid
to come in closer. He yearned for a pair of binoculars.

The two men spoke for almost five minutes, then rose,
apparently getting ready to part. Suddenly the shorter man
turned, full-face, toward him. Gordon strained his eyes. Yes,
it was Knudsen! The journey of 12,000 miles had finally
borne fruit. The "Beekeeper," as Davidson had called him,
was obviously in Berlin on some mission for the Baptist.
Could it also involve Mussad, the North African leader who
was visiting the German capital?

He had little time to contemplate answers. Gordon raced
down the hill and headed straight for the twosome, who
were shaking hands and just about to part.

"Hold up, Davidson!" he yelled, arriving at the bench winded. "I've got to talk to both of you."

Surprisingly, Davidson and Knudsen held their ground.

"Welcome to the Tiergarten, Mr. Gordon," Davidson said. "I see you finally arrived. Was the U-Bahn travel too exhausting for you?"

Gordon was nonplussed. Did Davidson want to be tracked to the park?

"I don't know exactly what's going on," Gordon answered in frustration. "But I do know that this guy is Alex Knudsen, and he's here on federal expenses from the White House— and involved in some crazy CIA plot. In a few minutes I'm going to call my office in Washington and see if they can't get Senator Chase of the Intelligence Committee to put a stop to it. Whatever it is."

Davidson shook his head. "No, that would be quite impossible at this stage, Mr. Gordon. In fact, I've been waiting for you so we could make this adjustment."

"What adjustment?" Gordon asked nervously.

Davidson glanced at Knudsen, who jammed his Beretta into Gordon's side.

"Take him to Withers's apartment," Davidson ordered. "Tell Sam to keep him locked up until this is all over."

Davidson turned, as if addressing the sky. "That's all I need. The U.S. Congress on my back in Berlin."

— 57 —

DAVIDSON was exultant. Horstmann had left a cryptic message on his phone recorder: "Tell Mr. Tiergarten that I'll be at the Munich Beer Bar on the Ku-Damm. Tonight at six."

He didn't get the message until 5:15, after his return from the run-in with Mel Gordon. Davidson borrowed the Ambassador's shower, then put on the spare gray herringbone he kept in his office closet.

By taxi, it was less than ten minutes from the Embassy. The Beer Bar was just that: noisy, raucous, the smell of fermented hops everywhere. Liquid remains overflowed tables, even onto the floor. Gaiety, in a minor alcoholic note, was in full spate. Not the usual habitat for this Intelligence man.

He scanned the room and saw Horstmann, looking larger than ever. Two metal steins of draft beer were in front of him, and his fattened hands encircled a willing waitress.

"Baptist, over here," Horstmann called, spilling some beer as he rose. "Please, *Fräulein*, clean it up."

Horstmann's smile told Davidson everything as he approached.

"My Ami friend," he said, hugging the Baptist. "I'm so glad you've come. We have business together. No?"

"Ja," Davidson said, humoring the ex-Stasi Communist turned Nazi, now apparently converted to Capitalism.

"Good. Sit down, Baptist. If you have the deed, I have the information."

Davidson produced the deed, and held it tantalizingly in front of Horstmann. He could read it, but not touch. "As soon as our work is done, you'll again be the Count—the *Graf*—of Raven's Nest, mortgage free."

"How do I know that you'll keep your promise?" Horstmann seemed skeptical. "In such a case, I would be in fearsome trouble."

"I understand. Normally I'd say you'd have to trust me, but I've arranged for the deed to be held in escrow by an attorney, Max Frisch, a member of the Berlin City Council. As soon as he reads the newspaper account of the other deed, he'll give you this one. You can verify it with him as soon as we're finished here."

"*Gut*. I have smelled around myself, Baptist. Even your enemies—and you have a few—tell me you are a man of your word. Let's get to it."

Horstmann drew a breath. When exhaled, it turned Davidson's sensitive stomach.

"The security around Mussad's Hilton penthouse suite is airtight," Horstmann began. "No chances are being taken. But I'm sure you knew that. In all, there are eighteen guards—BND, the city *polizei* and Mussad's own men in suit jackets, with automatics in their shoulder holsters. A few are even disguised as waiters. The front of the hotel and the downstairs lobby are heavily defended too."

"When is he going out to meet people, especially Bessinger?"

"Mussad's not going anywhere. All the German bigshots who want to see him will have to come up to the penthouse. That includes the Chancellor."

"My key man, whom you'll meet, told me he expected that."

"Glad you have smart people working with you. Neither one of us can afford to make a mistake on this."

Davidson pumped Horstmann extensively on the political state of Al Rashon. "Is there anybody who can take Mussad's place? Fill the breach if he's gone?" the Baptist asked.

"He has plenty of cronies who'd like to take over, but none has popular support. He has one political rival who is less anti-Western and who might be able to put together a regime."

"Who's that?" Davidson asked, surprised by Horstmann's savvy.

"Hassam Ali, a Cambridge-educated rival, head of the Democratic Forum. He's in exile in Cairo but he has many friends in the army, especially General Karadi, a Sandhurst graduate and former Commander-in-Chief. With Mussad dead, there might be a chance for a coup."

Davidson didn't think he needed to tell Horstmann that Hassam and he were old friends, or that Hassam had been a Middle Eastern consultant for the Agency.

"But all of that is conjecture unless you get Mussad," Horstmann stressed. "Do you have a plan?"

"Yes, and we think it's a good one, Wolf. All that's missing is one key player."

"Who's that?"

Davidson smiled knowingly. "You."

58

"I'D like a room, a single on a high floor if I could," the man in the loud Hawaiian shirt asked the registration clerk at the Berlin Hilton. "Just for two or three days." The man smiled ingratiatingly. "The cheapest thing you have. I'm traveling on a tight expense account."

The clerk worked the computer reservation system with German efficiency. "We have only two rooms available and they're not very cheap."

"How much?"

"Four hundred and seventy marks a night."

"Four seventy? That's about four hundred dollars American?"

"That's right."

"OK, I'll take it. I have only this one duffel bag. If you don't mind, I'll carry it myself. It has some expensive electronic equipment."

The room was on the 39th floor, in the rear, just three floors below the penthouse. Once he had settled in, the Beekeeper began his surveillance. He had less than twenty-four hours before the act, and the time was best spent in browsing, in absorbing the ambience and security details of the hotel. It was all part of the intuitive equation that had made him so invaluable to nations and political movements. And now, apparently, to the President of the United States.

Knudsen began by testing Mussad's 42nd floor redoubt. He took the elevator from the 39th and touched the 42nd floor button. The elevator rose on soft cushions. Within seconds, the light indicator registered "42." The elevator stopped, but the doors stayed shut. Obviously, they had been closed off to the public.

From there, he descended one floor, to the 41st, and exited onto the carpeted hallway. He walked the full length, following arrows marked both "Penthouse" and "*Dachwohnung*," and pointing in both directions to the extremities of the building. As he reached each exit, he was faced with a large, brass door that was double-locked. There was no ingress or egress from that route either.

Quickly, Knudsen searched about for a cleaning woman. Two doors down he found one working in a vacated room.

"I wanted to walk upstairs to the penthouse, but the doors are closed."

"Oh, yes, *mein Herr*. There's a staircase behind them, but they're all shut now because of the official visit."

By elevator, he descended to the lobby, an enormous ultra-modern space, replete with large crystal chandeliers of abstract design, all set against a thick red, yellow and blue Mondrian-like carpet. The furniture was of Italian design, light and bold. Approaching the special Tower-Penthouse elevator, he made a motion to enter.

"I'm sorry, sir," said a burly German, probably a Berlin policeman working undercover, Knudsen thought. "No one is allowed up to the penthouse without a special police pass. Security, you know."

The Beekeeper had no reason to press the point. He moved on, meandering, apparently aimlessly, through the almost block-square lobby. At the street entrance, he walked up to the double set of revolving doors. Here the guards were not disguised. Four Berlin policemen with semi-automatic sidearms cast continuous glances at the crowd. Knudsen gave them his best American tourist smile. He had already seen the rear service exit, where several trucks and two Berlin police radio cars were parked. Directly alongside was a rear pedestrian exit, with a couple of policemen on foot.

Returning to the lobby, he visited the newsstand where he bought a copy of the *International Herald Tribune* and some sugar-free gum. The Italian armchair looked inviting. He relaxed into its stuffed interior and started to read, hoping for a touch of serendipity.

It was not long in coming. Almost directly opposite him was a heavyset man, chewing on an unlit Meerschaum pipe. *Rauchen Verboten*, Smoking Prohibited, signs were posted in key places in the lobby.

Knudsen stared at the man, a faint sense of recognition tapping at his brain. The man was short, white-haired and professorial looking. He too was reading a newspaper, the *Berliner Morgenpost*. Probably not a tourist. Straining, Knudsen tried to reclaim the past. From where did he know this man?

The Cold War, of course. He was looking at a renowned member of his own trade, his counterpart in the Red world. A former East German Stasi consultant, "Bismarck" as some called him, had never earned fees as large as the Beekeeper's, but he had prospered by equalizing the playing field.

But the Stasi was now out of business. Who was his new employer? Besides Mussad, who else could be a target in Berlin? Of course. German Chancellor Bessinger, who would be visiting the terrorist leader the next morning.

This playing field would not only be equal, but busy. His and Bismarck's path had crossed more than once, but never with such deadly proximity.

59

"THE lady with the hat," Davidson had begun to call her.

Intrepid, determined, resourceful, were all words he would apply. Especially "secretive." He had no idea who she was, or why she was intent on following him, especially since her mission had often proven unsuccessful. And why the telltale chapeau, in such unmistakable colors as violet, kelly green or fuchsia? Always with a fine feather stuck in the tall crown.

He had no one to ask, except her, and she had been elusive.

Davidson boarded the S-Bahn, the fast commuter line, and took it toward Wannsee, about fifteen miles from the Embassy, to meet Sam at his apartment. Withers was complaining about playing nanny to Mel Gordon, who was screaming like a banshee over his imprisonment, threatening to jail both of them for kidnapping when he got back to the States.

He needed to talk over some last minute arrangements with Sam for tomorrow's meeting of Mussad and Bessinger, and also wanted to let Withers know that President Briggs had called again, with discouraging word on the hostage situation. All roads led to the Beekeeper's execution of his assignment tomorrow.

There she was. Not five minutes after boarding the

train, the woman, now wearing a black pointed hat with a white feather, appeared. She was not standing on the platform, but had seated herself at the end of his car. The woman caught Davidson's eye and smiled, not sardonically, but lady-like, almost warm. Davidson smiled back, but as he made an initial move toward her, she rose and started back toward the next car. As soon as Davidson retreated, she did the same. It was a dance of espionage.

She had apparently decided that reasonable proximity was all right, but that she would avoid actually meeting, or speaking, to her target. The woman, he guessed, was middle-aged, and had one great advantage. She knew who he was, but he only knew that she was attractive, that the feathers appeared to be ostrich, and that she had a mature, somewhat lined, long face and a dagger chin that complemented her pointed hats.

They rode in slightly embarrassed silence for twenty minutes, then exited the train together at the Wannsee stop. Davidson couldn't tell her intentions. Either it was her destination as well, or she was still "following" him. The woman made no attempt to disguise her moves, walking down the platform only ten yards behind him.

Davidson was about to mount the stairs when he was rudely jostled by a man—short, burly, with amorphous features and smoking a large white pipe.

"Oh, excuse me, *mein Herr*. I am so sorry," the man said, pressing his pipe almost into Davidson's face. "Could I have a light, *bitte*?"

Davidson reached into his pocket for a lighter he carried for an occasional pipe of his own. But his hand halted abruptly. His eyes had focused on the carved gargoyles on the pipe bowl. My God, Withers had told him about this man. He was the contract worker for Red Swastika.

"One second, I have it here somewhere," Davidson said, stalling, calculating whether he had time to unholster his Beretta.

"No sweat, as you Americans say," the short man responded. In that instant, he pulled a Mauser 7.65 from his parka, swiveling and raising it to aiming height in one swift, almost graceful, sweep.

The gunshot exploded into the air. Davidson staggered from the sound and stared at the burly man with the Meerschaum. The gunman stood there, surprised and immobile. His gun had been shot out of his hand and was laying uselessly on the ground. Without reaching for it, he turned and raced into a departing train, never looking back.

Davidson realized that the shot had not come from the pipe smoker's gun. His own pistol was still only halfway out of its holster. He looked up. Only a dozen feet away stood the "lady with the hat," a spent short-barreled pistol—a pocket-sized .25 caliber—in her hand.

"I suppose we finally had to meet, Mr. Davidson," she said in a husky accented English. "Detective Sergeant Langer sends his regards, and asks you to be more careful, *bitte*. The Berlin *polizei* prefer that you leave our city alive."

60

SERGEANT Kurt Langer sat at his desk in precinct headquarters near Budapester Strasse and weighed his options.

Koller had been killed by Major Niemann of the BND in what was probably an internal hit ordered by Red Swastika. It would be comforting to think that the organization had been fatally injured by Koller's death, but he knew otherwise. There were other Nazi sympathizers ready to take up the mantle, and Friedrich, apparently the "Fuehrer" of the organization, was still totally unknown.

He wanted to talk it over with John Davidson. Lichtenstein at the BND had told him of the old spy's prowess, and it was obvious the Americans had a vested interest in tracking down Swastika—if only because of its probable ties to Mussad. Yes, he'd call Davidson at the Hilton, and maybe share a beer. Or, in the Baptist's case, more likely a glass of Trockenbeerenauslese '71, a good—if expensive— white Rhine wine.

"Sergeant Langer, what a privilege," Davidson said as they met for lunch at the Scharnhorst House, one of Berlin's better restaurants.

"No, I think I'm ahead, Mr. Davidson. The cost of this lunch—about two hundred marks—is as much as I make in a day. We police are not used to such luxury. Unless, of course, we're on the take, which is not my style."

"I wouldn't think so, Sergeant. Shall we order? I'll let you do the honors. You're more familiar with German cuisine."

The young detective eagerly examined the menu, then waved to the waiter.

"We'll have two of each," he explained. "First we'll start with an appetizer, a small order of *Gansepokelkeule*—pickled leg of goose. Then *Ochsenschwanz mit Teltower Rubchen*, oxtail with Teltow small white turnips and *Bruhkartoffeln mit pikanten Beilagen*—potatoes cooked in broth with piquant trimmings, and a side order of *Aal grun*—young eels with cucumber salad. To drink, we'll have a Berlin beer, *Weissbier*, with a *Schuss*—a shot of raspberry juice. Serve it in a wide glass, please. For dessert, a *Kranzkuchen* cake. And please make sure it has plenty of currants. I want to impress my American friend with our Berlin cooking." Langer paused briefly. "Oh yes, if you'd like wine, too, I'll save you a little money, Mr. Davidson. We'll have a fruit wine from Werder for local color. That's made right here, near Potsdam, you know."

Once the waiter had left with the order, Langer laughed at a startled Davidson. "Don't worry, Baptist. The whole lunch is not more than three thousand calories."

They spoke as they ate. "Mr. Davidson, I think I have an idea of how to get to Friedrich," Langer began.

"Why, have you learned any more about him?" Davidson asked, encouraged.

"No, I don't even have a suspicion," Langer admitted. "But that's why I wanted to meet with you. To figure some plan of attack, some method of discovery."

"I'd like that, Kurt," Davidson said. "If we could reveal the top Swastika leadership, especially if it proved to be someone inside the German government, there'd be world-wide media coverage. It would be most embarrassing to Chancellor Bessinger. Maybe so much so that the Germans, officially and unofficially, would break their ties to Mussad, and rein in their more dangerous exports." He stared at the young detective. "Do you have any ideas?"

"As a matter of fact, I do." Langer quickly checked over his shoulder to insure their privacy. "I'd like to smoke Friedrich out—I think you Americans call it a 'sting.' "

"Yes, but how?" Davidson asked. Langer could see he had gotten the intelligence man's attention.

"The way I see it is this. If we feed them a piece of information that is startling and could be very useful to them, then they'll make a move. And in doing so, expose themselves. Especially if the information was important enough for Friedrich to show his hand. You know, get the itch to become personally involved."

Davidson listened, obviously impressed. "What kind of information, Kurt?"

"Oh, Mr. Davidson, that's up to you. If you're convinced Swastika is tied to Mussad, then I suppose it should be something that both Mussad and Friedrich would want— even find irresistible. You know what I mean? If you had something to offer them like that, then maybe Friedrich himself would come forward."

Langer guessed he now had the former CIC chief hooked. "You would need a middle man you could trust, probably some American who could pose—or be—a nefarious character, someone to lead the sting. I could help, too."

"How, Kurt?"

"I can get your sting information placed into police channels and into the BND. I have an undercover man in *Ganzfakt*. Only a clerk, but he can tap into and out of their computer operation. That way, any leaks will bring it to Friedrich's attention. Good idea, *nicht wahr*?"

The Baptist contemplated hard. "Excellent, Kurt. The plan is good. Now all it needs is some attractive bait. And I think I know just what that is."

"Yes, Mr. Davidson? Tell me. I am most curious."

"No, no, Kurt. The most important thing about a sting is that no one knows. Otherwise it stops being a sting and becomes a boomerang. No, I'll tell you when it's all over. But I want to thank you for your suggestion. I can see it all happening now."

Langer smiled wanly through his disappointment.

"Well thank you anyway for the lunch, Mr. Davidson. It was excellent, and much too expensive for a mere sergeant. And I'm glad I may be of some help in your operation. Even if I don't have your full confidence."

"You do, Kurt—under normal circumstances. And you deserved more than this lunch. Please, join me in a toast."

The men lifted their *Schuss* of raspberry juice.

"To Frederick the Great," the Baptist said. "May his reign be short-lived."

61

"SO I wasn't on a wild goose chase after all," Mel Gordon taunted Withers. "I started out with a lousy expense check made out to somebody nobody ever heard of, a New Jersey bee-farmer, and now I'm a kidnap victim in Berlin, held prisoner in an apartment by some wild CIA man with a crazy crewcut arranging an assassination."

"Mel, if I may call you that, why don't you calm down and take it easy," Withers tried to console him. "Carrying on is not going to get you anywhere. You're tied up proper and we're going to feed you and no one is going to hurt you. Only it would be nice if you'd shut up. I'm stuck here with you myself."

"SHUT UP? You've haven't heard a third of what I'm going to say when I get back to the States—if I get back. Do you intend to destroy the evidence after you kill Mussad?"

"What evidence?" Withers asked, somewhat innocently.

"Me! Of course. I'm the only one outside your unholy trio—I suppose a quartet counting President Briggs—that knows what's going on."

Withers laughed. "No, Mel. Nobody's going to kill you. Unless you try to escape and screw up our assignment. Thousands of lives could depend on that, and then we'd sac- rifice yours. But once it's done tomorrow morning, you're as free as a bird to leave here and get back to Washington. With our blessings."

"You're going to let me go after you kill Mussad?"

"Why not? We're not murderers you know. Mussad is not really a member of the human race."

"Oh, so now you and Davidson and the President are God. Well let me tell you, crazy ex-Marine. When I get back to Congress, I'm going to hang all three of you, and put you away for a zillion years. And the President? Well he's going to be an ex-Prez. Remember Executive Order 12333. That makes it illegal for any federal employee—and that includes him—to engage in or conspire to engage in assassination. High Crimes and Misdemeanors, bub. It's called Impeachment, with a capital 'I' and that rhymes with 'T' and stands for Trouble."

Mel paused only briefly for breath. "How in the hell did you expect to get away with it, anyway?"

"I'm not admitting anything, Gordon, and what you're saying is only hearsay. You don't think the Beekeeper would do such a thing—if he did it—without a full disguise, do you? Sure, you've got an expense check, but the President sending somebody to Berlin is no crime. Knudsen's just a consultant. You have plenty of those on the Hill, don't you? No, I don't think it's going to be so easy to prove anything as you think."

Withers paused, staring down Gordon.

"Doesn't it bother you that that bastard Mussad is torturing and raping our kids, and taking over his neighbors by armed subversion, and preparing for a deadly neutron war?" Withers asked rhetorically, aggravated by anyone who didn't have his clarity or patriotism. "And with Mussad alive, it could cost thousands of American lives to defeat him. Doesn't that bother you at all?"

Gordon smiled, almost patronizingly. "Sure, kill everybody you don't like. Break any damn law you want. Sure, a jungle. Is that what you want?"

"Well, we have a democracy back home," Withers answered, feeling worn by Gordon's attack. "We'll let the American people decide, won't we? That is, if we ever get the job done. Your coming here hasn't helped out, you know."

"Withers, old buddy. I don't give a shit about you ánd your supposed patriotic rhetoric. But like you said, we'll let the people decide. And as the top of my class at Brooklyn Law, I can guess what they're going to say."

"What's that, Mel?"

"Hang the three murdering bastards, and kick that so-called President out of the Oval Office, right on his fat Arkansas ass."

62

DER Tag had come.

Chancellor Bessinger and Mussad the Great were scheduled to meet within minutes on the 42nd floor penthouse of the Berlin Hilton. In addition to the principals and their staffs, about twenty in all, there were two members of the press, a pool reporter from *Der Spiegel* representing the German media and a staffer from *Al-Haqq*, The Truth, part of Mussad's controlled press.

Gunter Miltz, the thin bespectacled *Spiegel* man, wearing a worn corduroy jacket, seemed wary from the outset. He expected a quiet morning, filled with some conventional accolades from Mussad for his German benefactors, and from Bessinger, brilliant obfuscations that would make Mussad happy yet keep his American friends from getting apoplexy that there was a meeting between them going on at all.

The morning began with refreshments, a rather heavy German smorgasbord. The food was picked at by the guests, but got the most attention from the security people who, undercover, were scattered throughout the forty-foot-long living room.

Security was the hallmark of the meeting. The penthouse elevators were locked from the inside, and no one could come up without two guards, one of Mussad's own men, the other from the Berlin *polizei*. The German contingent was headed by Detective Sergeant Kurt Langer, who was ultimately responsible for the lives of both national leaders.

The procedure was simple. If someone wanted to come up to the penthouse, he called on a special house phone in the lobby, itself guarded by Berlin police. A close-circuit television camera displayed the situation below to Langer, who had to approve the guests. If accepted, the two guards were dispatched from the penthouse to pick them up. The 42nd floor elevators were closed after the guards left and not opened again until the password—Adenauer—was given.

Thus far, Langer was pleased with the operation. The informal part of the meeting had begun. The two Presidents were standing in the center of the opulently furnished room, talking. Bessinger wore his typically unfashionable three-piece worsted suit, but Mussad was dressed in a theatrical Berber outfit, a flowing red robe and black and white headdress.

"Herr Bessinger," Mussad was saying in English, the *lingua franca* of the meeting, "we are thankful for all your technical help in the building of a modern state. Only as the Germans can do."

"You flatter us too much," Bessinger said while his hands pulled at his collar, only one sign of his discomfort. "Any of the Western nations, even little Belgium, could do the same."

"Yes, Herr Chancellor, but there's the rub. *Only* Germany was willing to help us. And we are grateful." Mussad smiled confidently at the Chancellor. "But of course it is not a one-way street. You have a twenty billion dollar trade surplus with us and our friends. I suppose little Al Rashon makes a big difference in Berlin."

Bessinger displayed still more discomfort, hoping to drop the subject.

"Oh, yes, Chancellor, your trade is so vital to us that I've named a German specialist to my staff," Mussad added. He turned toward the giant of a man standing alongside. "This is Count Wolf von Horstmann, from a distinguished old Bavarian family. Surely, you've heard of him."

The Chancellor muttered some pleasantry. The conversation continued, but not a word was said by either leader about the neutron bombs or the American hostages. But the two men did joke, in a macabre way, about the reported threats on their lives.

"My security people say the threats are not just idle talk, Mr. Chancellor. In fact, I hear the Americans have even signed a contract on me. But of course that may only be espionage talk, which the Americans are fond of. Have you heard any rumors?"

"President Mussad, I'm quite sure we're safe here. I expect you'll be returning to Al Rashon tomorrow in the same condition as when you arrived in Berlin."

After some formal pronouncements, mainly for the media, and hand-shaking all around, the meeting started toward its conclusion.

"Would you like some refreshments, some wine or food, before you leave?" Horstmann solicitously asked Mussad, who was known for his appetite.

"Yes, good idea."

The two men excused themselves and moved toward the buffet table, where Mussad picked at the hors d'oeuvres while Horstmann poured himself a drink.

"Oh, *mein Gott*! Look what I have done."

Horstmann had tripped on the rug and poured half his wine on Mussad's red robe. The North African grimaced as Horstmann tried to wipe it clean. "Oh, you should be more careful, Horstmann. Now, I think we'd better go to the restroom so I can freshen up. I smell like an alcoholic. That's not part of my religion."

Horstmann apologized profusely as he accompanied Mussad to the restroom at the far end of the spacious penthouse. Meanwhile Chancellor Bessinger, who had seen the minor accident, had moved toward the elevator. He stood there, waiting for Mussad to return. Once they received security clearance from Langer, they would descend together to the basement, where their armored-plated Mercedes limousines were waiting. Mussad had arranged one outside appointment, at his embassy, before leaving Berlin.

Mussad and Horstmann entered the small restroom, decorated in black and white marble, with silver wallpaper and a plush red rug.

The only one in the washroom was the attendant who quickly wiped Mussad's robe as clean as possible with a damp cloth. Then both the North African leader and Horstmann stood side by side at the urinals.

"I think the meeting went well, don't you?" Horstmann asked his employer, hoping to divert him from the *faux pas*.

"Yes, it did. But do you believe Bessinger was being sincere? After all, he has enormous pressure from the Americans not to bother with me."

The two men adjourned to the wash basins to freshen up.

"I'd say that his appearance here this morning proves his sincerity," Horstmann answered. "It took political courage for him just to show up."

Horstmann's comments seemed to please Mussad, who moved toward the bathroom attendant.

"Please," Mussad said, extending his dripping hands for a linen towel.

The attendant, a short, almost wispy figure of a man, with a mustache, answered in English with a heavy German accent. "In a moment, sir," he said. Horstmann waited by the exit, drying his own hands with a paper towel.

The attendant reached into his linen basket and took out a folded, fresh linen towel. Opening it with a flourish, he handed it to Mussad.

"Here you are, sir, nice and clean."

As Mussad dried his face, the attendant's hand scrounged under the towels in his basket, looking toward Horstmann. "Won't you have one too, sir?"

"No, it's not necessary. Thank you anyway."

Mussad dried himself and reached out to return the towel to the attendant, who took his right hand from the basket, as if to accept Mussad's soiled linen. But instead of a towel, the attendant's hand held a gun, an M-9 Beretta 9mm, with silencer.

"WHAT . . . !" Mussad began to scream. But his words were drowned out by the short, muted booms of three successive shots from the semi-automatic.

Mussad's eyes fixed as he fell to the floor, his head striking against the marble, the blood trickling from the wound. The washroom attendant's bullets had meticulously punctured Mussad's body—one to the heart, another at the carotid artery in the neck, the third between his eyes.

"All right, Mr. Horstmann," the attendant called out, his fake German accent having vanished. "You're my passport to freedom. Raise your hands and walk outside in front of me. Do exactly what I tell you. This Beretta—I think it was once yours—will be nestled in your back."

The strange duo, with more than a foot in height and a hundred and twenty pounds of difference between them, moved cautiously out of the washroom. In spite of the silencer, the Beekeeper feared that someone might have heard the shots, or even the sudden thud of Mussad's skull against the hard marble. Or, perhaps people were waiting to enter the washroom, whose door the Beekeeper had nimbly locked from the inside before the shooting.

As the Beekeeper and Horstmann—with the German in front—walked into the main room, they were startled. A loud noise, more a bomb than a pistol shot, rattled the other end of the penthouse. An orange flash, like a magician's illusion, lit the whole area as the brass door from the penthouse to the floor below exploded open. A short man—the Beekeeper immediately recognized "Bismarck" the Stasi killer—rushed through the opening. His Mauser was aimed at Bessinger, who waited at the elevator, his face drained in fear.

The other security men had been frozen into position, but Langer had left Bessinger's side at the first sight of the flash. He hit the carpeted floor and rolled over into a flanking position, his gun aimed at the smoking open portal. As the rotund assassin raced through, Langer fired six consecutive blasts, one striking the center of Bismarck's neck. The assassin discharged his weapon but the fatal shot threw his aim off enough to send the bullet harmlessly into the elevator door.

"In here!" a Berlin policeman suddenly shouted from outside the restroom at the other side of the penthouse. "Mussad's dead. Been shot three times!"

The Beekeeper made quick use of the diversion. He moved himself and Horstmann to the elevator bank alongside a doubly startled Bessinger.

"Don't anybody fire at anybody!" Langer screamed as he saw the Beekeeper point his gun at Bessinger.

"All right, officer," the Beekeeper ordered. "I want you as a hostage too. Just in case nobody cares about Horstmann. Drop your gun or the Chancellor is finished."

Langer hesitated only a second, then lowered his gun onto the rug.

"OK, men, step back," he shouted. "There's been enough killing for one day. We can't risk the Chancellor's life. I'll let you through with your hostage, but Chancellor Bessinger stays here with my men."

The Beekeeper nodded his assent.

"OK, let him through," Langer called out.

As Chancellor Bessinger was pulled away, a clearing opened in front of the elevator bank.

"All right, Wagner," Langer called to one of his men. "Get the elevators open. I'm going down with them. I want to make sure there's no bloodshed in the lobby."

The strange threesome—Langer, the Beekeeper and Horstmann—descended together. As the elevator doors opened, they faced a half dozen Berlin police carrying UZIs at the ready.

"Hold it where you are, men," Langer shouted. "This man

is armed and has me and Count Horstmann as hostages. Make room for him to leave peacefully. Give him my car and the keys. Please don't try anything, and don't follow us. He's serious about killing us both unless we cooperate. But he's promised to free us once we're outside Berlin."

An aisle of security was instantly created by the Berlin police. The Beekeeper walked down its center, the two hostages directly in front of him. The fifty-foot walk to the curb and Langer's car seemed like an endless path, the guests scurrying for safety behind the heavy Italian chairs.

A small BMW stood at the curb. With a wave of his gun, the Beekeeper forced Langer into the driver's seat, while Horstmann got in alongside. The Beekeeper dove into the back, quickly lowering himself below the window level, his gun still aimed toward the front seats.

"All right, move out. NOW!" the Beekeeper ordered.

A half dozen Berlin policemen stood at the curb watching, frustrated as the assassin of the Great Mussad moved smartly away from the Hilton.

BOOK
—4—

— 63 —

THE White House phones would never stop ringing, Les Fanning feared. On second thought, she hoped the calls would continue forever.

Jubilation over Mussad's death was in the air throughout the nation. The tally of phone calls to the President—6,000 in just an hour after the announcement of the assassination—told that story.

Fanning received a regular fifteen-minute report, broken down into various categories. There was no evidence from the press, or from official sources, but almost all the callers automatically assumed the President had ordered the deed. And of these, over two-thirds approved, despite the violation of Executive Order 12333. About one-third disagreed, ranging from simple disapproval to outright anger. Some spoke of the "outrageous reversion to jungle tactics," but they were in the minority.

Overall, the nation was relieved. Now that Mussad was dead, they could await the return of the teenage hostages. A by-product of the assassination, most seemed to believe, would be a new administration in Al Rashon, with more peaceful intentions. There would be no 444 days of agony as in the era of Jimmy Carter.

Had the President really been involved in the assassination? Les asked herself. He usually confided in her, but she hadn't heard a whisper about this, although his private security advisor, John Davidson, had been in the Oval Office several times in the past weeks. She wasn't the only one with that query. Tim Calhoun, the White House Press Secretary, had been besieged by the media. "Did the President order the hit?" they asked. "If so, hasn't he broken the law?"

He was not about to ask the President, Calhoun told the reporters. He liked his job too much. But Les thought she might try, not for public consumption, but for herself. After all, she was working in the White House at a historic moment.

In the midst of the public jubilation, Fanning still feared the backlash from Speaker Kembeck and his cronies. What did the President think of the political danger to himself in spite of voter approval?

As Fanning entered the Oval Office, she could see the President standing, staring out the window toward the Rose Garden, his face illuminated by a smile.

"It's good news, isn't it, Mr. President?" Fanning began.

"Yes. I hate to see anyone die, but in this case, decency is probably advanced. However it happened."

Fanning took the next step carefully, her voice tentative.

"We're getting an overwhelming amount of phone calls, Mr. President. Almost seventy percent are pleased as punch. And . . ."

"Yes, Les. And what?"

"And almost all assume that you ordered the assassination. They believe it's against the law, but they don't seem to mind. They also think that the hostages will be let go, and that Mussad's successor will be easier to deal with."

Les waited for a response, but none was forthcoming.

"Yes, Les?"

"Well, sir, I was wondering if there was anything you could tell me. You know about the assassination. Just for my own curiosity."

Briggs hesitated. "It's best left unsaid, Les. But I sure hope the people are right in their optimism. It's a first step, but I don't know if the country's out of the woods yet. One thing I am sure of: I'm not. That SOB Kembeck has been waiting for something like this. I can hear him now, starting the rumblings about impeachment."

"Do you think he has the power to do it?" Les was now almost sorry she had broached the subject.

"God knows, Les. But sure as hell he's going to try. He'd like nothing better than to have me join Mussad, at least in political purgatory. We'll just have to wait and see."

"OK, call in that GAO gumshoe now," Congressman Kembeck roared, leaning back into the leather chair in the Speaker's chambers, an elaborate suite of rooms in the House side of the Capitol that he had inherited from his predecessors, going all the way back to Joe Cannon, for whom a House office building had been named. In spirit, he had inherited the mantle from Henry Clay, who became Speaker on his very first day in the House in 1811.

"What's his name? Oh, yeah, Mel Gordon, that sassy New York boy."

The GAO was informally the Speaker's fiefdom, some 5,000 people he could command to investigate not only budgets and executive waste and fraud, but his nemesis, the President of the United States, whoever the hell that happened to be at the time. He had been Speaker through the terms of three of them now, and he expected to outlast, and outfox, at least three more. Briggs had his spooks, and he, Kembeck, had his too. Now one of the best, he had heard from Danny Reiger, an ex-FBI man and the head of the GAO's Office of Special Investigation, was here with news.

"Super-urgent," the kid had said. Well, he'd see.

"Come on in, Gordon, and put your little ass down on this antique chair. But not too hard. They tell me the damn thing's worth twenty-five thousand dollars of the taxpayer's money."

Gordon had never been in the Speaker's chambers, which were directly off the House floor. He glanced around the office, an elegant room filled with a crystal chandelier, antique fireplace and brocade-covered furniture. This was one room of a suite of eight, Gordon had heard. Next door was the enormous—perhaps fifty-foot-long—historic Rayburn Room, named after the legendary Speaker Sam Rayburn, which was used for formal receptions. More like a small ballroom, Gordon thought. As a snooper of waste, Gordon had learned that the Speaker also had his own private dining room. No wonder the Congressional budget had now topped three billion dollars a year.

He had never met the Speaker and he found himself subdued in the presence of the bombastic South Dakota Congressman. If not a great man, at least a great politician, with a great voice and vast powers.

"So what's up, Gordon?" the Speaker asked.

"I've just come back from Germany, sir. I was in Berlin, in the clutches of the President's henchmen. One of them was the hit man who took out Mussad. It was an official assassination ordered by President Briggs."

"WHAT?"

Rusty Kembeck forgot the protocol of his office and rose from his leather chair. He came around and slapped Gordon on the back, his approximation of warmth.

"Why, that's just terrific, kid. I knew that Arkansas fatback did it. I just knew it!" He turned back to Gordon. "Mel, I heard you were a super sleuth. Now take yourself a drink and tell me everything. Naturally, you have proof."

Gordon nodded, smiling confidently.

Kembeck paused, then banged the red leather desktop. "I'm going to hang that Arkansas lizard by his hide. Yes siree, just like I said, from the top of the Taft Campanile."

Gordon reached into his pocket and took out the original $1,273 check that had started his trek back and forth across the Atlantic. He proudly handed it to Kembeck. The Speaker looked at it, turned it over a few times, examining it as if he were sniffing a dead fish.

"What's this, boy? I know it's a White House check, but that petty cash is less than it costs to lease my limo for a month. Don't tell me that's the assassin's paycheck. Did he hire a boy scout?"

Gordon knew he'd have to talk quickly. In rapid fire order, he described his work in tracking down the owner of the check, who he figured was on some assignment for the President. It had led him to Berlin, and to the Tiergarten, where he had confronted John Davidson and his killer, who they called "The Beekeeper."

"Then what happened?" Kembeck asked, his curiosity fully aroused.

"Well, they pulled a gun on me and took me to the apartment of Davidson's CIA sidekick, an ex-Marine named Sam Withers, posing as Second Secretary at our embassy there. I heard them making plans for the assassination. Then, when it was all over, they let me go."

"Let you go?" Kembeck was incredulous.

"That's right. They said I was free as a bird. I didn't understand it either."

"Do you have any witnesses or did you tape record anything?" Kembeck asked, already building the impeachment case in his mind.

"No, sir."

"No, what?"

"No, all I have is my word that they kidnapped me in Berlin and planned the assassination. The hit man was the Beekeeper. I saw him and spoke with him. Plus I have his White House travel check, which you saw."

Kembeck rose and circled the office, picking his way through the nineteenth-century furniture. "Look, Mel, I don't mean to be critical, cause you did one hell of a good job. I got enough ammunition, just on your word, and that petty cash check, to get my buddies in the House and the Senate riled up. But I need more if I'm really going to nail that arrogant bastard Briggs. Your job's not over, boy. And now you're working directly for me. Do you understand? This is the most important thing that's happened to both of us. I'm a politician. A damn good one, but I need a gumshoe to finish this off. And you're it."

Gordon swelled with power as he listened.

"Do we know how much they paid this Beekeeper for the hit?" Kembeck next asked. "Any word on that check?"

Gordon shook his head. "No. The Beekeeper—he uses the name Alex Knudsen now—has two bank accounts that I know of. One is in Zurich, the other in the Cayman Islands. I checked both and he hasn't deposited a nickel since. I also checked the White House accounts before I came here. Nothing more for Knudsen. But, Mr. Speaker . . ." He hesitated.

"Yes, talk up, Mel. You don't impress me as a shy New Yorker. What did ya want to say?"

"Well, I didn't think I'd find another check for Knudsen. I overheard them kidding about Knudsen giving Davidson a 'freebie.' "

"A hit man not being paid? Come on, Mel."

"Yes, sir. I heard Knudsen once mutter, like in a joke, 'This one's for the Gipper.' He had his Presidents mixed, but it was the spirit, like he owed Davidson a favor and this was it."

Kembeck fell silent, circling the room, his hand massaging his beardless face, an inheritance from his Sioux great-grandfather.

"I'm not going to give this up, Mel. There's got to be another link. Could there be an inside man on Mussad's side who got the payola? Maybe that's it. What do you think?"

Gordon reflected, for only a moment. "Mr. Speaker. You should have been a gumshoe yourself. That's a good thought. The German press announced the killing was done in the restroom of the Berlin Hilton penthouse. Yes, there had to be someone on the inside helping out. Yes, I'm sure that's it."

"OK, kid. If that's the case, the evidence is back in Germany. Get your Bronx ass on a plane to Berlin today, and call me as soon as you get anything."

A smile, satisfied and sardonic, returned to the Speaker's face.

"I'm just itching to lynch that Arkansas bastard."

64

"OK, Baptist, what is it now? Can't you see I'm making a buck as a real businessman. I don't need a front anymore. I'm it."

Davidson offered him a reluctant smile. "Mike, you've done some good jobs for me and the Agency, but this one's the most important. It involves Red Swastika."

Mike Kennedy had been a Berlin expatriate for twenty years, and spoke German almost as fluently as he did Boston Irish-English. An itinerant asset for Davidson over the years, he made his living as an export-import advisor for German firms, specializing in American and Latin American business. He had been successful enough to build a staff of ten, housed in the giant Europa Center opposite the Decayed Tooth church on the Ku-Damm.

This morning, he was serving Davidson coffee in his private office, with a panoramic view of Berlin in front of them.

"Red Swastika? Sounds interesting." Kennedy's blue eyes, a soft contrast to his full head of white hair, a marker of old Eire, became iridescent. "Who are they?"

"You've heard of the Fourth Reich? And of course, Mussad."

Kennedy nodded. "Sure. It's that pro-Nazi party that's running a slate for the Bundestag. But Mussad? Why, the bastard's dead. Someone must have put out an expensive contract on him."

Davidson let the innuendo pass.

"Well, Mike, both are connected to Red Swastika," he said, explaining that it was the neo-Nazi organization that controlled both the Fourth Reich party and Mussad's neutron armament, which was being stockpiled in the North African desert. "Using their right-wing connection to German industry, Heinschmann to be exact, they've even built underground bunkers that are immune to our smart bombs," the Baptist added. "And all this is centered here in Berlin."

Kennedy's head shook in surprise. "John, I'm afraid I've been out of the game too long. I've been hearing right-wing rumbles, but I never knew they had become so active. What can I do for you?"

"Well, I need someone like you to handle a sting, to smoke out a man code-named 'Friedrich' who heads Swastika. My idea is to offer them a cache of radioactive tritium and nuclear triggers for more neutron bombs, material supposedly stolen by you and your buddies in the States from the Nevada stockpile. We'll ask for a hundred million dollars, which will only make the offer more attractive."

Davidson explained Mussad's whole operation, including the delivery of raw material from the Russian nuclear-scientist wing of Swastika, and the Brazil-Heinschmann operation in assembling the neutron shells.

"I'm betting that not only will Swastika be interested, but that Friedrich himself will be intrigued enough to come forward. Then we'll learn who he is and maybe take him."

Kennedy's mass of white hair moved.

"And I'm the guy you're thinking of? The schmuck American who'll stick his neck out to get your Nazi honcho. Right?"

"Exactly, Mike. And our government will make sure it won't cost your business anything in the process. A kind of unofficial insurance policy."

"Backed by the President?" Kennedy asked.

Davidson swallowed hard. "Backed by the President."

Kennedy rose and walked to the glass wall, staring out over the Berlin scene below.

"How about bona fides? How do I get these people to believe me—if I took the job?"

"We'll make sure of that. I promise you some good gossip in local papers and some planted intelligence info that will get to Swastika. Don't worry, by the time they make contact with you, they'll believe you're the real thing."

Kennedy continued to stare out the window. "You know, John, I've gotten to like this city. Next to Boston, it's my home. I've even raised my kid here—sort of half American, half German. I really don't want to get back into the game, and I don't need the dough, even if you offered it. So, I suppose I'll do it. What the shit. It's for both my countries. These people can't take another Nazi regime, no matter how much they might like the glory."

He turned back to face Davidson.

"So Baptist, when do I begin the sting?"

65

IN the two key capitals, the main protagonists heard the news at the same time, with the same emotional kick in the stomach.

In Washington, President Briggs got the word first, in his morning's intelligence summary, placed on his desk at 7:00 A.M., as usual.

The brief was succinct, and devastating:

NEW AL RASHON LEADER ABDUL LAKIM, MUSSAD'S NEPH-EW, TAKES OVER FOR MUSSAD. SAYS HE WILL FOLLOW HIS DEPARTED LEADER'S PROGRAM IN EVERY WAY. HE ACCUSES THE AMERICAN PRESIDENT OF HAVING ORDERED MUSSAD'S ASSASSINATION. THERE WILL BE NO RELEASE OF AMERICAN HOSTAGES, WITHOUT RANSOM, AND NO LET-UP IN THEIR CAMPAIGN TO DEVELOP AN INDEPEND-ENT PAN-AFRICAN FOREIGN POLICY TO COMBAT THE PAX AMERICANA.

Briggs fell, more than leaned, back into his enveloping leather chair.

Had it all been in vain? Had he risked impeachment only to replace one madman with another?

He could hardly blame Davidson. But he did need the Baptist to do something—dramatic—to change the political course in Al Rashon, to make the death of Mussad pay off as planned.

"Les, come in," he called into the intercom, gaining the instant attention he so relied upon.

"Get our Embassy in Berlin on the horn. I need to talk to John Davidson. Right away."

In Berlin, Davidson sat at his desk, making what looked like small doodles on a blank yellow pad. Step by step, he was outlining Kennedy's job of making contact with Friedrich. It had been a hard decision, but he had concluded that not even Sergeant Langer should know about Kennedy, or the details of the sting. Like Langley, Berlin was too much of an intelligence sieve.

The knock on the door was insistent. He hoped it wasn't a trivial interruption.

"Who's there," he asked, almost intemperately.

"John, it's me, Sam. I have news. Just came over the coded telex."

Davidson unlocked the door and Sam sat, almost folded himself, into the mock Barcelona chair alongside his desk.

"Yes, Sam, what is it?"

"Hold onto your non-existent hat, John. The new honcho in Al Rashon, Abdul Lakim, says he's following Mussad's policy all the way."

Withers outlined the new situation, adding that Al Rashon had signed a unity pact with the United African Republic, the country Mussad had taken over, aiming eventually at a single state.

"And I hear there's the beginning of another so-called 'indigenous rebellion,' equipped by Al Rashon, starting southward from the UAR into two black former French colonies that Mussad had his eyes on. Things are getting serious, John."

Davidson circled the small room in tight steps.

"I sort of expected this, Sam. We had to get rid of Mussad, but it's obviously not the final step. I know that things are not that solid for his people in Al Rashon. Many in his army would like to avoid a bloody war with the US. All it needs is a good push, and I think I know how to do it. As soon as I get this Friedrich thing launched, I'm off to Cairo."

The White House phone call to Davidson came minutes later.

"John, I suppose you've already heard about the new regime in Al Rashon. Not good is it?"

"No sir, but now's the time to hunker down and hold everyone at bay."

He could hear a ripple of hollow laughter.

"I'll do what I can. But as soon as the networks gave out the announcement, the tide of my phone calls turned—against me. The people want action, and I think they mean war."

"What about the impeachment talk, Mr. President?"

"For a while it died down, but I can already hear Rusty riling up the natives on the Hill."

"Mr. President, things are progressing in order," Davidson said, mustering all the confidence he could. "As soon as I get the final leg of my Red Swastika plan moving, I'm off to Cairo to meet with the opposition leaders to build support for a coup."

"Hurry up, John," the President simply said.

On the other end, Davidson could hear the phone click off. Not hard, but with a soft touch of resignation.

66

MEL Gordon felt like a commuter. His Lufthansa flight from Dulles International, non-stop on an Airbus 310 to Tegel Airport in Berlin, brought him in at 8:30 A.M. Not exactly a red-eye, but he had left at 6:30 P.M., and it was more like 2:30 in the morning by his biological clock.

He had only slept a few hours and had no time for self-pity, though he hated flying. An antagonist of exercise of any kind, Mel viewed jet vibrations as an unwanted drain of his energy, something akin to aerobics and even more tiring. What everyone called the mysterious "jet lag," he was sure was a simple, unscientific case of physical exhaustion.

At 9:45, he was to meet his contact at the Berlin Hilton, the site of the recent mayhem, for breakfast.

On the taxi ride, Gordon arranged his thoughts. Operating on the theory that the Beekeeper had inside help, the best lead should come from the inside as well. But the informant had to be someone loyal to Mussad and his heirs—someone who had the same goal as he. To find the killers.

By phone, he had set up an appointment with Kamel Ibrihim, one of Mussad's Lieutenants, serving as Chargé d'Affaires at the Al Rashon Embassy in Berlin. Though they had a common goal, Gordon was no *aficionado* of the North African gang. He had refused to meet at their embassy. Thus the neutral ground of the Hilton.

Kamel was pointed out to him by the maitre d'. He was waiting at a table in the Sans Souci Room, a breakfast and lunch nook named after Frederick the Great's palace in Potsdam. As he approached, Gordon was surprised. Instead of an Arab in flowing robes, he was staring at the model of a European gentleman, wearing what he guessed was a silk Armani suit, a two-part blue collar and white-striped shirt, a paisley tie, unostentatious gold cufflinks, and sporting the sophisticated smile of a man who either had, or thought he had, everything.

"Mr. Gordon, I presume," Kamel said in the broadest British diction, gallantly jumping to his feet as Mel approached.

Gordon cast a quick, disapproving glance at himself. He really looked like a schlep in his $95 Bond suit, crushed worse than usual by the Airbus. He had almost a full day's scrubby growth on his face and, despite a package of Clorets, he was afraid his breath smelled. Well, this was no GQ contest anyway. He had come for proof of an illegal assassination, and to prosecute those involved. If he could stand Kamel's politics, Mussad's man would have to suffer his appearance.

"Excuse the way I look," Gordon mumbled. "I just got off a plane."

"Please don't apologize. It's a pleasure to meet such a distinguished member of the American government," Ibrihim said in lilting Mayfair tones. For a moment, Gordon felt like Eliza Doolittle, comparing his own flat New York diction with the Arab's English public school rhythms. The only similarity in their speech was that both had a kind of singsong quality. One on key, and the other, he confessed, discordant.

"I've been reading up on the General Accounting Office. People don't realize how well you ride herd on your Presidents," Kamel continued.

"We try, Mr. Ibrihim." Flattered that the GAO's reputation had spread across the ocean, he smiled and picked up the menu.

"Try the grilled herring," Kamel suggested. "An excellent local dish."

After the ordering was done, Gordon stared—he was afraid maybe a touch too intently—at his contact.

"Yes, a number of people wonder about me, Mr. Gordon," Kamel said, noticing his curiosity. "But it's really quite simple. My father, who was a wealthy oil merchant, sent me to school in Britain as a youngster. First to Gordonstoun in Scotland, Prince Philip's and Prince Charles's old school, then to Cambridge. I returned to Al Rashon and I have been, until the other day, in Mussad's employ ever since. I enjoy the diplomatic service very much you see."

Kamel paused to sip his espresso. "And what could I possibly do for you?" he asked.

Gordon had to play nervous poker. He needed to elicit information, but he didn't want to seem anti-American, to play to the propaganda of the Mussad people.

"Well, as I told you on the phone, the GAO is doing a routine check on the assassination of your leader, Mussad. Nobody in the States—you'll excuse me—cries for him, but it's my job, as a Special Investigator assigned to oversee the White House, to check out your country's allegation that our President was responsible." Gordon took a deep breath. "We don't believe it for a minute, but like I said, I have to check it out."

"Well, check away."

"Whoever hired that gunman to do the job, I figure he needed someone on the inside to set it up, to make it go smoothly, which I understand it did. Can you think of any of Mussad's men who might have been an accomplice?"

Kamel laughed. "My God, no. If anyone in his group had been suspected, his hands would be cut off first. Then he would be executed by slitting his throat, probably in front of his family. You know, these old traditions are a bit bloodthirsty."

Gordon feared he had wasted four thousand miles of traveling. But no questioning ever went right in the beginning. "Well, let's look at it differently. How many of Mussad's men were with him at the time he was killed?"

Kamel thought, his chin pensively supported in his hand.

"All told, I'd say there were fourteen actually in the hotel."

"And what's happened to them?" Gordon asked. "Think about them, one at a time. OK?"

"Mr. Gordon, you really are pressing me."

Mel pulled back, smiling. This wasn't the first time someone had accused him of pushing his point. Nor would it be the last.

"I understand," Gordon said, his tone now softer and slower. "It's just that I'm trying to help us both. But why don't we hold up a little, so you can collect your thoughts. OK?"

Ibrihim laughed. "You win, Mr. Gordon. I've already done the work."

"Yes?"

"Well, of the fourteen, nine have been flown back to Al Rashon. Three are working at the Berlin Embassy, and the last . . ."

"Yes, what happened to him?"

"Well, the poor man wasn't a traitor. No, he paid the extreme penalty only because he was negligent. He'd been assigned to follow Mussad everywhere, even into the restroom. But he was busy talking and drinking at the time. Nice chap, too."

Gordon sighed along with Kamel, then did a quick mental double take.

"But that's only thirteen. What about the fourteenth one?"

"Oh, he wasn't from Al Rashon. A German fellow, a Count Wolf von Horstmann. One of Mussad's top advisors."

"A Count? Where is he now?"

"He went home right afterward."

"And where's home?"

"Well, it had been nowhere. Horstmann had lived in East Germany when he was a Colonel in the Stasi. Then he stayed with Mussad from the time of unification in 1990, until now."

Gordon leaned forward, his self-computer booting up. "And where did he go this time?"

Kamel looked at him quizzically. "Lucky fellow got back his family estate—they hadn't had it for almost fifty years. A place called Raven's Nest, in Bavaria. Seems some relative in the States became rich and bought it back for Horstmann. Lucky guy."

Lucky! Gordon waved for the waiter, his mind racing. From the figures he had, Davidson had spent less than ten thousand dollars on the Beekeeper's operation. That was no price for a professional assassination. There had to be more money spent somewhere, greasing some key palm. Now, he was sure he had found it. Horstmann must be the inside man. Rich relative in the States, baloney. Davidson was the sugar daddy and he didn't have a drop of German blood.

"Mr. Ibrihim, you've been most helpful. I just have one more question."

"Yes. Shoot, as you Americans say."

"Where in Bavaria is this Raven's Nest? Where can I find Horstmann?"

"I've never been there, but I know it's in a small valley in the Bavarian Alps, a place called Mittenwald, not far from the Austrian border. And not far from . . ."

"Where, Kamel?"

"Not too far from the other Nest, Eagle's Nest, Hitler's old place at Berchtesgaden."

IN Berlin, Davidson had gotten permission from Mike Kennedy to use him, in a manner of speaking, in a "planted" story in a local English-language paper, *Ami News*. It was well read not only by expatriates in the Zehlendorf district near Lake Havel called "Little America," but increasingly by Berliners looking for color on the States. The Baptist assumed that the Swastika leadership would either see it, or be told about it.

An ex-Agency CIC man, Charlie Spector, had done the job for him. Davidson wondered how he could repay him. Would a plug with the President be of any value? Surely, it wouldn't have any weight with the IRS, the only federal agency Spector was in regular contact with.

In any case, the little touch of gossip was deftly inserted in the "Newspeople" column:

"What important American export-import man with

*offices in Berlin's Europa Center has become inadvertently
mixed up with some West coast 'wiseguys' peddling a giant
pile of nuclear material? Federal officials in Washington
hint that heavy hydrogens are missing from a storage basin
in the Nevada flats. He vehemently denies any involvement
in the deal but rumors are that a hundred million dollars
will clear up his memory."*

The Baptist had only to wait until someone made contact
with Kennedy. Meanwhile, he had put Withers to work
tailing Foreign Ministry official Paul Dollop, whom both
he and Langer suspected of knowing the real identity of
"Friedrich," the Fuehrer of Red Swastika.

Now that Davidson and Kennedy had met, they had to
avoid each other, except through a simple drop system.
Davidson used the main public library, the Staatsbibliothek,
or the "Stabi," near the Opera. The messages were placed
in a copy of Heinrich Heine's collected short stories, in the
center of "The Rabbi of Bacharach," a tale that takes place
in that Rhineland town where many German Jews lived in
the Middle Ages.

Davidson was to check the stacks every day at noon.
If a message, in the form of a blank yellow-lined paper
bookmark, was inserted in the short story, they were to
meet at 3 P.M. that same afternoon in the pre-war abandoned
railroad station at Nollendorfplatz, which had been converted
into a *Flohmarkt*, or flea market, with stalls where the trains
had run.

Meanwhile Withers had been active.

"John," he called into the Embassy one morning just after
eight. "This fellow Dollop has a dozen years on me, but he
has the energy of three young men. I've been trailing him
all over Berlin. First, it was just one government meeting
after another. But about ten minutes ago, he met someone
whom I don't know, but whom I recognized."

"From where?" Davidson asked.

"From the first meeting at Koller's place, when I saw his examining room and . . ." Sam's voice choked, " . . . learned that Marieanne was there. In any case, he wasn't one of the guests. He was standing with the housekeeper, like some kind of retainer. Today, this fellow—a thin, scar-faced guy—met Dollop at the old castle at Charlottenburg, in the front lobby." Sam was speaking of the Charlottenburg Palace, built in 1700 by Friedrich, the first King of Prussia, for his wife, Sophie-Charlotte.

"What makes that suspicious?" Davidson asked.

"Well, first off they didn't go through the museum or the royal apartments. And second, I could tell the guy—he called him Stoecken—was wearing a shoulder holster. I think he's a gunslinger for Swastika, maybe a replacement for Bismarck."

"Good. Maybe you can get someone to watch this Stoecken guy while you stay with Dollop. How about the kid clerk at the Agency, the one who helped us with the light in Koller's alley?"

"Good idea, John. Any luck with Kennedy yet?"

"No, not yet. But I'm hoping for something soon. I keep checking the Stabi. See you, Sam."

Davidson didn't have long to wait. That day, at noon, in "The Rabbi of Bacharach," Davidson found the yellow bookmark.

At three, Davidson and Kennedy met at the old station, next to a stand selling Victorian "estate jewelry."

"Yes, Mike, who made the contact?"

"A fellow named Kreutzer. Claimed he was talking for the German government, for an investigative group in the Foreign Ministry looking into rumors of stolen nuclear material smuggled into Germany. Do you know anything about him?"

"No, but it's easy, Mike. He's a cover for Paul Dollop, the guy we need to lead us to Friedrich. What's Kreutzer want you to do?"

"He's going to set up a meeting with his principal and me tomorrow morning at the Charlottenburg Palace."

"Good. And how did you like the publicity I got you?"

"John, it's like being known for the bubonic plague. I could do without it, but I see that it worked. When it's all over, would you get me an apology from the paper?"

"I'll see what I can do. Meanwhile, thanks. Your government appreciates it."

Kennedy could only emit a soft moan.

Davidson tried to be his most casual, walking up and down the main floor exhibits of the Charlottenburg Palace, waiting for a familiar face.

They came in rapid order.

"John, I didn't expect you here. Looks like a convention," Sam Withers said, sidling up to Davidson in front of an eighteenth-century vase.

"Where's the convention, Sam?"

"Over there. Dollop and his henchman. I just followed them here. I told the kid to go back to the Embassy. Who are you expecting?"

"Mike Kennedy. He has a meeting to set up the sting. We had better keep our distance. Do you think you were spotted?" Davidson asked a winded Withers.

"I hope not. I'm not in shape to trade insults, or worse, with Dollop's gunsel."

"Kennedy should be here any minute," Davidson explained. "They made a three o'clock appointment." Before the sentence was finished, Davidson swiveled toward the entrance. "There's Mike now. Let's pull back to the next wing. Maybe we can watch them without being spotted."

With the protection of a giant Ming-dynasty vase, they observed as Dollop and Kennedy shook hands, then spoke animatedly for a few minutes. Davidson strained to lip read. He caught a few words of Kennedy's dialogue in English. But most of the conversation was in German, and lip reading was impossible.

Davidson wasn't sure he should have intruded into Mike's meeting in the first place, but curiosity had pulled him. At least he had learned that Dollop was involved. One step closer to Friedrich. Now, he decided it was best for all parties to retire gracefully. No sense muddling a good beginning.

"Sam, let Dollop go for today," Davidson said in whispers. "We don't want to give away our covers. We'll just wait here until they leave, then head back to the Embassy by U-Bahn. I'll set up a meeting with Kennedy at the flea market to find out what's happened."

Withers nodded in acknowledgment. Ten minutes later, Kennedy and Dollop shook hands. Dollop departed with Stoecken.

Davidson and Sam prudently waited a few minutes, then exited the palace, into the giant courtyard flanked by enormous wings on both sides. They were headed for the main gate when Davidson sensed steps closely behind him. He started to turn but halted abruptly.

"Good, Baptist. You should take care. I have a Mauser in your kidney, so walk slow and cautiously. And you, Mr. Withers—walk in front of Mr. Davidson casual-like. If you make a move, I'll do surgery on the old spy's kidney. Am I clear?"

"Yes, Stoecken," Sam said.

"Walk out the front gate, then turn toward the U-Bahn station. Just do as I say. We've had both of you too much on our necks. Now you're interfering in an important business deal."

The threesome walked toward the station, but a few hundred yards before their goal, Stoecken barked another order.

"All right, in here. *Machen sie schnell.*"

Davidson turned into the courtyard of an abandoned building under demolition. The crew had finished for the day and the grounds were deserted, the stillness foreboding.

"OK. Now both of you walk ahead, right up toward that demolition crane and ball. When you get there, turn and face me. I don't like killing people in the back. Now move—quick."

Davidson caught Withers's eye as they walked, seemingly poised, even stoic. Both men knew the only possible maneuver. Slight chance, but some. To hit the pavement simultaneously at Davidson's signal and roll, one to the left, the other to the right and draw their guns. If one escaped Stoecken's barrage, the other might get him.

They walked, but slower than ordered, toward the demolition ball.

"I said *schnell*. Otherwise, I'll shoot you in the back right now."

Davidson gambled that Stoecken would hold his fire until they turned.

"Now!" the Baptist screamed, both men hitting the ground and reaching for their guns at the same instant.

But before they could fire, a volley of shots rang out, echoing through the courtyard.

Prone, they looked up at Stoecken, whose gun had left his hand. His body, tottering toward the ground, was riddled, blood spilling from a dozen holes from his skull to his feet.

"Baptist! Up here!" Davidson could hear.

They pulled themselves off the pavement and looked up. There, on a parapet of the abandoned building, was Sergeant

Kurt Langer and three of his men, all waving their UZIs.

"You follow them and we follow you!" Langer yelled, his youthful face lit with an Olympic smile. "But please, Baptist. Take it slower. You're wearing us out."

Davidson waved back in appreciation. Langer didn't know how right he was. He had better husband himself, or his Cairo engagement with Hassam Ali, which he had planned for tomorrow, would never come off.

— 68 —

MEL Gordon landed at the airport in Munich. Here, in the heart of Bavaria, Hitler had first made his name in the Beer Hall Putsch of 1923, when he and his Nazi Brownshirt cohorts were arrested after an aborted coup. He served less than a year in jail, was treated much like a political celebrity, and used the solitude to write *Mein Kampf*, which brought him not only fame but the greatest financial rewards of his life to that time.

Now, over seventy years later, a relative of some of Hitler's victims was landing in the same city, looking for another Nazi, a former Communist named Count Wolf von Horstmann—paradoxically, not to arrest him, but to get the goods on an American President. History and time play strange games, Gordon was sure.

The very name "Munich" intrigued him. All over, he saw signs saying "München," the German name of the city.

How in the world, he wondered, did other countries misname foreign cities. If it was München in German, why Munich in English. If the capital of Russia was Moskva, why Moscow? And why was Wien, Vienna?

They weren't translations or even transliterations, so he supposed there was no answer, except perhaps in the untutored minds of early map makers. But there had to be an answer to his conundrum. Did the once-impoverished nobleman, Horstmann, get paid off by Davidson to set up the kill in the Hilton? And if so, how much did it cost the American taxpayers, who had never authorized it? According to the Constitution, and Gordon loved every word of that law of laws, the only chamber legally able to appropriate federal monies was his boss, the House of Representatives.

In his mind, and when anyone would listen, he loved to recite Article I, Sections 7 and 8 of that august document, which gave the Congress the right to originate bills for raising money, and the power to regulate the use of same. The President? He could only spend what he was told to. Apparently, Hawley Briggs had never learned that lesson.

At the airport, Gordon rented a car. First, he scanned the availables, shopping for points on his frequent flyer program. Then, suddenly seized by the sight of a red Porsche Carrera II turbo sports car, he was taken by an uncharacteristic impulse—maybe tied to the expansive feeling of his foreign travel. He signed up for the sleek car for the day at 150 marks, or over $100, plus gas. He was surprised at himself, but if Congress balked, he was prepared to rebate the difference between that and the cost of a Ford Escort.

He hadn't bought a driving cap. With the top down, the air riffled his thinning hair, but Gordon enjoyed the sensation almost as much as the expectation of finding Horstmann.

The drive out of Munich on Autobahn 95 took him due south in the direction of the winter resort of Garmisch-Partenkirchen, up into the Bavarian Alps, with one mountain peak—the Zugspitze—over 9,000 feet high, the tallest in Germany. The distance was not far, only fifty miles, but the landscape was breathtaking. Some of the trip was reminiscent, in its long, high views, of the Haute Corniche on the French Riviera. But this drive, now along the German Alpine Highway, was even more majestic, with its green valleys below and its gray, snowy peaks above.

It was, Gordon feared, also more dangerous. The raciest car he had ever handled was a Ford Taurus. Despite the initial thrill of the Porsche, he felt uncomfortably like an amateur, maybe even a poseur, behind the wheel of the 315-horsepower vehicle.

The winding road from Garmisch to Mittenwald was only ten miles, but it held dizzying turns. From a distance, he could barely make out Mittenwald below, a green village nestled alongside a river, with forested hills on two sides and mountains on the others. From his Baedeker guidebook, he remembered that the river was the Isar, and that Mittenwald—literally "In-the-Middle-of-the-Woods"—had been an important trading post on the ancient road from Augsburg, Germany, through Austria, which was only a few miles away, ending up in Verona, Italy.

The traffic on the high Alpine road suddenly heated up. Gordon started to watch his turns, nervous that the German drivers seemed indifferent to speed. He tried to focus on the road ahead, but simultaneously watched both sides—the steep drop at his left and the cliffside to his right—staying close to his lane for safety. Driving on these roads, he realized, was not his forte.

He watched every car anxiously. One in particular, a large black Mercedes sedan, seemed to be encroaching on his lane, nibbling away at his rear, trying to pass him. In no mood for chicken-in-the-sky, Gordon edged closer to the cliffside to accommodate the Mercedes, moving onto the narrow shoulder within two feet of the cliff. But the closer he came, the more the Mercedes, now alongside him, pressed inward. He slowed, hoping the black sedan would pass quickly, but it hovered in place.

My God, Gordon realized. The Mercedes was after him! Its driver was trying to force him against the mountainous edges of the road, and sure death. Now he could feel the pressure on both sides. The rear right fender of the Porsche was scraping the stone ledge, the sparks plainly visible in his mirror. On the other side, the Mercedes was pressing against his left front fender, giving off the frightening sound of crinkling metal. A mad thought entered his mind. Had he paid the extra fee for a collision damage waiver?

Gordon knew he had to do something, inexperience or not. He had not learned to drive until he was twenty-seven. It had to be something he didn't think he was capable of. What would a James Bond-type do if he was being crushed to death on an Alpine road by a Mercedes three times the size of his car?

His mind quickly focused. The Porsche's power was his only escape. He hunched down into the seat, and just as the Mercedes moved to the left a couple of feet to prepare for another onslaught of sideswiping, Gordon half-closed his eyes and pushed the accelerator to the floor. The speedometer registered one hundred, one hundred and twenty, one hundred and forty kilometers an hour, the wind coming in above the side windows, attacking his face.

In seconds, he had punched a hole in the road space and had pulled ahead of the Mercedes. Gordon behaved as if he knew what he was doing, driving down the center of the road, giving his attacker no room to pull up on either side of him—all the while watching nervously for oncoming traffic. The Mercedes came on toward him, almost catching up, but Gordon pushed the Porsche to the limit, soon losing the black sedan in his rear-view mirror.

Not until he came down into Mittenwald itself did he relax, slowing down and advancing into the village at a normal speed. The Mercedes had disappeared as suddenly as it had appeared.

His Baedeker had sung the praises of the village. It had not exaggerated. The fronts of the old houses boasted hand-painted frescoes, with a backdrop of the decorated tower of an old baroque church. He had heard that the village had once been a violin-making center. The fiddle had been his companion since the age of ten, and he enjoyed playing it badly. But today he had no time for pleasure.

Parking the car, Gordon walked into a food store.

"*Sprechen sie Englisch?*" Gordon asked in crude neo-German.

"*Ja*, I speak it some," said the portly proprietor. "Can I be of help to you?"

"Yes, I'm looking for a large estate, Raven's Nest. Do you know where it is?"

"Rabenhorst? Yes. It is the large place beside the river. Old manor house built maybe two hundred years ago."

"Who owns it?"

"Oh, was some crazy rock star, but I understand the Count now returns. His family has been away ever since the war."

The proprietor sold Gordon a map of the area, and marked the small country road to Raven's Nest.

Gordon drove almost two miles into the forested area, then saw the sign, burned into a wooden slab—RABENHORST *LANGSAM FAHREN*—Drive Slow. He approached careful-ly, going through the old stone posts as if he belonged, then started up the lengthy driveway, curving continuously as he went. His eyes were focused on the manor house at the crest of a small hill when he slowed to begin what looked like his final turn.

His wheels had just followed his steering when he heard, and saw, it. The whoosh of a fast-moving vehicle reached his ears at the same time that a car sped down the driveway as if it were the final leg of the Grand Prix de Monaco— passing within inches of his ascending Porsche. Gordon turned quickly to see a black Mercedes sedan. It was the same one which had tried to cripple him on the Alpine Highway! Was Horstmann himself the avenging villain?

Mel chilled at the thought. Would Horstmann still be after him? It frightened him, but he was heartened that someone in Mittenwald knew he was on his way to Raven's Nest.

Gordon brought the Porsche into the landscaped gravel courtyard and parked. He walked up to the double door, a carved oak entrance with heavy iron hardware, and rang the bell. He waited. Even though he kept telling himself he was safe, he felt anxious. But after three minutes he despaired of an answer. Apparently no one was at home. A BMW was parked out front, but Horstmann had probably left the house, using a second car. Or the menacing black Mercedes could have been his own.

Gordon had half turned back toward the Porsche when he saw it. At the center of the double door, a small crack of light was peeking through. Maybe the door was open. He tried the brass lever handle. It turned with ease. Someone had left the door unlocked. Should he go in, or come back another time? Perhaps there wouldn't be another time. Despite his uneasiness, he decided to walk in.

"Count Horstmann!" Gordon quickly called out. He waited at the threshold, but there was no answer. The large foyer was laid out in checkerboard black and white marble, with a center curved staircase, also in marble. A delicate wrought-iron balustrade curved up to the second floor landing.

"Count Horstmann!" he called out again, as he tentatively took a few steps upward. When he heard no response, he started up two at a time. The stillness of the mansion intrigued, and unnerved, him. He felt driven by mystery.

At the landing, there were two paneled doors partially open before him. In one room, he could see a large bed. Probably Horstmann's bedroom. He knocked again to be polite, then entered.

He approached the bed, suddenly bashful that he had intruded into someone's room. The bed was unmade and ruffled, as if it had been slept in the night before. He circled the bed, then halted.

On the floor was a giant of a man, stretched out, his mouth agape in surprise. Between his eyes was a single, almost bloodless, shot, like one made by a 9 mm bullet. It was Horstmann, he was sure.

Gordon turned quickly and raced down the stairs. One thought drilled into his mind. Had he uncovered more than he hoped for? Had Mussad's men taken out Horstmann because he had betrayed them to Davidson? Or had the Beekeeper, on orders of the President of the United States, eliminated the evidence of his earlier assassination?

69

THE Egypt Air plane, once an indirect flight through Munich, was now non-stop from Berlin to Cairo International Airport. The trip was urgent, Davidson was sure. Action on the Red Swastika sting in Berlin would be moving ahead while he made this vital one-day detour.

When Davidson served in Cairo as Chief-of-Station for a few years in the 1950s, fighting an intelligence war against Gamal Abdel Nasser, he had enjoyed the city, and had not expected to return under the present conditions.

In 1952, shamed by Israel's victory in the 1948 war, Nasser had started a Free Officers movement in the Egyptian Army, which then overthrew playboy King Farouk—launching Nasser as the first Pan-Arab leader with ambitions to unite the Middle East.

Nasser soon nationalized the Suez Canal, prompting the British, French and Israelis to invade Egypt in 1956 in retaliation. Davidson then found himself in the awkward position of intervening on behalf of Egypt when the UN, America and the USSR pressured the Allies to withdraw on the eve of their victory. In 1958, Nasser joined Egypt with socialist Syria as the United Arab Republic, a union that was short-lived.

He moved increasingly into the Soviet orbit, stockpiling enormous caches of arms and becoming their client state, virtually turning his secret police into a communications network for KGB spies. In 1967, Egypt, Syria, Iraq and Jordan began a take-all invasion of Israel, but the surrounded country won the brilliant Six Day War, instead occupying large parts of Egypt and Arab territories for itself.

After he died, Nasser was replaced by Anwar Sadat, who had his own agenda. On Yom Kippur Day in 1973, Egypt and several Arab nations invaded Israel, the Egyptian Army surprisingly cutting through the Israel defenses at the Bar-Lev Line in the Sinai. Syrian tanks threatened Israel proper, but with last-minute American aid—in the form of on-line jet fighters flown in from American bases in Germany— the Israelis held, although their fate was problematic for a few tense days.

Now history had turned full circle. Within three years after the Yom Kippur War, Sadat had traveled to Camp David and Jerusalem and made peace in exchange for return of the Sinai, bringing Egypt into the Allied fold. Its participation in the Iraq war had only solidified that position, making modern Egypt the logical nation from which Davidson could start an internal campaign against Al Rashon.

Egypt had shared America's hatred of Mussad. Their enmity against those who followed him was equally strong. Thus their hospitality to the dissidents of Al Rashon, who were welcomed, even financially supported, in Cairo.

Davidson had settled into the Ramses Hilton on Corniche El Nil, overlooking the Nile, a relatively quiet spot in the noisy city. In moments, he expected to meet with Hassam Ali, an old friend and leader of the Democratic Forum, the Al Rashon movement in exile. Ali had been tortured in one of Mussad's prisons, escaping only after an elaborate inside-coordinated scheme. His halting speech and a limp, which he tried to disguise, were souvenirs of Mussad's cruelty.

"My old friend, the Baptist," Hassam said as Davidson opened the door after a quick security call from the lobby. "It must be almost twenty years since we've met. The last time in Khartoum in the Sudan. Am I right?" He stood back a pace. "You look none the worse—the hair a little whiter. My God, John, the same suit?" he laughed.

"Yes, the same suit. And just a little wiser, I hope," Davidson said, embracing Hassam.

They talked of old times, then Mussad's assassination inevitably came up.

"John, that was a lucky stroke—or was it luck made in Washington?" Hassam said. "Whatever, it was a boon to the world. He was potentially more of a Hitler than Saddam Hussein, you know. Not more evil. In that they were evenly matched. But smarter. Knew when to keep a low profile as needed. He had already taken two African countries, with more on his menu, all without the world saying a word. Now that he's out, we have a chance to topple his government, secret nuclear arms and all."

"You know about his neutron bombs?" Davidson asked, surprised.

"Oh, yes. I have people in his main bunker. The new head of the government, his nephew, has been accelerating the shipments from Brazil. Yes, I also know about the German connection. It was a logical match—German industrialists hungry for money and pro-Nazis looking for power. They and Mussad made a good team. And his nephew is carrying that on."

The conversation was suddenly interrupted by a knock on the door.

Davidson reached for his Beretta, stuck casually in a table drawer.

Hassam waved him away. "No need for that, John. I took the liberty of calling room service for a light lunch. The hotel makes a delightful lamb cooked on a brazier."

The waiter, a tall, bearded, muscular man, his head fully draped in a thick turban, entered with a wheeled cart.

"We can continue to talk, John. I checked the waiter out beforehand. He's a mountain refugee from the Afghan war, a *mujaheddin* guerrilla warrior. Speaks only Pashto. Doesn't know a word of English."

As they ate, Davidson paused and stared at his partner.

"What's our next step, Hassam? When will you make contact with a likely coup leader? My President is getting flak to get the hostages out and to justify the assassination. I know you've kept up contact with General Karadi. Is he one of us?"

"Absolutely, John. He has a strong following among the command officers, particularly the younger ones who fear a war with the United States. They don't want Al Rashon to become another Iraq."

"Good, good," Davidson exclaimed, speaking both of the lamb and his hopes for a coup. "But how do you get in to Al Rashon to meet with him? Or can Karadi come to Egypt?"

"That shouldn't be too difficult, John. I've already taken the first step."

Hassam turned to the waiter and mumbled a few quick words Davidson didn't understand.

"What did you say, Hassam?"

"Only that we're among friends."

As Davidson watched, transfixed, the tall waiter removed his false beard and started to unwind the burdensome turban.

"Mr. Davidson of the United States," Hassam said in courtly fashion. "Meet General Achim Karadi, Sandhurst, '54, retired Commanding Officer of the Army of Al Rashon."

70

"YES, there's been a recent change in ownership of Raven's Nest," the municipal clerk explained to Mel Gordon. "Back to the people who owned it for almost two hundred years, the von Horstmanns. Now, we have to find the family heirs."

The small town hall in Mittenwald was being accommodating. After Gordon had reported the murder and produced his credentials as a Special Agent for the US Congress, the land records were made available. Gordon didn't reveal his suspicions about the murder. That would make world headlines, and he was not prepared for that—yet. Nor did he have any proof. His immediate objective was to connect Horstmann to Davidson, and thus to the President.

"How did the Horstmanns lose Raven's Nest in the first place?" Gordon asked.

"Oh, it was after the war. A matter of debt, I understand. But I don't think that was the whole story. They had trouble refinancing it, I believe, because the family had been Nazis. The old man died in Spandau, you know." The clerk paused, to recall some detail. "Oh, yes, the present—I mean the late—Count would come here every few years, just to look at the place. It changed hands several times, last time to a rock star, some maniac with a group called 'The Gestapo.' Just a short time ago, someone put a deposit on the place, then Count Horstmann showed up and filed the deed. It was all paid for. No mortgage at all."

"How much was the transaction?"

"One minute, I'll look that up." The clerk pored over the large record book, then came back, smiling. "It was a big price, especially for this area. Yes, Horstmann paid 2.4 million marks, about 1.8 million dollars, to get Rabenhorst back."

Gordon knew he had hit pay dirt. There was no way a Stasi agent could muster up that kind of money. Behind it, he was sure, was the fine Virginia hand of John Davidson, and behind him—illegally—the Treasury of the United States.

"Who handled the deal?" Gordon asked, his glands smelling out a lead.

"A real estate firm in München, Stieber Associates. Joseph Stieber was the broker."

Gordon thanked him profusely, then drove back to Munich, traveling like some obsessed German motorist, hitting over 100 mph, some 150 kph, once he reached the Autobahn after Garmich.

Stieber's office was in a baroque eighteenth-century townhouse on the elegant Brienner Strasse near the obelisk commemorating the 30,000 Bavarians who died fighting with Napoleon in Russia in 1812. He opened the door to a glossy black-and-white modern interior, furnished in severe Bauhaus style.

"Could I see Mr. Joseph Stieber?" he asked the receptionist in English, discarding his lame use of a few German words.

"I'm afraid he's busy negotiating a sale," she answered in English. "Could you come back tomorrow morning?"

"Lady, tomorrow's no good," Gordon pressured. "I hope to be back in Washington then." He held his gold SPECIAL AGENT badge directly under her eyes. "Just tell him the US

Government is afraid he's been involved in a giant fraud. Maybe even a murder."

'The receptionist, a tall blonde with a full figure, jumped out of her chair. She returned within two minutes with Joseph Stieber, a short round man, pink-cheeked and balding, looking quite unlike Hitler's mythical Aryan.

"My God, you have scared the life out of my receptionist." Stieber spoke excitedly, his German accent tripping over his English. He seemed unsure whether he should be angered or fearful. "What do you want? And who has committed a fraud? And murder? And who are you, may I ask?"

Gordon smiled patronizingly. Now that he felt in command, he tried to slow down the rush of emotions.

"This is my ID. I'm a Special Investigator for the United States Congress and I'm here trying to track some illegal government expenditures, which we believe went through your office," Gordon said forcefully. "Now do you understand?"

Stieber sat down and motioned Gordon to do the same.

"I don't know what you are talking about. So explain yourself."

"It's about the sale of Raven's Nest to Count Wolf von Horstmann, who incidentally has just been killed in his manor house. I understand you were the broker for the sale."

"Oh yes, but what is illegal about that?"

"Well, we believe the money was misappropriated from the U.S. Government. Do you remember who initiated the deal, and how?"

Stieber thought for a moment, then nodded.

"Yes, an American came in here and put down a deposit, fifty thousand marks. He said he hoped to close the deal later, but would do it by bank draft from Berlin. Which he did. There was nothing special about the deal. The check came and we had a closing here in Munich with representatives of the Berlin bank and the local bank in Mittenwald who handled the seller—that crazy rock star. So, that is all."

"You say an American put down the binder. Do you remember his name?"

"Yes, it was a Herr Marshall. David Marshall. A very nice courtly man. Maybe in his sixties."

"Did he have a full head of white hair, and black bushy eyebrows? Medium height, about a hundred and fifty pounds?"

"Yes, that sounds like him."

"And please think, Mr. Stieber. Was he wearing a gray herringbone suit?"

"Ah, yes. I remember that because I liked the style. We Germans used to wear those English tweeds too. Ah, yes. He told me he had it made on Savile Row. Yes, that is him."

"And the check for the final payment, what bank did it come from, and whose account?" he asked, the scent of the paper kill coming on strong.

"For that I will have to look at my records. One minute, please."

Stieber returned with a Xerox of a check, printed on both sides.

"Yes, it is from the Dresdner Bank, and both the checks are signed by this David Marshall. Here, you can see for yourself."

Gordon studied the check. Davidson—alias Marshall—had bought the estate with federal funds, bribing Horstmann to collaborate on the assassination. Maybe then he had the Beekeeper finish Horstmann off. The crime was complete but far from perfect.

"Mr. Stieber, could I have a copy of that check?"

The rotund German looked at him, his eyes fearful.

"I don't know if I can do that, Mr. Gordon. You see, this material is broker-protected and I have my reputation—I assure you a good one in München—to think about. I really . . ."

Winning through intimidation, Gordon said to himself.

"Mr. Stieber. I know you're a good German citizen and don't want any bad publicity. So, I'm asking you—no, warning you—to give me a copy of that check. Otherwise, the Mayor of München will be subpoenaed, as will you. The U.S. Congress will demand that you appear *personally* before a Congressional hearing on the matter."

Gordon slowed for only a second. "You know about our hearings—Joe McCarthy, Watergate, Iran-Contra. Well, I promise you that this one is going to be the biggest of them all. And unless you cooperate, you're going to be a main witness. Lights, television, notoriety, suspicion of fraud, and all. Now do you understand?"

Stieber's smooth, pink cheeks first turned gray, then a bloodless sallow.

"Here, Mr. Congress, take your damn check and never let me see you again!" Stieber half-screamed.

Gordon's stern expression was replaced by a smile.

"My pleasure, Mr. Stieber. And thanks for your cooperation. I appreciate it, and so does the United States government."

71

"I CAN hardly believe it, Baptist," Manfred Lichtenstein was saying at BND headquarters immediately on Davidson's return from Cairo. "To think that an official of the Foreign Ministry would get involved in such a sleazy affair."

Davidson shook his head in sympathy. "I'm sure Dollop's guilty, but Langer has no proof yet—except that he was consorting with that gunman Stoecken, who almost wiped out yours truly."

Davidson had carefully avoided mentioning Mike Kennedy to Lichtenstein. That part of the hunt was his and Withers's, exclusively. Even Langer was being kept in the dark. After the shooting, the Sergeant had casually asked what the meeting in the Charlottenburg Palace was all about. When Davidson pleaded ignorance, the young detective offered a skeptical look.

"Langer tells me that Dollop says he only hired Stoecken as a bodyguard. He was recommended by a reputable security agency," Lichtenstein said, his head still bobbing in disbelief. "He claims he had no idea Stoecken was a gunman. So there we stand."

"Can you help out, Manfred?" Davidson asked, feeling pressed by the rush of events back home.

"Not much. You seem to be in good hands with the Berlin

police. But we can watch Dollop as well, if you'd like."

"Any other ideas?" Davidson tried not to sound desperate.

Lichtenstein circled his office, then pensively stared out at the calm waters of Lake Havel, and at the moat that isolated the Citadel.

"I do have one thought, John."

"Yes, Manfred?" Davidson knew Lichtenstein was a competitive, even brilliant, strategist.

"Why not send out a fake story? You know, a sting. Something Friedrich would find irresistible. It's worked before."

Davidson was taken unawares. Surely Manfred didn't know about the operation. Then a reverse thought struck him. Why not use Manfred to unknowingly give his sting greater credibility—assuming it would find its way into the BND network, then back to Swastika?

"No, Manfred, Friedrich's too smart to fall for a fake story. I can't tell you the details, but I have set up a *real* offer that Swastika can't refuse."

"What's that, John?"

"Manfred, I have to hold that confidential—even from you."

"Does Langer know?"

"No, nobody. It's a giant risk for our side. What we're offering is valuable beyond money. One leak might chase away Friedrich. But as you said, he'll find it irresistible."

Davidson needed to reach Kennedy immediately. At the Stabi, he placed the blank yellow bookmark in "The Rabbi of Bacharach," then met Kennedy at the flea market stall in the abandoned railway station.

"Mike, I have an idea for us."

"Before you say anything, Baptist, I have news. I think good."

"Yes?"

"I was contacted through an anonymous letter on plain computer paper saying that my prior lead was invalid. We were to start over, without any dangerous preliminary moves like before. I'm to make arrangements for the delivery of the neutron bomb material. The money will be placed in a numbered account in Geneva, with a good-faith downpayment on the spot. I'm to respond by placing a classified ad in the *Morgenpost* saying 'Go ahead' in English. They'll contact me."

"Good." Davidson's face brightened. "Maybe now we'll be dealing directly with Friedrich."

The news was rapid in coming. Kennedy reported back that after he had placed the ad, he'd received a call from a pay station. The man spoke in English, with only a slight, somewhat cultivated, German accent.

The goods mentioned by the previous contact were to be placed in a van, painted yellow like a BEWAG truck, and left on the shoulder of Autobahn 2, exactly fifteen kilometers north of the Berlin city line, on the right-hand shoulder of the road. Flares were to be placed around it, as if it were disabled.

Only Kennedy should be with the van. No one in the Berlin police or the BND were to be told. If so, his contacts in those agencies would let him know and the rendezvous would be canceled.

The van should be parked at 9:00 P.M. Someone would arrive at 9:30 in another false BEWAG vehicle to pick up the material. At the point of transfer, they would deliver $10 million in gold as a sign of good faith. The remaining $90 million would have already been deposited in a Swiss bank, the passbook to be exchanged for the material.

The Red Swastika people would arrive with equipment capable of testing the tritium and the nuclear triggers for authenticity and radioactive strength. No attempt should be made to fool them. Otherwise, Kennedy would pay, personally.

"What did you say to the terms?" Davidson asked.

"They told me that it was yes or no, right then. So I told them 'yes.'"

"Good, Mike. That was the thing to do."

"Sure, that's great, Baptist. But where on God's green acres do we get our hands on a vanload of radioactive heavy hydrogen?"

72

SPEAKER of the House of Representatives Frank L. (Rusty) Kembeck was ecstatic.

Stamping his tooled boots deep into the Oriental rug of his chambers, he let out a whoop, a cross between a cowboy roundup call and an Indian war chant.

"Gal-don it, kid, you've done it! I told the Whip just the other day. Said he could have all our FBI people and their fancy guns and fingerprints. I'll put my money on this New York kid with his brains and chutzpah. And you've done it, Mel. You've done it!"

Kembeck held the copy of Davidson's check for $1.85 million over his head and turned it over and over.

"David Marshall, bullshit! The President shifted a few million from some phony White House account, and the Baptist paid off that German no-good Count to set up Mussad for the kill. And now, we've got Davidson—and the President—dead to rights. Come on, kid, we're going to see the Honorable Mr. Craver, the man who can cause them so much trouble they'd rue the day they ever thought about assassinating anybody, even a swine like Mussad!"

Gordon stared in awe at the overwhelming politician, whose balls were bigger, he knew, much bigger, than his own. If he had chutzpah, Rusty Kembeck was a case of unmitigated gall.

Quietly, he got in line behind the Speaker, who stormed down the hall in the general direction of the House Judiciary Committee.

Congressman Lucian Craver, a near-imitation of Gary Cooper, a tall, taciturn Representative from Wyoming—the only Congressman in the House from that sparsely populated State of only 482,000 souls, about the same as the small borough of Staten Island in New York, and in an area larger than the entire United Kingdom—sat leaning casually back in his high-backed leather seat of authority.

His handful of voters exercised a lot of power in the House of Representatives when Craver presided in the Rayburn House Office Building, specifically in Hearing Room Number 2141, where he was holding forth in Executive Session as Chairman of the House Judiciary Committee. It was the place where Presidents could get in, as he had warned others, "a passel of trouble."

Since this was a closed Executive Session, there were no spectators or press. Just twelve of the full thirty-five Committee members, two staffers, including one counsel, and Speaker Kembeck had gathered to hear Gordon's evidence, in private.

"First off, let me tell everybody that this is no Star Chamber, but I don't want a word of what we hear to get out of this room," Craver said in opening. "Not to Evans and Novak or anybody. Is that clear? Having said that, could the man of the day, GAO Investigator Mel Gordon, tell us what he's learned?"

Gordon sat in the stiff-backed witness chair, just as if this were a formal hearing, and told his story, beginning with that day he audited some White House expenditures and found the $1,273 check. He finished it with Horstmann's murder and the *big* check of $1.85 million used to purchase Raven's Nest.

The members listened, spellbound, to a story that justified all their paranoia about the secret machinations of the Presidency and his private games of espionage and derring-do—some within and some outside the CIA—which the non-executive House of Representatives envied, and despised, at the same time.

"Some tale, Gordon, and I wouldn't believe a word of it, even your kidnapping, if you didn't have those checks," Craver commented. "I assume you're going to get hand-writing specialists to verify that this fake 'David Marshall' is indeed John The Baptist Davidson."

"There's no doubt in my mind, sir, but yes, we'll have it checked."

The microphones had been shut off, so aging Silas Penford, the liberal New Englander from an old-line Puritan family, leaned forward to speak.

"Mr. Grossman . . ."

"Gordon, sir."

"Oh yes, Gordon. Do you really believe that the President himself ordered this assassination, or is it just the work of that spook Davidson? You know his name has come up several times over the past quarter century in connection with adventuresome Presidents."

"Congressman Penford, I know that Davidson and his sidekick Withers, and his assassin, the Beekeeper, who calls himself Knudsen, are personally involved. They're the ones who seized me at gunpoint. The President? Well, he's obviously involved because he paid for it—handsomely. We're going to check all the White House accounts again. I assure you we'll find that he used some phony foreign aid fund, and had the cooperation of some friendly country to launder the money. From the White House to Panama or Taiwan or Saudi Arabia, then to Davidson's account in a fake name at the bank in Berlin. Of that I'm sure."

The twelve members set up a buzz, ominous just in its length, sidetalk replacing the questioning.

"Tell me, Mr. Gordon," Chairman Craver finally asked, returning to the witness. "Do you have a recommendation to make to this committee? What would you personally like to see us do about it?"

Gordon suddenly felt the unaccustomed emotion of stage fright.

"Well, Mr. Chairman, I have a private opinion but I don't think it's my place to make such a suggestion," Gordon said. "I'm the investigator and I think I've presented you with good and sufficient evidence of illegality. You gentlemen, as representatives of the people, are here to make those decisions. That's the law."

House Speaker Rusty Kembeck, a member of no committee, and *ex officio* part and parcel of them all, jumped to his feet. He half pushed aside Gordon at the witness table.

"Well, as duly elected Speaker of this House, I sure as hell have an opinion," he shouted.

"Rusty. Sit in that chair and get it off your chest," Craver said, unwilling to stir the ire of the Speaker.

"Well, it's as plain as the face of an old farm spinster in Dakota. President Briggs has broken Executive Order 12333—against assassination—which he and five other Presidents have signed. He's misappropriated money, hired an international hit man, and bought some turncoat Nazi a mansion in Bavaria. If you fellows can't add, I'll do it for you. He's violated Article II, Section 4 of the Constitution by committing 'High Crimes and Misdemeanors' for which the penalty is uncomplicated."

Kembeck paused for a sip of water.

"It's impeachment. The Constitution says so. We've tried it before in this House, and almost done it twice. There's no better time than now and no better case than Briggs's to do it with. And this Committee is the legal place to start. All you've got to do is get the full thirty-five members together, hold a hearing, vote a majority, then bring it to the House floor for action on impeachment. Once they vote, that Arkansas dirt farmer who's too big for his overalls will stand trial in the Senate. Then our job will be done."

The buzzing started up again among the Congressmen, magisterially seated in the imposing room which had been the setting for the Watergate hearings of the 1970s, among other historic proceedings.

"Impeachment, you say!" shouted back committee member and Majority Leader Happy Rider. "I don't know if the President ordered that killing of Mussad, and to tell you the damn truth, I don't care. Remember, Mussad's the SOB who took our kids as hostages, and they're still rotting in his country. And his phony guerrilla armies are gobbling up one black country after another in the sub-Sahara."

He stared down at Kembeck. "And what would *you* do, Mr. Speaker? Start a war and lose first our teenagers, then thousands of Marines?" He halted short of revealing what Briggs had told him about the neutron weapons. "No, I repeat. I don't know if Mussad was taken out by us, but if so . . ." Rider suddenly halted.

"Yes, Mr. Rider, what did you want to say?" Chairman Craver prompted.

"What I *will* say is—maybe it was the right, the cheapest, and the best way to handle a bastard like Mussad. I think the American people think so too."

"Now hold off, Happy." Speaker Kembeck had grabbed the dead mike for emphasis. "Don't use the name of the American people so glibly. First, this ain't a democracy run by the Gallup poll. This is a *representative* democracy. We represent the people, and we vote their voice. I don't know if the people would have voted for the impeachment of Nixon in some damn public opinion poll. But your Committee voted it, and chased him out of office. Remember?"

Kembeck stared defiantly at the Chairman. "Well, we don't even know what the people really think this time," he continued. "Sure, when Mussad was killed in that hotel, they cheered Briggs like hell. But what about now? The bastard's dead, but our kids are still hostages and being abused. Maybe even raped again. And there's still the chance of a bloody war. Do you think the people like that?"

Again a loud buzz. The Chairman softly banged the gavel for silence.

"Gentlemen. We're not going to settle this right now. But I'll tell you what we are going to do." The Chairman stared at Gordon. "You're going to finish your investigation, working with our staff and Chief Counsel. Then we're going to get up a list of witnesses, including that Davidson and his sidekick, and even that guy you say was the hitman, if we can find him. And we're going to subpoena them to a formal hearing, open to the press and the public, on

Executive Order 12333 and the whole question of High Crimes and Misdemeanors."

"You're what?" Happy Rider shouted.

"That's right, Mr. Majority Leader," Craver answered in a deepening Western twang. "And we're going to subpoena one more witness, too. Just to get the damn record straight."

"And who's that?" Happy asked.

"Well, none other than the President of these United States, Mr. Hawley Briggs, himself."

With that, Craven banged the gavel, this time with emphasis, as the hearing room fell into a stunned, uneasy silence.

—— 73 ——

"COME HOME SOONEST. PLEASE RECOMMEND SPECIAL COUNSEL. SITUATION EXPLOSIVE. BRIGGS."

The coded cable had arrived at the American Embassy in Berlin only eleven hours before. It exuded urgency.

Davidson was worried that it was a bit premature to leave Berlin for Washington, but as he leaned back into Lufthansa's First Class lounger (he didn't feel guilty because the Embassy had arranged the tickets) he tallied what he had lined up for action.

The coup possibility in Al Rashon had been left in good hands with Hassam Ali. In addition to General Karadi, two brigadiers on active duty with Mussad's mechanized divisions had been smuggled into Cairo as well. The five men had spent hours in Davidson's hotel suite laying plans for a military takeover that would quell their nation's aggressiveness.

The Berlin operation on Swastika was also advancing. He had left Withers and Kennedy in charge of that sting, with the rendezvous with Friedrich all set. He hoped his decision to freeze out both Lichtenstein and Langer was a sage one.

Now as he flew non-stop to Dulles airport, he tried to imagine the agenda that awaited him in Washington. It took little foresight. Mel Gordon and impeachment would surely be the topics at hand. After Mussad was taken out, the Beekeeper suggested putting the GAO investigator in "protective custody," meaning holding him in the Bavarian Alps for a few months. But Davidson had vetoed the plan.

From Berlin, he had already called an old friend, Charlie Samuelson, Professor of Constitutional Law at Harvard, and told him to contact Les Fanning at the White House. She would know what to do.

As soon as the plane landed at Dulles, Davidson called the White House.

"Come as you are, Mr. Davidson," Les Fanning anxiously told him. "Professor Samuelson is on his way."

Davidson hopped in a taxi and in thirty minutes was in the anteroom of the Executive West Wing.

"The President's waiting," Fanning said hurriedly as she met him. "Professor Samuelson's already here."

From the doorway, Davidson could see Briggs and his guest standing by the fireplace chatting. Samuelson was tall and quite thin, his face ascetic. His expression suggested intellect.

"John, welcome," the President said. "Glad you could make it back so quickly. Thanks for calling in Professor Samuelson."

"Charlie, good to see you," Davidson greeted the prominent attorney. "I hope you appreciate this. Could be your biggest case yet."

Samuelson smiled. "I'm sure both myself and President Briggs could do without the pleasure. I understand it's quite serious."

"Yes, John, that's for sure," Briggs explained once they were all seated near the fireplace. "This is going to be a constitutional crisis to top them all. Happy Rider tells me that Kembeck has already brought the House Judiciary Committee into special executive session. He's riling up the troops about an impeachment proceeding—both on the assassination and unauthorized use of money. Rusty seems to have an ally in Craver, the Wyoming cowboy who runs Judiciary. He's going to subpoena a ton of witnesses, including you, John. And guess who else? Me."

Briggs turned to Samuelson. "What do you think of that, Professor? What's the precedent on Presidents appearing before Congress?"

Samuelson pondered his answer. "Mr. President, the Constitution doesn't mention it at all, but so far no President has agreed to testify before Congress or the courts, citing executive privilege. But they keep trying to push them. Jefferson was subpoenaed by Chief Justice Marshall to testify at the treason trial of Aaron Burr. Jefferson refused but agreed to supply some papers. And if you remember, the Supreme Court ordered Nixon to give up his tapes."

President Briggs was all ears. "But what could the court have done if he didn't agree?"

"They have little power to do anything against a President. But the Congress can always impeach him. That would have happened in an instant if Nixon had balked. But every case is different."

Davidson's mind took it all in. "But isn't a lot of it

political?" he asked. "If the President is strong, it looks like he can probably get away with almost anything. And if he's weak, as Nixon was, he can't do a damn. Am I right?"

"Exactly, John." Samuelson's response was definite. "Look at Reagan. Nobody really considered impeachment on the Iran-Contra because he was a popular President. Congressmen don't want to vote for something that will come back to haunt them at the next election. So they waited until he was out of office and settled for a videotaped testimony in the Ollie North case."

The law professor turned to Briggs. "Mr. President. How strong are you politically on this Mussad thing? Will the people back you up and scare away the impeachment hounds in Congress?"

"I'll let John give that one a try."

Davidson hesitated, aware that his answer was important to the President's case.

"Taking out Mussad was a popular move," he finally said. "But the people are a little disappointed now. They thought it would immediately lead to freeing of the hostages and the end of Mussad's threat to his neighbors. That hasn't happened, so people are waiting and seeing. Meanwhile, the political vultures will try to pick the President's bones."

"I agree, Professor Samuelson, and that's why I'm going to need good counsel," the President responded. "And I'll tell you this. I did the right thing as far as I'm concerned. As Commander-in-Chief my job is to protect our citizens and the peace of the world. I won't admit to Kembeck or his cronies that I did anything at all, but I'm not sorry for what I did. Not for an instant. I'd do it all over again if I had to. And I'll fight them, in the Judiciary, in the House, even in a Senate trial if I have to."

The President paused, his eyes looking worn by the thought of the travail.

"So, Professor Samuelson, how do you stand on the whole issue?"

The Harvard lawyer stood up and paced, as if he were addressing a court, then halted and faced Briggs and Davidson.

"Mr. President, Congress is a sometimes foolish institution. They are mistake-prone—I remember they passed the draft by only one vote just before World War II. But without them, our system would be endangered. Even though Presidents are elected by all the people, if they didn't have checks, we could have a tyrant in the White House. But in the general battle between Presidents and Congress—in times of crisis—I lean toward strong Presidents. Where would this country be without Jefferson or Jackson or Lincoln or Teddy Roosevelt or Wilson or FDR or Truman, men who took the executive reins in their hands? No, a strong—and wise—President is a mainstay of our freedom. I don't know the whole story but, in this crisis, I side with you."

"Then you'll take my case?"

"Yes, Mr. President. As my first order of business, what will you do with the subpoena to appear before the House Judiciary Committee? From what you say, it's coming."

"Oh, it's coming all right. And I'll tell you this. I'm looking forward to seeing Rusty Kembeck's face when he finds out what I'm going to do."

74

SAM Tomasino had taken a taxi, paid for by the Judiciary Committee, all the way up Pennsylvania Avenue, right from the Rayburn House Office Building on Independence Avenue on the Hill, to 1600 Pennsylvania.

Nervous was hardly the word for what he felt. Judiciary Chairman Craver had approached him just that morning with that determined look on his face. As the youngest member of the Committee staff, Sal had often been given onerous jobs, but this one, he feared, was going to be the worst.

"Sal, I want you to do something that will put you into the history books," Craver had told him.

The idea sounded appealing at first, especially for a twenty-four-year-old law graduate from St. John's University on Long Island, still waiting to take his bar exams. "Yes, sir, what is it?"

"Well, I want you to serve this subpoena on one of our witnesses."

That hardly sounded historic to Tomasino. Congressional staffers did most of the subpoena work and he had even served a few himself.

"Surely, sir, who is it?"

Craver started to laugh. Not loud, but in a kind of insidious way that frightened Sal. The Chairman, a spare six-foot-four Westerner who hardly cracked a smile, sounded more ominous when he was laughing than when chewing out a staffer, which was frequent. Tomasino had so far been spared that, but only, he was sure, because he hadn't yet come to the attention of the Chairman.

"Your subpoena victim, Sal, is none other than the President of these United States, Hawley Paul Briggs. We're inviting him to his own impeachment hearings. How does that grab you, kid?"

Not too well, Sal said to himself when he took the document. The form was the same as usual, a single page signed by Chairman Craver and the Clerk of the House, along with the House seal. But this time, the impact was different.

By the authority of the House of Representatives of the Congress of the United States, To: *Hawley P. Briggs, President of the United States.* You are hereby commanded to be and appear before the House Committee on the Judiciary of the House of Representatives of the United States, of which the Honorable Lucian Craver is Chairman, in Room 2141 of the Rayburn House Office Building in the City of Washington on June 4, at the hour of 10:30 A.M., then there to testify touching matters of inquiry committed to said Committee, and you are not to depart without leave of said Committee. Witnessed by hand and the seal of the House of Representatives at the City of Washington.

As he left the cab and approached within a few feet of the Executive West Wing, Sal felt queasy. The paper, tucked into his inside pocket, was burning a hole in his mind. Who in the hell was he to get mixed up in such a monumental affair? He'd just as soon be back at the Committee working on some insignificant brief. Tomasino, still-not-a-lawyer, up against the President of the United States? No way.

But, of course he knew he had no choice if he wanted to keep his job.

As the guard at the West Wing blockhouse examined his House ID, Sal told him he had come to see President Briggs.

"So you want to see the President? Well I'll let you talk to his assistant, Les Fanning." He handed Sal the phone.

"Miss Fanning," Tomasino said, his palpitations almost out of control. "I'm a staffer on the House Judiciary Committee. I was told to give what I have personally to the President in the Oval Office. What should I do?"

"We've been expecting you. Come on in."

He walked down the edge of the driveway to the West Wing building and into the anteroom, where he was met by a Secret Service man. The agent winked at Sal knowingly. He seemed to understand something he didn't, Tomasino thought, which only increased his *agita*.

"Come right this way," the agent, a tall man with a bulging jacket, said, leading him down the corridor, then to the left, toward the Oval Office.

As he approached, the agent abruptly turned around and departed. Tomasino stopped dead in his tracks.

In front of the closed double doors stood two Marines, both seven-stripe Sergeant Majors in full dress uniform, their chests decorated with the combat ribbons of a dozen engagements. M-16 rifles, topped by open bayonets, were in their hands, half-poised in the direction of Tomasino.

His breath had left him. Only with maximum effort could Sal put his hand inside his jacket and extract the subpoena.

"I'm from . . . the House . . . Judiciary . . ." he began, his voice coming in short, halting gasps.

"We know," one Sergeant Major interrupted. "Now I'll tell you what to do."

"Yes, Sergeant?"

"Take your crappy piece of paper and get out, quick. The Commander-in-Chief didn't say so in these exact words, but you can tell your Chairman just where he can shove his subpoena. Get it?"

At that moment, a flash of light shot through the hallway. Sal turned in shock to see a photographer recording the scene on film, including the two Marines at bayonet-ready and himself, his hand outstretched, his face whitened, displaying an unearthly expression.

Sal pushed the subpoena back into his pocket and started to walk backwards, clumsily, down the hall. After a few hesitant steps, he turned fully around and ran toward the front door. He raced out of the anteroom into the fresh air, only seconds ahead of the Secret Serviceman's laughter.

If he was making history, like Chairman Craver said, it wasn't the kind he wanted anyone, especially his folks on Long Island, to ever read.

75

THE audience in the hearing room hushed as Congressman Lucian Craver of Wyoming entered and took the Chairman's seat—its buttoned leather back a significant few inches higher than the other thirty-four.

All were arranged on a double dais overlooking the witness table. The spectators, over 100 strong, and a small army of media, crowded forward. Four television networks were airing the proceedings, live, to an audience of some one billion.

Seats to the hearing, a kind of Beltway gladiators' battle, were on a first-come first-serve basis. Some people had been waiting in line since 6 A.M., spending four hours in anticipation of a historic event. Interest had been sparked by the incident at the Oval Office, especially the photo of the two Marines blocking the Congressional staffer from serving a subpoena on the President.

The picture had been splashed across the front pages of every daily in America. The *New York Times* gave the story a full eight-column banner: "PRESIDENT USES MILITARY TO BLOCK CONGRESSIONAL SUBPOENA; SAYS CHIEF EXECUTIVE IS IMMUNE TO LEGISLATIVE TESTIMONY." New York's *Daily News* said it simpler: "PREZ GIVES HILL THE FINGER." Even *Pravda* gave the story first-page play.

The nation was excited and titillated by the upcoming contest of the White House versus the Congress, one that had now taken on dramatic overtones. The television news programs and talk shows were buzzing with the controversy. No one wanted to be left out.

Neither did any of the thirty-five members of the House Judiciary Committee want to miss this showcase event in Hearing Room 2141 of the Rayburn House Office Building, the newest and most expensive of the six House buildings. It was in this room that Representative Peter Rodino of New Jersey chaired the hearings that led to President Nixon's probable impeachment—had he not resigned in time to stop it.

Chairman Craver had the same goal in mind for President Hawley Briggs, Davidson was sure.

Only one member of the committee was absent—Josiah Fremd, 89, who was near death in Bethesda Naval Hospital. Another infirm Congressman, Maxwell Lake of Minnesota, 83, had insisted on attending and was now rolling down the aisle in his motorized wheel chair, helped up to the dais by federal police.

Davidson had wrestled all night in his four-poster in Leesburg, deciding how he should handle the House inquiry. He finally decided to accept the subpoena, served at about the same time as the President rebuffed his own. He was not the President and he had the simpler remedies of a citizen, including obfuscation and his Constitutional rights. He'd do what he could to provide a buffer for the President, between himself, the press and the President's enemies in the House.

How had the people reacted to the Marines blocking the Oval Office? Davidson sensed that most had enjoyed the idea. It was a sign of the President's macho independence, the trait they seemed to like in their Chief Executives.

Some, of course, thought it overly theatrical. Still others understood that it was Hawley Briggs's way of dramatizing the separation of powers, that in the nuclear age, he—as Commander-in-Chief—had greater responsibility for war and peace than did the slow-acting Congress.

To exercise that responsibility he also needed authority. And that included not being dragged before every Congressional committee that would like to question, second guess, or pillory him.

Of course, in the back of his mind, Davidson thought that if he were cited for contempt of Congress, or convicted of a crime, the President could pardon him, a power granted in the Constitution by Article II, Section 2. It covered all crimes and all violations, except that a President couldn't use his pardon in cases of impeachment, including himself. But one President could pardon another, as Ford had done for Nixon in 1974. Davidson didn't count on it, but it was a reassuring thought.

Now he sat in the witness area, awaiting his call. There was no rehearsal on his part, even mentally. Perhaps it was best to be spontaneous and instinctive. But one thing he wasn't going to do. He wasn't going to give Rusty Kembeck any ammunition with which to impeach the President.

The Baptist listened as the Chairman began, explaining that this was a public hearing regarding the question of Presidential High Crimes and Misdemeanors. This was not a trial, only a hearing. But there were questions of violations of the Constitution that could lead to a Judiciary Committee vote recommending impeachment of the President, which would then become a matter for the whole House.

It required only a majority vote in that body, Craver reminded everyone, to impeach—or some might say "indict"—the President. After that there would be a trial in the Senate, presided over by the Chief Justice of the

Supreme Court. There, a two-thirds vote was needed to convict. The Vice-President, who was usually President of the Senate, was purposely omitted from the impeachment procedure by the Constitution. After all, he'd have the most to gain if the President was convicted.

In the past, as in the case of President Nixon, the issue was first heard by a subcommittee, Craver explained. But he had decided that the importance of this matter required the attention of the full committee. And so this hearing.

"We had intended to have the President of the United States as a witness," Craver said straightforwardly, "but he has refused a subpoena. We find that action uncooperative at best, and obstructionist in fact. We're dealing here with serious charges—the assassination of a foreign leader, the illegal use of funds unauthorized by Congress, and of bribery on a massive scale. We shall hear a number of witnesses to clarify the truth."

Craver paused briefly. "Our chief counsel is Albert Sardino, and he'll do most of the questioning. But as Chairman, I, and any of our members, may query the witnesses as well. Now, I call the first witness, Mr. John Davidson. Is he present?"

Davidson raised his hand and moved forward to the witness table. After taking the oath, he sat, he thought without much anxiety, facing the Committee.

"Mr. Davidson, do you have a statement to read for the record?" Sardino, a thin, mustached man resembling former New York Governor Tom Dewey, asked.

"No, sir. I do not."

"Then we'll get to the heart of the matter. Mr. Davidson, were you given an assignment by the President to perform some duty for him?"

"Yes."

"Can you tell us what that was?"

"I promised the President confidentiality, so naturally I cannot tell this Committee, or anyone, what it was. That would destroy my value to the White House. Would it not?"

"Were you offered immunity by this Committee from later criminal prosecution if you cooperated and told us everything you know?"

"Yes."

"How did you respond?"

"I told them I didn't want immunity. I'll take my chances with the system as it is. I don't believe in the whole idea of immunity—letting somebody off the hook for incriminating his colleagues. It breeds immorality, of which we have enough."

"Are you one to talk, Mr. Davidson?"

"I think so."

"Now to get back to the main line of inquiry. Are you a federal employee?"

"No longer. I was Chief of Counterintelligence for the Central Intelligence Agency for a number of years, but I am now retired."

Sardino offered a sarcastic smile. "Isn't it true that you were forced out of the Agency for, some said, excessive suspicion of the CIA leadership?"

"I can't comment on people's motives, Mr. Sardino. But I am retired."

"Then in this matter you served as a private consultant for the President, is that right?"

"One can assume that, yes."

"And were you paid?"

"No."

"You are a wealthy philanthropist and patriot then?"

"No sir. Not wealthy nor a philanthropist. I just use my pension and my farm earnings to do what I can for my country in certain emergencies."

"Then this is not your first secret expedition for the White House?"

"Hardly. I have served several Presidents, this one included."

"Now, Mr. Davidson. I understand they call you The Baptist. Is that right?"

"Yes, sir."

"Now, I'll repeat my earlier question so there is no misunderstanding. What assignment did you undertake for President Briggs? Was it to assassinate the leader of a foreign nation in violation of Executive Order No. 12333, which was first issued by President Ford in 1976, then agreed to by Presidents Carter, Reagan and Bush, before the present President? Did you also bribe a foreign national with 1.85 million dollars to help you carry out this assassination? And did you hire an infamous political assassin to do your dirty work for you? I ask you this, with the reminder that you are subject to charges of contempt of Congress should you refuse to answer."

Davidson breathed in. "Mr. Sardino, do you consider any of these charges to be criminal in nature?"

"Why absolutely. Wouldn't you?"

"Well, then I have to quote the Fifth Amendment to the Constitution, passed you may know, in December 1791. Part of it simply states that 'No person shall be compelled in any criminal case to be a witness against himself nor be deprived of life, liberty or property without due process of law.' I'm sure they taught you that at law school."

Sardino half-rose out of his chair, his finger pointed accusingly at Davidson.

"So you're taking the Fifth?" he barked.

"In the vernacular, I suppose, yes. In any case, I stand on my constitutional right not to be forced to incriminate myself."

Sardino rose and walked over to Chairman Craver. The two were soon engaged in energetic whispering.

"Need I warn you, Mr. Davidson," Chairman Craver interjected, "that you could be held in contempt of Congress for refusing to answer that question? If so, you could go to jail. Now, I'll give you one more chance to purge yourself. Will you answer the question?"

"I already have, sir, quite properly and constitutionally. You know I can hardly be placed in jail for exercising my legal rights as a citizen. No, I will not answer out of respect for the Fifth Amendment, one of the most brilliant devices invented by the Founding Fathers. Specifically, if I recall, by James Madison, who became our fourth President."

Craver growled some Western epithet under his breath.

"All right, Mr. Sardino, call your next witness. Maybe he'll be less hostile."

The next witness, Mel Gordon, was hostile all right, but not to the Committee. Dressed in his best Bond discount suit, with a yellow dotted tie, and a handkerchief to match in his breast pocket, Gordon detailed for twenty minutes everything he had learned in Germany and Switzerland and the Cayman Islands about the pay-off to Horstmann and the assassination in Berlin. He painted, Davidson thought, a quite accurate picture of the whole operation. If he were back as CIC of the Agency, he'd snatch Gordon right away from the GAO.

The audience broke into animated chatter as soon as Gordon was finished. The television cameras zoomed in, focusing on Gordon's constantly tapping fingers, then switched to Sardino's sarcastic expression, then back to Davidson's satisfied smile—the commentators racing with the details of the plot to kill Mussad.

Ezra Jenkins, a network reporter, kept speaking of the "historic hearing that could settle, for once and all, the two-hundred-year-old battle for power between the President and the Congress."

Davidson doubted that.

The Committee broke for ten minutes, the Congressmen buzzing back and forth, chatting with their colleagues about the case. Davidson was afraid he had no reading on what they were thinking.

The next witness after the break was his friend, Charles Samuelson, Professor of Constitutional Law at Harvard.

"State your name, occupation and address," the clerk asked.

Samuelson did, then interjected: "But there's an additional piece of information the Committee should know about up front."

"What's that, Professor?" Chairman Craver asked, perplexed.

"Well, I've been asked by President Briggs to provide him with legal counsel in case of an impeachment hearing such as this, or an actual impeachment and trial."

"And what did you say?"

"I've signed on."

"Do you think that this relationship with the President will prejudice your opinions at this hearing?"

"Well, if you mean will my answers be different now than they would have been two weeks ago, the answer is 'No.' But does that mean that I may not agree with the Committee's concept of constitutionality? Then I have to plead guilty."

"I'll accept that caveat, Professor. Now you can begin, Mr. Sardino."

The prosecutor stood for a moment, as if in court, then realized that he wouldn't be heard without his mike. He retook his seat and focused in on Samuelson.

"Professor Samuelson, do you think the President had the constitutional right to refuse our Committee's subpoena? Does the Constitution itself give the President any such immunity?"

"Absolutely not."

Sardino smiled.

"But," Samuelson continued, "the Constitution is a living document, as the Supreme Court has shown us. And precedent is entirely with President Briggs. When Jefferson was subpoenaed by Chief Justice Marshall to appear at the treason trial of Aaron Burr, he refused. But he did give the court some documents. The Supreme Court also ordered President Nixon to turn over his tapes. But no President has ever accepted a *personal* subpoena to appear. You can see how destructive that would be to our democracy. Every court and every one of our hundred and fifty Congressional subcommittee chairmen might try to hold him in contempt. Jefferson said it best when he told Marshall that his duties were 'superior' to those of the inquiry. So I suppose, using precedent as law, you can't effectively subpoena a President."

Sardino shifted uneasily in his chair.

"To get to this specific matter at hand, Professor, wouldn't you say that if Mr. Gordon's testimony is accurate and that President Briggs ordered the assassination of Mussad—and we've had no testimony to counter that evidence—that that itself is a prima-facie violation of Executive Order 12333 and therefore an impeachable offense?"

"Based on the Executive Order itself?"

"Yes."

Samuelson sat silent for an instant, in thought.

"No, not on that alone. You see, an Executive Order is signed by the President, and is not a legislative law of the land. It is a federal policy only. Federal employees must follow it or be subject to discipline. But the President himself? . . . Well actually, since he put it into use, he could just as easily take it out of circulation. That is, Order 12333 could now be no more if President Briggs says it's no more."

"Are you telling me that the President is exempt from his own order?" Sardino asked, incredulous.

"In a way, yes. Since it's his own creation, it's probable he can destroy it at will. I would guess that it binds others but not him. That's my legal interpretation, as strange as it sounds."

"Even if he were an accessory to murder?"

"Well, that's a different story. Then he'd be subject to criminal penalties as a citizen since murder is against the common law. But first you have to arrest the President. No one has ever done that. I presume you'd first have to impeach him, which I don't think you can do on violation of his own Executive Order."

Sardino first blanched, then flushed in anger.

"Are you telling me the President is above the law? I can hardly believe that. What is he, some kind of superman? Are you excusing Oval Office fever? Just because he has a finger on the nuclear button, does that make him God— even if he thinks so?"

"No, hardly. But at the same time the President is surely not an ordinary man under our law. First, he is Commander-in-Chief of the armed forces, and he also has the constitutional right to pardon anyone for any crime: Mr. Davidson, for example, if he did what Mr. Gordon claims he did. And, as we know, he can *make* war and kill thousands of our troops and foreign troops, and civilians, as well."

"But the Constitution says that only Congress can declare war. Isn't that true?"

"Absolutely. The Commander-in-Chief can't declare war. That's up to Congress, as you correctly point out. But he can make war, and he's done much more of that than Congress. We've had military hostilities about two hundred times—maybe twenty of them serious, and Congress has only declared war five times. Andy Jackson took Spanish Florida without Congressional approval. We had invaded Mexican territory for three weeks before Congress approved it. Truman made war in Korea without Congress. Roosevelt started a sea war with Nazi U-boats before World War II. It might interest you to know that the Monroe Doctrine was never authorized by Congress. Reagan made war in Grenada, and I suppose the bombing of Libya was war too—and Congress did nothing about it. Bush did the same in Panama, and I think he would have made war against Iraq whether Congress agreed or not. No, Mr. Sardino, the President is far from an ordinary person."

"But we've seen President Briggs operating here in secret, in a sneaky manner, assassinating and bribing, without letting anyone in Congress—not even the Intelligence Oversight Committees or the Speaker—know what he was doing. Is that constitutional?"

"Before I answer the last part, let me say that Presidents have always been sneaky. In a crisis they generally try to do what they can before Congress can get their hands on them. President Tyler made a secret deal with the Republic of Texas to get them into the Union, and he almost got impeached for it. President Jefferson swiftly grabbed the chance to make the Louisiana Purchase, about a third of our present country, from a hungry Napoleon for fifteen million dollars. When Congress complained they hadn't authorized the money, Jefferson asked if he should give back the land. The sneakiest was Abe Lincoln. Before Congress could meet in the Civil War, he raised an army, spent money on arms, even eliminated habeus corpus, a sacred legal right. No, Presidents are not ordinary men."

"What about the constitutionality of all of this, Professor Samuelson? How do you stop this Imperial Presidency, these God-like powers the Presidents seem to like?"

"Ah, there's the rub, Mr. Sardino. I sometimes think the Founding Fathers made the separation of powers of the President and the Congress somewhat vague so that this battle—a political one really, of public support, or lack of support—could go on. We've never impeached a President, although Andy Johnson only escaped by one vote, and Zachary Taylor was brought up on charges but the House failed to vote a majority. And President Nixon resigned beforehand."

"Are you, as a legal scholar, saying that anything goes if the people support it?"

"I wish you hadn't asked me that question. I have my reputation to uphold as a Constitutional lawyer."

"That's nice, but what's the answer?"

"The answer is that the Constitution settled the question by providing for impeachment. Outside of impeachment, where the people's representatives speak, loud and clear, the President has been able, and therefore I assume will always be able, to do whatever . . ."

"Yes, Professor Samuelson, do what?"

"Whatever he can get away with. If you want to stop him from assassinating people, using bribery, making unauthorized war, Iran-Contra, Watergate, covert action without a finding—whatever—you'll have to impeach him. I understand that's why we're here."

"And if he's not impeached?"

"Then, by default, it's apparently legal. And, I hate to say it, constitutional on a practical level."

Samuelson paused, searching his mind for an example.

"Yes, Mr. Sardino, Jefferson said it again. It was his Great Occasions speech. It was pertinent then and I think it holds up today. Let me quote it. I scribbled it down before I came here."

Samuelson reached into his inside pocket and took out a torn envelope. "Yes, here it is. Jefferson said: 'On Great Occasions, every good officer must be ready to risk himself in going beyond the strict line of the law when the public preservation requires it. A strict observance of the written law is doubtless one of the high duties of a good citizen, but it is not the highest. The laws of necessity, of self-preservation, of saving our country when in danger, are of a higher obligation . . . To lose our country to a scrupulous adherence to a written law, would be . . . ' "

Samuelson looked up at the Chairman, then turned, only for a second, to address the spectator audience.

" ' . . . Would be to lose the law itself.' In this case, if it can be shown that President Briggs ordered an assassination, I would presume that he firmly believed that Mussad was a kidnapper of teenagers, the probable *provocateur* of aggression and a bloody war, and thus a menace to our liberty and law. Thus one of Jefferson's 'Great Occasions.'"

The room first hushed. Then many in the audience and on the dais started to speak, chatting animatedly. The Chairman banged his gavel.

"So what good is the Constitution?" Sardino blurted out.

"Oh, young man, the Constitution is perfect, the most perfect document ever written by man. Everything we are stems from it. It rests in the people. And the people rest not only in the President, the only one elected by us all, but in their Congress as well. So, Congress can always kick out an evil President. That's what makes the perfection."

"So, the Constitution is therefore a political document, not a legal one."

"No, it's both. In a democracy, legality and politics are often one and the same. The people's will, within a framework of law."

Samuelson took out a handkerchief and coughed into it to clear his throat.

"I think I can best sum it up this way. If you impeach President Briggs, then what he did was illegal. If you don't, it was sanctioned by the people and, by default by the Congress. Therefore what he did is presumably legal and constitutional. I know that doesn't sound too scholarly, but it's the truth. And as a professor, that's my obligation. To learn and explain the truth."

"So when, Professor Samuelson, do you think this whole thing will be settled—the question of what a President can or cannot constitutionally do?"

Samuelson smiled, his eyes glancing purposefully across the dais of thirty-four Congressmen.

"Never, Mr. Sardino. If God grants us continued liberty, somebody like me will be sitting in this same chair a hundred years from now, arguing out the same battle, searching for the right answer. That's the genius of our government."

The audience stilled as Samuelson rose and left his chair.

"On that note, we'll adjourn until tomorrow," Chairman Craver called, banging his gavel, this time a bit more softly.

76

SAM Withers squeezed his full 130 pounds and five feet six inches into the false partition that had been built between the driver's cab and the back of the fake BEWAG van, now painted yellow.

The partition, with holes for air and two small gun slots, had been fabricated at a service shop that handled the cars of the American Embassy. The owner, Karl Meintz, could be trusted to keep the alteration confidential.

Before he left, Davidson had improvised the "radioactive tritium" for the exchange with Red Swastika. The Air Force had loaned him several small lead containers that had once held nuclear material, but were now filled with radioactive waste. Davidson knew that any expert would spot the fakery after a few minutes, but a quick detection sweep would probably give Sam enough time to carry out the plan. If all went as hoped, Friedrich himself would be on the receiving end of an unwelcome sting.

Withers was armed with an UZI hidden in the partition, and a semi-automatic 15-shot Beretta in his jacket pocket. Kennedy had a Mauser 7.65. They had worked out a protocol to outfox the Swastika people, but it required good timing. And equally important, good luck.

At 8:18 P.M., Kennedy, dressed as a BEWAG driver, and Sam, stuffed in the hidden compartment, left the Embassy garage on Friedrichstrasse and headed out of town, traveling through the Berlin streets at an average speed of only forty kilometers per hour. When they picked up the Autobahn in what used to be East Berlin, it was 8:48.

"OK, Mike," Withers said on the small walkie talkie they had set up between the hidden compartment and the van's cab. "Watch the mileage. We have to slow down at about fourteen and a half kilometers from this spot, then let the van struggle a little—hit the accelerator, pull off it, then go back on, as if the engine's in trouble. When you get down to five kph, pull over and stop dead on the shoulder. The trick is to make it happen at exactly fifteen kilometers. We don't want to blow it because our arithmetic stinks."

"Will do, Sam. You're right. We've got to pull this off like a ballet. Otherwise there'll be two dead Americans on the Autobahn."

Night had fallen, and their travel on Route 2 northward attracted no attention. The odometer had read 18,725 kilometers before they left, and now was registering 18,745. Kennedy kept staring at it, almost obsessed as each tenth of a kilometer clicked off. Five, six, seven. Each one, he quickly calculated, took forty-two seconds at their speed.

The Autobahn was not busy and Kennedy craned his neck to look for another BEWAG van. The Swastika van was not scheduled to arrive until a half hour after them, but they had to be prepared for a false switch in time. Exactly following the schedule might make Swastika vulnerable if a police ambush was planned, which he was sure it wasn't. Following Davidson's orders, Langer was told nothing about the rendezvous.

Once the BEWAG van was parked, Kennedy hopped out and quickly surrounded it with flares, lighting them to signal that the vehicle was disabled. He got back into the truck and waited.

Five minutes later, he could hear the sound of a car coming behind him. He peered into the rear-view mirror. Oh, no, it was a highway policeman, coming to a stop. That's all they needed now was police interference.

Kennedy spoke rapidly in German, watching his accent. His role as a BEWAG driver had to hold up.

"No problem, officer. A little mechanical trouble, but I called it in on the emergency road phone. Another BEWAG van with a technician is on the way. They'll be here in about fifteen minutes. I'll just wait."

The officer said nothing, just circled the van as Kennedy held his breath. He assumed Withers was equally tense, perhaps more so, in his tight compartment.

"All right," the officer finally said. "I think they'll take care of you." He turned and drove away.

Kennedy knew the chanciest part of the scenario was yet to come. He was right. Less than five minutes after the patrol car had left, the second BEWAG wagon pulled up directly behind him. Kennedy waited, a minute then two and three, before someone left the other van and approached.

Two men, wearing black jump suits, one with a ski mask covering his face, walked up to his driver's side window.

"You are the American with the tritium, I presume," the leader said in well-spoken English. "Please get out of the van so we can start our inspection. Open the back door. Is that where the material is?"

"One second, please, *Herr* whatever," Kennedy complained. "We were supposed to pick up ten million dollars in gold as a down payment. Don't you remember?"

"Surely, and we are good at our word. The gold is in our van. As soon as Ernst, my fusion expert, authenticates the products, we'll make the transfer. Now get out of the van."

This time he waved the order with a PM, semi-automatic
Pistolet Makarova 9.25, the favorite handgun of the KGB.

Kennedy got out as told. The plan was still intact but
all depended on Withers in the back—to get as many of
their men into his gunsight before taking action. Or, if the
Swastika men were busy outside, to quietly leave his hiding
space. At Sam's call, they would make their move simultaneously.

"All right, Ernst, now take a look at the containers in the
back. Tell me what you think."

While the technician headed toward the Air Force-loaned
material, the lead man crawled into the front cab and poked
around near the wall of Withers's partition. Kennedy could
see him from his spot on the shoulder. If they located Sam's
hiding place, not only was the sting a bust, but Kennedy
could imagine Swastika's response when they learned the
fusion elements were false.

"Ernst!" the lead man called out. "Drop what you're doing
and come here. Quick. I want you to look at something."

The minutes passed slowly for Kennedy as the men
banged and searched in the front cab, like carpenters
seeking a wall stud. Ernst then returned to the back of
the van and crawled inside. In a minute, he exited.

"You!" The lead man motioned to Kennedy. "Come
here."

He quickly obliged.

"Ernst has measured the van from your cab to the extreme
end, then inside as well. It doesn't jibe. There is an extra
space between the sections. Do you have something—or
someone—hidden in there?"

Kennedy's breath wouldn't escape. That damn German
efficiency. He just shook his head at the man in the ski
mask.

"No? Then surely you won't mind if I riddle it thoroughly

with my automatic. Ten or fifteen shots shouldn't hurt the wood too much."

Without a further word, he walked to the open rear doors and raised his pistol, as if for firing practice.

"OK! HOLD IT!" Kennedy yelled. "There is someone in there. Don't shoot!"

"Always games with you Americans. All right, whoever you are, come out. Your little plot has failed." He paused. "And first throw your guns out the trap door, or whatever. And I mean all guns. If I don't see at least two, I'll have to open fire."

Inside, Withers let out a groan of disgust. He tilted up the trap door, and threw out the UZI, followed by his Beretta.

"All right. Now yourself. Come out the same way you came in."

Moments later Withers extricated himself from the partition, his voice low, the expletives harsh.

"Good, now one of our men will drive your BEWAG wagon in front of ours. We'll go to our place in the countryside and settle accounts. If the fusion products are real, we may spare you—but I doubt it. But if they are false, as I'm beginning to expect, you will become human, not radioactive, waste."

At gunpoint, Withers and Kennedy walked to the second van, their expressions a model of dejection. Kennedy felt a twang of remorse. He really didn't need to get back into the intelligence business. And now . . .

The two Americans had been hustled into the rear of the van, Ernst sitting cross-legged in front of them, his UZI zeroed in. Kennedy could hear the engine of the van rev up, the beginning, he assured himself, of the end.

The two vans started to move out together, just beginning to leave the shoulder strip to reenter the Autobahn, when Kennedy heard it—loud and clear.

"*ACHTUNG!* BEWAG VANS. PULL OVER TO THE SHOULDER AND SHUT YOUR ENGINES. THIS IS THE BERLIN POLICE."

Through the small side window, Kennedy could make it out. Two police helicopters were hovering just fifty feet above the highway.

"All right, stop your engines and all come out with your hands up," the bullhorn blared. "THIS IS AN ARREST!"

Kennedy could feel the sudden lurch of the BEWAG. Instead of shutting the engine, the driver gunned the accelerator and the van raced forward from a standing start.

From above, he could hear the chatter of automatic fire. The van traveled a few hundred feet, then swerved off the highway. A tire, or two, had been blown by the gunfire. Now the engine was quiet.

Ernst walked out of the van and dropped his UZI on the shoulder strip. He was soon followed by the lead man in the ski mask and black jump suit, then by three others, all now unarmed.

"All right, push together in one spot where we can watch you. We're landing now. Look out for the rotor wash."

In moments, four Berlin policemen, three in uniform and one in civvies, had alighted from the two helicopters and were approaching. Kennedy and Withers rushed up.

Even from a distance, Sam could see that the man in civvies was Detective Sergeant Langer. "God, am I glad to see you, Kurt," Sam said. "I suppose I'm lucky you didn't listen to us."

"No, not for a minute did I let you alone," Langer said, smiling. "We've been watching you and Kennedy, and the BEWAG wagon, and Swastika all at one time. Now follow me, the most important part is yet to come."

Langer walked over to the grouped prisoners, the lead man waiting, his face still covered with the ski mask.

Without a word, Langer pulled it off.

"As I expected, Manfred Lichtenstein of the BND. Or should I say 'Friedrich' of Red Swastika?"

Withers was nonplussed, but pleased that Davidson wasn't there to see the unmasking of a once-trusted colleague.

"OK, Sam. I believe your tour of Germany as a State Department employee is over," Langer said, motioning for him and Kennedy to enter the police helicopter. "My boys will take them in and you can get back to the Embassy, then to Langley. But be sure to visit us in Berlin again. Only next time, please keep me informed of your whereabouts. We can't afford to lose any American diplomats."

Withers laughed. But only a little.

77

"MR. President, great news!" Davidson almost shouted as Les led him into the Oval Office.

Briggs half leapt off his chair and came forward to meet him.

"Yes, John?"

"I've just heard from Sam in Berlin. Withers and the Berlin police have nabbed Friedrich, the leader of the Red Swastika movement. He's under arrest, along with four members of the government. Looks like the Nazi movement, at least its leadership, has been crippled for now. The Germans are cleaning out the BND including my former friend Manfred Lichtenstein, and clamping down on Heinschmann and the neutron bomb deliveries. This should help you at home. Once the nation knows everything . . ."

The President shook Davidson's hand warmly, cutting him off in mid-sentence.

"Good job, John. But no, I can't use this for my own defense. The American people have only hints about the pro-Nazi movement in Germany, and know nothing about the N-Bomb deliveries. I want to keep it that way." Briggs started across the rug. "The hostages are still being abused, and if the American people learn about Al Rashon's neutron bombs, they're going to demand a war. I've got to resist the temptation to get myself off the hook and put the country in a jam. No, we'll just have to wait."

The President moved back toward his desk and stood alongside the long colonial window facing the Rose Garden. As he peered out, his expression reverted to one of near-depression. "John, what do you make of the hearings so far? Does it look like they're going to vote to impeach?"

"It's a tough call, Mr. President. Samuelson's testimony helped, but I'm afraid the evidence given by Mel Gordon was devastating. He told them everything that's happened. There's going to be one more round of testimony before the Committee votes. My guess is that the House will go the same way as the Judiciary."

On his feet Davidson now joined the President. "What about Happy Rider?" he asked. "What does he say? He's on the Committee too."

"About the same as you, John. He says we need some good news from Al Rashon if we're going to make it. Something to scare the bejezus out of the Congressmen. That if they vote against me, they're on the wrong side."

The President halted, then returned to his desk, seated at the old Teddy Roosevelt chair from the Sagamore Trust in Oyster Bay. He sat quietly, rocking, the motion seeming to have some soothing effect on his tattered emotions.

"John. I want you to know that I don't hold anything against you. What we did with Mussad was right—the only possible solution. And your job in Germany. Well, that was spectacular. The world couldn't use another Nazi government, especially with a Third World arming heavily and susceptible to seduction from a rich high-tech nation like Germany. So I want to thank you for that—even though I can't use it in this impeachment business."

Davidson took the President's subdued mood as a sign to leave. "Well, good luck, Mr. President," he said, moving toward the doorway. He slowed as he almost bumped into Les Fanning, who was entering the room, excited.

"Oh, Mr. Davidson! So glad I caught you. I have an overseas phone call for you."

"OK, I'll take it outside."

The President looked up from the busy work on his desk.

"No, John, take it right here, on the table near the fireplace."

Davidson moved toward the phone, glancing back at Fanning.

"Who is it from?"

"A man named Hassam Ali."

"Hassam? Good. Is he calling from Cairo?"

"No sir. I think he said he's in Al Rashon."

"AL RASHON!" the President shouted across the room.

Davidson picked up the phone. "Yes, Hassam, you're where? In the President's office in the capital? Wonderful, wonderful! And an almost bloodless coup? Congratulations all around!"

He listened for a minute, then enthusiastically signed off.

"Hassam, I'll call you back in an hour or two. Thanks again. Wonderful news."

Davidson turned, facing a beaming President.

"Yes, sir, that was Hassam. The two Brigadiers surrounded the Presidential palace with their mechanized units. And General Karadi called the commanders all over the nation, telling them to stand down. He was coming out of retirement to lead a military coup. The young officers, with three thousand men, took over the government in a matter of hours. Hassam Ali is provisional President until they can hold elections."

"What about our hostages?" Briggs asked, his voice exultant.

"Hassam says that's his first order of business. The airport has been secured and we can send in our C-5As any time we want. His troops are preparing the boys and girls for immediate release."

The President placed his face in his hands. "Thank God, John. Not just for me, but for those kids, and everybody."

"I suppose this will make a big difference in the impeachment hearings," Davidson offered.

"It won't hurt, John. But I really won't be off the hook until Kembeck cries uncle and tells his people not to vote against me."

The President halted as Davidson started out of the Oval Office.

"Where are you going now, John?"

"To the Hill, Mr. President. To see if I can't smoke a peace pipe—or, if I have to, to threaten war—with that big chief of the Sioux."

— 78 —

"DON'T tell me! The great Baptist has come to see a lowly pol of the people? How democratic can you get, Mr. Davidson?"

Davidson brushed aside the polished, patronizing tone of Speaker Rusty Kembeck, who had come to meet him at the door to the Speaker's elegant suite. He never knew servants of the people could work in such luxurious surroundings. In some ways, they rivaled the White House. Davidson supposed that's what Kembeck himself was, and would always be—a rival of the President. Unless, of course, he was someday elevated to that office, which many suspected was his secret ambition.

"Mr. Speaker, I've just come with some important news that could change the course of the impeachment hearings."

"Good, Baptist—if I may call a spook legend that to his face. Let's have a drink over it. Do you take bourbon and branch water? Inherited it from one of the great ones before my time, Speaker Sam Rayburn."

Davidson nodded and sipped along with Kembeck, who made satisfied noises as he drank.

"So, what's your news, Baptist?"

Davidson told him of the phone call from Hassam Ali about the change of government, the almost bloodless coup and the release of the remaining twenty-nine teenage hostages.

"That's great, John! Great news for the people and the country. But what does that have to do with the impeachment? My friend Hawley still had someone, with your damn help, pull a trigger on a foreign President, and used money only *we* can authorize to bribe some Kraut son-of-a-bitch. Get me?"

Davidson had another trump to play, and he could no longer hold it in reserve.

"Mr. Speaker, there are other things you don't know about."

"Such as?" Kembeck's face registered curiosity.

In detail, Davidson explained Red Swastika and the pro-Nazi German movement, especially its growing influence within the Berlin government and parts of the Third World. He described its support of Mussad and, most important, the shipment by Heinschmann of neutron bombs to Al Rashon, stored in bombproof bunkers also built by the Germans.

"So you see, Speaker Kembeck," Davidson said in his most reasonable manner, "the President was in a double bind. He didn't want to tell the people about the neutron weapons. He feared that a war against Mussad could mean a hundred thousand US casualties. Meanwhile, he wanted our teenage hostages freed. I told him assassination was the only way, and I think events have proven us right."

Kembeck rose and walked over to Davidson. His expression was serious, his smile warming.

"John, I had no idea there was so much provocation for the assassination," he said, placing an arm around Davidson. "You're a wise old coyote, and I suppose in your own old Virginia way, a credit to the union."

"Does that mean that you're calling off the impeachment dogs in the Judiciary?"

Kembeck reared back his head and roared.

"Davidson, just a minute before you walked in here, CNN announced the news from Al Rashon—the coup, the freeing of our hostages, the whole thing. I got right on the horn to my boys in the hearing room and told them to kill the impeachment, that Briggs was home free. Then I called Happy Rider with the news. You see, John, those teenagers back home are worth about ten million votes for Hawley. And an old Indian pol like me knows that if you can't count, you can't play in this democracy. And if there's one thing I can do, even with my shoes on, it's count."

Kembeck laughed again between breaths.

"But you didn't waste your trip here, Davidson. Now I know all about those Nazi bastards in Red Swastika and I'm going to send my personal regards to the President for what he did."

The Speaker moved toward the door, indicating that the meeting, and the incident of Executive Order 12333, was over as far as the House of Representatives was concerned.

"You see, Mr. Davidson, this democracy always seems to come up smelling. Sometimes it does it in a cockeyed way, and it scares the hell out of a lot of people before it's straightened out. But so far, at least, we've done it, close calls and all."

For the first time in many years, Davidson couldn't think of a thing to say. He just tipped his hand to his head and exited, smiling.

— 79 —

DAVIDSON was ushered into the Oval Office by an exuberant Les Fanning, who joined him, the President and Majority Leader Happy Rider in front of the White House's new 36-inch television set, one of the few American-made ones on the market.

"John, take a seat," the President said. "The C-5A will be landing at Andrews Air Force Base in a few minutes, and we'll watch it on TV. The plane's got all twenty-nine kids on board."

The President's face told volumes about his mood, and to Davidson, the emotional highs and lows that went with the job of the Chief Executive. He had never envied the position, with its hammerlock on one's life, an existence to be lived, in a way, in the shadow of the people he served. No President could lean too far in his own direction without having the voters pull him back to where they wanted him. No, being an intelligence man, fully employed or not, was a much more preferable experience.

He could see it in the President's eyes. They were shining and joyful now, but behind the celebration of the good news, he sensed a weariness that would never go away.

As they waited for the live television coverage, the President pulled his chair closer to Davidson's.

"Baptist. I thought you'd like to know what's happening—the loose ends of the things we started. Well, Chancellor Bessinger has finally clamped down on Germany's export policy and has fired a lot of people involved. Heinschmann and their boss, Klaus von Stimmel, have been fined a hundred million marks. Their partnership with Cotrell has been cut and they've been kicked out of the nuclear business entirely. Bessinger swears that no more developing nations are going to get poison gas, or bacteriological warfare materials, or nuclear reactors, or missiles from Germany. It's good talk. I know we've heard it before, but maybe now it'll be true. I'll leave it to you to monitor what you can." He paused. "And yes, Detective Langer has found the killer of Horstmann. It was ordered by Friedrich."

"What about Al Rashon? Any word on the neutron bombs, Mr. President?"

"Yes, Hassam has invited in some of our experts. They're preparing a demolition program to defuse the neutron artillery, and ship the tritium to the States for storage and control. Not that we need it, but this will keep it out of the wrong hands. Meanwhile, he's preparing for elections, and he seems resigned to maybe losing the race himself—sign of a good democrat, with a small 'd' that is."

"And the 'Red' part of Swastika?"

"John, the Kremlin is always a quagmire, but now that it's anti-Communist, they've arrested Barenchenko. And a new Inspector General appointed directly by President Malinovsky has uncovered the ring in Akademgorodok that stole the fusion products and the N-Bomb triggers for Mussad. Let's hope Russia stays stable enough to keep its nuclear arsenal safely under control."

The President looked up at the television set to see if the hostages' plane had arrived.

"It looks like another minute or so, John. I've got VP Morse out there to greet them along with guess who? None other than Chief Rusty Kembeck. He was flattered by the honor. I know I should have gone myself, but I confess the emotional strain would have been too much for me. I didn't want to cry in front of the whole nation."

"Here they come!" Happy Rider called out as the giant C-5A came into view, its wheels now extended for touch down. "Hawley, our kids are coming home."

The small group in the Oval Office watched, like a family anywhere in the suburbs, softly cheering as the plane landed, and the teenagers came down the stairs. The first group walked on their own, followed by one youngster in a wheelchair, and three others, gaunt and emaciated, on stretchers.

"Well, John, we did it. In our own way, but it worked," the President said proudly. "Those kids owe their lives to you."

"No, Mr. President, I'm just an instrument of the Presidency."

"While you're all taking and giving credit," Happy Rider chimed in, "let me tell you, Hawley, that you owe your political life to those kids, to that very scene we're watching now on television. To be honest, I didn't think that you and your spook friend here could pull it off, but you did and so we can all celebrate. But if you hadn't, you'd be leaving this office with your uncombed head between your long legs, headed for obscurity—maybe disgrace—in that bitty town in Arkansas. You know that, don't you?"

Briggs smiled at his political buddy of four decades.

"Happy, I know it as well as you. And not only that, I think that's the way it should be. Politics belongs to the people. We're only actors and we play our parts as well as we can, for as long as we can. Then we're discarded on the people's compost heap. Yes, sir, we're expendable as hell. And I don't forget that for a minute, especially when I came so close myself."

Davidson looked at the two veterans of the political wars and thanked his stars that he had never had the nerve, or the desire, to enlist in that select, troubled army.

"Mr. President," the old spy said, lifting his cognac toward the television screen. "This is for you, and for Mr. Jefferson. It's been almost two hundred years, but he knew that American politics wouldn't change an iota, and they haven't. He also knew that Presidents like you, who followed in his footsteps, would have the guts—or would find them—to do what had to be done. To recognize one of his 'Great Occasions' when it came their way."

"Gentlemen, to that toast I have only one response," the President said.

"What's that?" asked Davidson.

"Just simply Amen, John. Amen."

THE END